Hidden:Soulhunter
BETRAYER

COLLEEN VANDERLINDEN

Hidden: Soulhunter - Betrayer
Colleen Vanderlinden

For permission requests, email the author at
email@colleenvanderlinden.com.

Published in the United States
by Building Block Studios LLC

ISBN 0692492348
ISBN-13 978-0692492345

http://www.colleenvanderlinden.com
http://www.buildingblockstudios.com

CONTENTS

PROLOGUE

Hesiod, Theogony 211
(Greek epic 8th or 7th Century B.C.)

"And Nyx (Night) bare hateful Moros (Doom) and black Ker (Violent Death) and Thanatos (Death), and she bare Hypnos (Sleep) and the tribe of Oneiroi (Dreams). And again the goddess murky Nyx, though she lay with none, bare Momos (Blame) and painful Oizys (Misery), and the Hesperides... Also she bare the Moirai (Fates) and the ruthless Keres (Death-Guardians)... Also deadly Nyx bare Nemesis (Envy) to afflict mortal men, and after her, Apate (Deceit) and Philotes (Friendship) and hateful Geras (Old Age) and hard-hearted Eris (Strife)."

Nyx the Creator
(As told to the Fates by Nyx, Darkness Be Her Name)

How little the living know of Me,
From whom the beginning and all things arose.
I am unknowable.
I lay with none, yet gave Breath to all.
Aether, beloved Son of My Flesh. My only.
Nether, created to balance Aether.
And Nether and Aether together
created children, planets, stars.

Life requires balance, and so I created Death.
Hades, God of Death, to judge.
Furies, also named Erinyes, to punish.
Guardians, also named Keres, to escort the dead.
The Fates, also named Moirai, to observe and remember.

Balance.
Life and Death.
Good and Evil.
Happiness and Malaise.
Married forever, never one without the other.

My creations.
My design.

Existence.

Without balance, existence crumbles
Until there is only Me,
For, should everything else end, I will remain
And I shall create anew.

CHAPTER ONE

The soul of Boqin Chen ran from me, darting through stall after stall in the Silk Street Market in Beijing. A few minutes past, I had almost had him, when he had ducked into a narrow stall selling silk and cotton fabrics. This one knew enough about my abilities to know how to work against them. A crowded place like this one, full of people, made it so that the more useful of my powers, the ability to rematerialize in a different place, was nullified. Disappearing and reappearing among the shoppers would only cause panic and confusion, and, while that did not really matter overmuch to me, I disliked drawing attention to myself. I would save that handy little trick for when I would actually benefit from it.

So he stuck to the crowded areas, and I followed him, stalking quickly on foot like a mere mortal while he played his games.

I was beginning to lose my patience.

We had been playing this particular game for over an hour. In addition to what I already knew about Chen, it was all just giving me more reason to look forward to sticking my dagger into him.

Repeatedly, perhaps.

My phone vibrated in my jeans pocket again, and I suppressed my irritated sigh. It would wait.

Chen, like too many other souls I had dealt with of late, was on his way to developing a corporeal form. I now knew that a few of my own sisters, the other Guardians (who I had assumed dead) were partially behind the effort to raise an army of undead to use against my friend, my Queen, the Goddess of Death. She had no shortage of enemies, and we had learned that there was a concerted effort now being made to overthrow her. My sisters had been working with someone, or perhaps several someones, to use the very souls under Mollis's domain against her.

Undeath was an efficient way to do it; they fed the still-beating heart of a human to a soul. If they did that three times, the soul would have a fully capable, ridiculously strong, endlessly hungry living form. And, in the process, they created three new souls; those of the humans they'd murdered. Those souls were never given a chance to make their way to Mollis to be judged.

All of it weakened my Queen, and our enemies knew it.

I caught sight of Chen again, ducking into a stall off of the main thoroughfare. He caught my eye, grinned in a rather cocky manner. I stalked toward him. The shopkeeper saw me coming, and started selling me on his wares immediately, a fragrant array of spices that gave his stall a pleasant, warm aroma. I ignored him, eyes on that which I hunted. If I moved quickly enough, I could get a hand on Chen and rematerialize us elsewhere to finish what I needed to do.

Humans tended to panic when I stabbed at what looked like thin air with my Netherblade. I had learned that lesson the hard way countless years ago. It was best to do any stabbing that was required in private. And there was always stabbing required.

I made my move, sweeping my hand out while the shopkeeper continued chattering on, and Chen dodged to the side and did something I had never seen a soul do before: he stood in the same place as the shopkeeper, using the human's body as a shield against me.

She shopkeeper shivered and began rubbing his arms.

"Cold all of a sudden," he muttered.

I stared at the soul of Chen, whose face, to my sight, was like a transparent layer over the face of the shopkeeper. While the shopkeeper shivered and muttered, Chen grinned. It was an infamous grin, and I had to admit that, knowing that, I only found his smiling more disconcerting. Most of the souls I was hunting for Mollis were murderers. Serial murderers. Some had also been serial rapists, and usually they had murdered their victims as well.

Chen, though… Chen was different. In his day, he had been known as "The Happy Sadist." Torture, unspeakable pain and suffering. That had been his thing, and during his lifetime, he had abducted and tortured twenty-two people. Every one of his victims had lived, and he had set them free once he'd bored of them. Every one of them lived to tell the tale of the terrifying man who grinned while torturing them. The authorities had never caught up with him, and Chen had died, finally, of a heart attack. I had collected his soul in the first place. I was not at all happy to be doing it again.

"Did you just get cold? Must be a rain coming," the shopkeeper said to me, shivering slightly.

"Perhaps moving around a bit would help," I said in Mandarin, and the shopkeeper nodded, started pacing. The second Chen was exposed, I gave up on being subtle and not confusing the humans. I leapt forward, got a hold of Chen's arm, and rematerialized him in the next second to an empty stretch of alley in one of Beijing's red light districts. Most of these establishments were not open this early in the morning.

The second Chen and I reappeared, I plunged my Netherblade into the back of his neck, with no small amount of pleasure. He screeched, and struggled, and, thankfully, weakened.

One human heart. This one had begun his transition to undeath but thankfully would not be around to complete it. I was beginning to learn what the various stages of undeath felt like. During the past month, I had continued my work for Mollis in secret. There was a traitor in my friend's own family, and to attempt to draw them out, Mollis had exiled me. To the rest of the world, she and I were now enemies. The hope was that her traitor would eventually approach me, attempt to draw me to work with them against her. So we waited, and we played this game in which publicly we were at war, but behind the scenes, we were perhaps closer than we had ever been. Her mate, Nain, knew about our ruse, as did Brennan.

The only real complication (besides losing my home and the regard of many of the city's supernaturals, who now treated me as a pariah now that word had spread of the split between Mollis and I) was that I could no longer simply turn these lost souls over to Mollis's family in the Netherwoods. I was no longer allowed there. And that meant that the souls could not just be locked up to await their judgment.

In the end, what Mollis and I had come up with was that I would collect a soul and take it to an abandoned church in Detroit. Mollis was always able to feel when I had collected one, and she would meet me at the church as soon as she possibly could. Usually, it was mere minutes. She would work at the soul, and, finally, judge them, punish them, and send them to where they would spend eternity. We had to do all of this circumventing the Furies, Mollis's family. Right now, they were our primary suspects. Mollis understandably wanted more proof of their betrayal before destroying them. They were her family. Her aunt, and her own mother. She had come to love them, to cherish the connection she had to them.

But we both knew that the second we found evidence that they'd betrayed her, Mollis would destroy them. And her fury would be absolute.

So Chen had been helped by someone. Souls were not able to murder on their own, not until they reached full undeath.

"Who helped you?" I asked as he screamed, as my dagger leached the meager life he'd attained from him.

He lunged at me, and I raised my knee, catching him squarely between the legs. As he doubled over, I kicked out, landing a solid kick to his face, and he flew back, crashing into the cinder block wall behind him.

Of course, that only pushed my blade, which was still lodged between his shoulder blades, deeper. He screamed, and I was the only one who could hear it.

I stalked toward him, a cold smile of my own on my face. "I wonder if this is how your victims felt, Chen. Helpless as they screamed while you hurt them. How does it feel?"

I hauled him up, drew the second Netherblade I'd claimed from one of my traitorous sisters, and plunged it into his lower back.

I had not believed it was possible for him to scream any louder than he had been. I was wrong.

"Who was helping you, Chen?" I asked again. "All you have to do is answer, and I will start removing daggers."

He spit an expletive at me, then continued to scream.

"Very well. If you think this hurts, just wait a few minutes. It only gets worse," I promised him as I wrapped the thin chain that I used to bind the souls around his wrists and behind his back. Now, he would be unable to move without my assistance. No more running. No more hiding. No more using humans as shields.

There were few things I liked less than cowardice. And those who victimized others were always cowards at heart. That was something I had grown absolutely certain of in the thousands of years since I had come into existence.

I stood and watched him suffer, and it soon became clear that he either could not or would not talk to me. I shrugged, took his arm in my hand, and focused. It was time for me to go home, anyway.

We reappeared in a vacant church on Detroit's east side. The former Catholic church had been one of the many victims of the Detroit Archdiocese church closings that had begun in the 1980s. The building remained empty all these years later. Scrappers had long since taken anything of value, from the stained glass windows to the copper downspouts. Even the pews were gone.

This was where the souls I found were handed over to my Queen.

These souls were not going through the typical capture, waiting, judging, punishment process most souls went through. We could not simply just put them into a Nether prison, not when Mollis's relatives, the other Furies, were our prime suspects in who had betrayed her by releasing the souls in the first place. Not when they could talk, and tell someone about me. Not when we were unsure they would stay imprisoned for long, since they were obviously among her betrayer's pet souls.

No, there would be special consideration given to this soul by the Goddess of Death herself.

I let go of Chen, knowing he was unable to go anywhere. His screams had quieted, mostly because he was becoming weaker by the second. If my daggers remained in him much longer, he would be unable to stand. Eventually, he would lose even the ability to see.

Well. That would not do. He had to be able to talk and scream for my Queen, at the very least.

I walked over to him and tugged one of my daggers out of his lower back. It pulled out reluctantly, a wet sound accompanying it that I found comforting. One of the familiar sounds of my line of work.

He swore at me again, and I ignored him, pacing back and forth nearby. I looked around. The stone walls of the church wore graffiti, and the floor was littered with debris. Garbage, mostly. There were charred remains of a small fire. Someone had likely sheltered here during the winter.

My phone vibrated again, and I took a breath as I dug it out of my pocket.

"I am working," I said before the person on the other end had a chance to say anything. "You know this, because I already told you I was working today."

"Well thanks, but I don't care," Artemis's voice said over the line. I glanced at my phone in surprise. Yes, it was Brennan's number.

"Why are you calling me? Where is Brennan?" I asked her.

"My imbecile of a grandson got himself shot during one of those raids his department does. I thought you might want to know."

I felt my stomach turn over, came to my senses and decided to ignore it. He was immortal. He was fine. "How is he?"

"He is home, and resting. He was shot twice in the back. Luckily, I was able to get Asclepius to heal him quickly." She paused. "It was stupid, telling him he was immortal now. He has become careless."

"Careless is not a word I would use to describe him," I said.

"Says you. He is reckless with his safety. He can't keep doing this."

"He is immortal," I murmured, keeping my eyes on Chen.

"You don't know that. You assume that. There is no guarantee that he will live if he gets himself shot up." Artemis's voice rose a bit.

"He is your grandson. He was mated to Mollis. Asclepius has now healed him at least twice."

"And none of that is a guarantee. I keep trying to tell him that, but he takes your word over mine. Would you please reiterate to him that it is a theory and not fact? He has no business walking around as if he can't die." I did not answer, and she paused for a moment. "If he was still mated to Mollis, then yes. He would be immortal and I would not be worried. They broke their bond, and he weakened because of it. He is not all he should be. You know this."

"He is not lacking in any way," I argued, still watching Chen, but not seeing him.

"While your loyalty is touching, Guardian, loyalty won't save him if your little theory is wrong."

"Your blood, Mollis's blood, Asclepius's healing. It is enough," I said softly.

She sighed. "It is likely enough. I know. He has had Molly's blood, and that alone offers a protection I still do not understand. But we don't know for sure, and I am not in a hurry to see another of my descendants die. Losing his mother was hard enough, even though I did not know her. I knew of her. I checked in on her when I was able. It still hurt." She paused, and then, more quietly: "I hate to lose them."

Her voice thickened at the end, and I bowed my head. She still mourned her brother, Apollo. Of course. We had lost so many, I was beginning to lose track of who we still needed to mourn.

"Artemis, I will speak with him. I promise," I said, trying to soothe her. "You do know he has no intention of dying?"

"I know that. But we never do intend for it to happen, do we?"

At that moment, Mollis appeared with a "pop" in a spot to my left. I nodded at her, and she nodded back, then turned her gaze to Chen, who started crying.

Crying. For the love of Hades, he was pathetic.

"I know. I will stop by later. I need to finish this up first. All right?"

"Thank you. I will cook dinner, then."

I made a face at the phone as I ended the call. Artemis's cooking was its own form of torture.

"Hey," Mollis said.

"Did you know Brennan was shot?" I asked in greeting.

"I know. Asclepius took care of him," she answered. "Artemis isn't happy, from what Asclepius told me."

"So I gather," I said wryly, and Mollis gave me a sympathetic smile.

"Having the mother-in-law experience already, huh?"

I rolled my eyes, and she let out a low chuckle. Then she sobered. "So, dickhead," she said to Chen. "Are we going to do this the easy way, or do I get to have some fun?"

He started blubbering, crying, apologizing.

"All it takes is a name. Who helped you?" Mollis asked.

He laughed then, laughed, and lifted his chin in my direction. "She thinks she is helping you. One woman is nothing against us. We are legion," he said.

"Ugh. Really? We're at the 'we are legion' point in our deluded villain story already?" Mollis asked. She walked closer to Chen, slowly. His expression changed from haughtiness to fear, and I saw him swallow. Mollis took her time, walking around him, letting him lose sight of her as she went behind him. I knew this game, like cat and mouse. She stalked, and he grew more afraid, and every time he lost sight of her, his panic increased, sure that, this time, she would hurt him.

It was only proof that he and his cronies did not know my Queen very well. She always liked those she was punishing to see it coming, to know, without a doubt, that the pain is about to begin.

I stood, and nonchalantly twirled my dagger between my fingers, watching, waiting for any assistance my Queen might want.

"A name," Mollis said one more time. "Or anything else. This is your chance to lessen the pain you have coming to you." Of course, he still had plenty coming. But she meant what she said. She could make it hurt much worse, and much longer, if he did not try to be of some use now.

"She was like her," Chen said quickly, trying to stop Mollis before she started. "Longer hair, though. I haven't seen her in weeks. She was supposed to bring another one for me, and I was waiting where she told me to. She didn't come, but she warned me about this one," he said, nodding toward me again. "So when I saw her, I ran, the way the other one told me to. Though she did warn me that if you found me, I probably would not escape you," he said to me.

Well. At least my reputation as a zealot was still holding. How comforting.

"What about anyone else? Any others she spoke of, or that you saw?" Mollis asked and he shook his head.

"It was just her. Please," he begged.

It was quiet for several moments while Mollis studied him, while his sins washed over her. Undoubtedly, she was in his mind, sifting through the things he knew about his helper, sifting through memories, dusting off things he may have forgotten. He whimpered, shook his head.

After a few moments, Mollis seemed satisfied. She gave me a small nod; he had told us all he knew about our adversaries.

"I bet your victims begged while you hurt them, didn't they?" she asked quietly, still pacing behind him.

He let out a low whimper.

"And you liked it, didn't you?" Mollis continued.

He shook his head, hard, as if trying to deny it. It was of no use. Mollis had the ability, inherited from her father upon his death, to see everything about anyone who stood before her. There was no hiding your deeds from her, unless you were like her. Unless you were a Fury. The

12

Furies, being those who are tasked with punishing the dead, were, themselves, seemingly above reproach. Which, I imagined, was part of what made Mollis's father so content around her mother, the Fury Tisiphone; she was the only one whose deeds were not constantly broadcasting, forcing him to see every sin she'd committed. I knew Mollis could see everything about me. Happily, she is the only one I have no urge to hide myself from. Mollis had told me that when she first realized she had her father's powers, she had been with Tisiphone and Megaera, and all of their past deeds had hit her. It had not happened that way since, and the only theory they had for why she had seen their pasts in that moment was because her new power had just flared to life and the three of them were close, unguarded, raw in their grief over the death of Hades.

I knew she wished, now that we very obviously had a betrayer in our midst, one who could well be her own aunt or mother, that her power still applied to them the way it did to everyone else. It would have provided instant answers to the questions that plagued us.

I turned my thoughts away from problems I, as yet, had no answers to, and back to my Queen and the soul she was judging.

"I won't take any joy in this," Mollis said. "Though it is satisfying when evil shits like you beg." And it began, and I knew it would be a while before I would be able to check in on the shifter. With as many sins as Chen had, Mollis had her work ahead of her.

CHAPTER TWO

A few hours later, Mollis had satisfied herself that she had punished the soul of Chen enough. Most of Mollis's punishments were of the mental variety. She used their thoughts, their deepest fears, against them. Of course, she punished them physically as well. She hadn't needed my help at all, though I understood why she liked having me there. Having another being standing ominously off to the side only made him more afraid.

We had been doing this for a few weeks now. I would hunt, now looking for just about any missing soul I could, and I would bring it directly to Mollis, who would learn what she could from it, punish it on the spot, and then release it into the Everafter on her own. For those who had done horrid things, apparently the Everafter was not a nice place. Mollis's punishments were usually their introduction to what they had ahead of them, their own personal version of the mortal concept of hell. If they were good people, their Everafter was peace and love and being reunited with loved ones.

It was not the easiest way to handle things. It meant

that Mollis was pretty much on call, because she did not want me to have to stand around with a soul for hours until she was able to come. She also had to hide the fact that she was seeing me, due to the fact that we supposedly hated one another.

Really, I hoped her traitor would be discovered soon.

My small group of New Guardians, souls who had started following me when I had begun my hunt for lost souls, were essential in helping me find as many souls as I had. We were in a race against whoever Mollis's adversary was, it seemed, each side racing to claim a newly-deceased soul before the other side took it. Quinn, who had taken the worst of the injuries when my sisters had attacked, was back on his feet and relentless as ever. He had started to show some interest in learning to rematerialize, despite the fact that it still made him nauseous. Claire seemed to have become my second-in-command, and kept track of the movements of the other three New Guardians, reporting their successes, and, more often than we liked, failures, to me.

I had tried, gently, because I know Mollis would rather not talk about it, to suggest that she look into her mother and aunt's minds. She could do that. And this whole mess would be at least partially reconciled within minutes. So far, she had demurred, with the excuse that she would have to sift through thousands of years of memories, and there were things in her mother's mind she did not want to see again. She had torn her way into Hades' mind once, when she was captive in the Nether, and apparently had learned a hard lesson about the things one sees in the mind of a death god.

I understood that, but in this case, it seemed worth the risk. Why would you not want to just know, for sure, whether someone had betrayed you or not?

As I watched Mollis send the soul of Chen to the Everafter, which only took seconds after she was finished punishing him, I considered broaching the subject again. A

15

look at her eyes, at the razor edge of madness there, made me swallow the advice I was about to give. The souls we were missing still weighed on her. Nether still fought her for control.

Instead, I took her hand, gave it a small squeeze. "Another one down, demon girl."

She nodded. "Too many still out there, though."

"We are working on it," I said, trying to soothe her.

She gave a small smile. "I know, E. Thank you. It would be pretty handy if you discovered a few more New Guardians out there somewhere, though."

I gave a short laugh. "That it would. Though Quinn does the work of three Guardians on his own."

Mollis nodded. "Thanks for this. The only one he ever saw was Delo."

I nodded. "About her…"

Mollis sighed and shook her head. "I'm still working at her, as well as your other sisters we have in custody." She paused, looked uncomfortable. "There is still that blank space in their memories, and I know whoever is pulling the strings is there. I just wish I knew how to undo whatever was done to them to make them forget. At the same time, I really don't want to risk whoever was working with them somehow managing to help them escape."

I nodded.

"Nain has been watching their cells almost non-stop since you kicked Anthousa and Delo's asses back in Tokyo." That fight had been brutal, even beyond the loss of my wings, and I had believed, at the time, that I had killed Anthousa, at least, on the mortal plane. As it was, despite it looking as if her body had turned to dust, Mollis had found her, weakened and unconscious, not far from the building in which we had battled. I did not quite understand it, but I was glad my Queen had been able to take another enemy to interrogate. "We don't want to risk them getting out again," she continued. "But he has other work he needs to do too, and it's coming to the point where having them there and accessible is more of a liability than a help."

I could see where she was going. "So you want to end them?"

She nodded.

"I think you should do it. If they have nothing of use to offer you, do not risk keeping them around."

"You're sure you don't mind…"

"Mollis! As far as we all knew, you killed them once already. It did not pain me any then, and it certainly will not pain me now. Even less so, this time around."

She studied me. "Do you want to be there when they end? Do you want to say anything to them?"

"I have nothing to say to them. If you would like me to be there, I have no problem doing that."

"They're your sisters, E," Mollis said softly.

"They are traitors. I have seen the things they have done. I feel no loss or pity for them, only regret that they have failed so completely in what they were created to do." I paused, changing my mind and deciding to say what I intended to say earlier. "Speaking of familial traitors," I began, and Mollis shook her head. "Have you made any headway with your mother and aunt?"

She did not want to believe it possible of either of them. Truly, neither did I. But Furies are not above petty backstabbing and other betrayals. It had already happened once, with the third Fury, Alecto, whose name was no longer spoken; everyone, especially the Furies, wished they could make it so that she had never existed at all.

Alecto had betrayed her sisters, Hades, and, most of all, Mollis. She had worked directly with the demon Astaroth, Nain's oldest enemy, to get to Mollis. It had all ended badly, with Nain dying in the mortal realm. Mollis's blood in his veins, thanks to the demon marriage bond they'd performed, had been the only reason he had resurrected in the Nether. Like many beings who had been imprisoned in Tartarus, Alecto was now trapped in the Nether, the gateway between the worlds having been destroyed by Mollis and then permanently closed by Mollis's grandmother, Nyx, who was the Creator of everything known to man and god alike.

"I'm keeping an eye on it."

I repressed a sigh, but she felt my irritation anyway. "We're not all as uncomplicated as you are, E. I know. You just want me to break in and be done with this."

"Obviously," I answered. "Obviously, I want you to do that so we actually know something instead of guessing. You need to get into their minds, Mollis. Do you really want to keep going on this way?"

"Are we already falling apart here, E?" she asked me quietly.

"I am not the one falling apart," I said, looking her squarely in the eye. "You know there is nothing I would not do to help you. You know this. So take what I am about to say in the light it is meant: you need to stop being so soft about this. You need to get into their minds and have this question answered."

She sighed. "I know." Her shoulders slumped, and she looked up at the night sky. We'd walked out of the church, and were standing on the front steps. "I don't want to just force my way in, E. I do that when I have to, and if we can't figure this out, then I'll do it. But this is my family."

"It is tearing you up inside, wondering which one, or if both, betrayed you," I reminded her, and she nodded.

"It is. You haven't had that done to you, though, have you? Had someone break into your mind?"

I shook my head.

"It's an assault. An invasive, violent, terrifying assault. The only way I can explain it that truly expresses how wrong it is is that it's like mental rape. I have done that. I have broken my way into people's minds, back before I inherited my father's powers. Now, there's no need, except for these cases in which I'm trying to uncover what has been hidden from us," she said with a grimace. "This is my family, E," she stressed again. "My mother. My aunt. I don't want to do that to them. Not unless I have strong evidence to suggest that it needs to be done. Because if I'm wrong, and I do that to them... there's no way to come back from that."

We stood in silence for several long moments. "And I know that our theories point to it being at least one of them, because of the missing memories in the lost souls and your sisters. I am being careful. But you also recommended that I look at every possibility before leaping to the conclusion that it had to be one of them, remember?"

"Yes," I said. "You know, you could ask them to let you into their minds," I said.

"If it comes to that," Mollis said. "I will."

She had closed up on me, which I knew meant that our conversation was over. She would not budge on this, and I did not know how to make her see that she was only making it more difficult on herself. The illogical nature of the way she was about her family truly baffled me.

"Well. As I said before. If you desire to end my sisters, please feel free to do so. I have no remorse for traitors," I said.

"Touché, E," Mollis said wryly. "You think I'm weak."

I shook my head. "Not that. Never that. I just hope you do not end up regretting the loyalty and respect you are giving them. They may not both deserve it."

"That makes two of us, E," Mollis said softly. Then she disappeared, most likely returning to her palace in the Netherwoods to be with her mate and children.

I stood there alone for a few moments longer, and looked up at the night sky, at the puffy clouds passing over the tiny sliver of a moon. For just a moment, I felt my wings flex under my leather coat.

But of course, they hadn't. It was the memory of wing movement, the phantom reminders of what it had been like to be able to soar.

These were the times I needed it most. These were the times I needed to feel free and weightless, just for a few moments.

My mind flashed back to that day in Tokyo. My New Guardians and I had believed ourselves to be tracking prey, tracking a soul that had eluded us. We had made our way into one of the love hotels in Tokyo, and found ourselves beset by too many enemies, including two of my sisters.

Memories passed through my mind, images I would not likely forget.

My New Guardians, lying weak and injured.

The bodies of the goddesses of autumn and winter, chests ripped open, their hearts taken from them.

My wing, falling, torn and bloody, to the filthy floor.

I shook my head and closed my eyes, trying to will the images away.

It was not just the fact that I missed flying. It was the knowledge that I was now less than I should be. That I was not fully able to do the things I knew I should be able to. I had always considered myself to be a fairly even-keeled being, especially for an immortal. But the emotions that had stormed through me since waking a few weeks ago and realizing my wings were gone, for good… those were things I had not expected. I was, at turns, depressed, angry, mournful.

Frankly, it was irritating.

I forced my gaze down, away from where I longed most to be, reminding myself that I had a ridiculous shifter to reprimand. And Artemis's cooking to suffer through.

CHAPTER THREE

I rematerialized in the backyard of the cozy bungalow where Brennan had moved his small family after Mollis had "exiled" us from her inner circle. I had lived there with Brennan, his son, and Artemis for only two days before deciding it was more than I could take. I still visited most days, but it was a relief to know I did not have to live in Brennan's home.

It was not that I did not enjoy my time with the shifter. I did. Likely, I enjoyed it too much. It was very easy to forget myself when his eyes met mine, or when we sat, side by side, his strong thigh pressed to mine. The kisses we had shared in Japan, that beautiful flight we'd taken together still haunted my dreams and memories. Both of us, likely for our own reasons, had drawn back from what had started between us. There had been no more kisses once I had fully recovered, and though he still often watched me in a way that made my heart race, he had made no further advances.

I did not know whether I was grateful or irritated with him for that.

The back yard of Brennan's home, the place he had lived as a child before his parents had died, before he hd gone to the loft to be raised by Nain, was the perfect place to raise his son, Sean. It was an ideal place for a little boy to be able to call his own. A large expanse of lawn, surrounded by a chain link fence and gate (absolutely necessary for a shifter child) and it was littered by all manner of climbing, swinging, and sports equipment. There was a large apple tree, which Sean had already taken to climbing. Near the house was a brick patio with a small wooden table and two chairs.

That was where Brennan sat, and I repressed a sigh. It was always much easier when I was ready to see him, when I could prepare myself mentally for whatever confusion he caused in me. Yet there he was.

"You are a complete idiot," I said, walking toward where he sat.

He laughed. "I love you, too, Tink."

I stood, resting my hands on the back of the sturdy wooden chair across from where he sat. "I am not joking around. That was a theory, about you being immortal. I did not intend for you to go out and test it."

"Believe me, I didn't intend to get shot, either. That hurts like a son of a bitch," he said.

I felt whatever ire was inside me lessen, just a bit. "Does it still hurt?"

He shook his head. "Asclepius does good work."

I nodded. "He does. Are there still wounds?"

"No. I have a couple of new scars, but that's it."

I did not respond.

"How was your day?" he finally asked. I merely looked at him, slightly raising my eyebrow in response. He laughed. "That good, huh?" He gestured to the chair I was leaning against. "Take a load off and tell me about it. You must have pissed Artemis off. She insisted on cooking for you."

"I know," I grumbled, settling myself into the chair. "She called to blame me for you getting your fool self shot," I said. I focused, sensing. "Is Asclepius still here?" I asked, feeling the power signature of the healer immortal.

Brennan nodded, then leaned forward, gesturing for me to do the same. "I think he and Artemis are... you know..." he said.

"What?" I asked, genuinely confused.

"Oh, come on. You know what I'm saying," he said.

I shook my head.

"They're messing around."

"What, now?" I asked, glancing toward the house.

"No! Not right this second. I mean, in general. They've gone out every night I didn't need Artemis to watch Sean."

I leaned back and shook my head. "You are such a gossip," I said.

"That doesn't seem like a weird pairing to you? The kindly healer and then Artemis, who pretty much wants to put an arrow through anything that moves in a way that annoys her?"

"They are both immortals," I said.

"And, what? That's enough?" he asked.

"They understand one another in a way very few would be able to. It is difficult for someone who has not lived as we have to understand it. Most of the immortals who are interested in having relationships, sexual or otherwise, have paired with just about all of the others at one point or another. Except for Hephaestus," I added. "And the Furies. And me." I shrugged.

He did not respond, and I felt the stupid urge to keep talking. "Zeus has been with everyone who showed the slightest interest, and many who did not want him at all. Artemis seems to like the quiet types, and I do not think she ever involved herself with Zeus or Ares. There was a period of time when Apollo and Hestia lived quite happily together," I said, remembering.

He laughed, shook his head. "The immortals almost sound like Nain's team."

I tilted my head questioningly. "How so?"

"It was pretty much the same with them. For example,

when my mom met my dad, she was dating Nain. She, Ada, Ada's husband, a couple other women, and Stone were all on Nain's team. Nain had dated Ada really early on, I guess— "

"Ada?" I asked in shock, envisioning the stately older witch.

"I really do have to show you some pictures. Ada was hot."

"I do not doubt it. She is a beautiful woman. Aging is a strange thing," I said.

He grinned, then continued. "So Nain dated Ada, and they stopped but it ended on good terms. Then she started dating the man who she eventually married. Her first husband," he clarified, and I nodded. "And Nain started dating my mother but that ended after a while, too, and my mom and dad started dating. Stone dated Ada for a while too, before Nain did," he said, remembering. "I think it was likely kind of for the same reason. They all understood one another better than anyone else could. Really, I guess that trend didn't end with them."

I nodded, realizing it was true. Not only had Mollis been with both Nain and Brennan, but Shanti had dated a teammate, Levitt (a demon who we had unfortunately lost), and then Zero. Ada had married Stone a few years past.

I blushed a little, and he noticed, and once again I damned his preternatural senses.

"What, Tink?"

I shrugged.

"Tell me."

"I had been wondering if anyone would be looking at me strangely for the way I have been... involved with Nain, and then with you."

He shook his head, grinning. "Thanks for admitting we're involved."

I glared at him.

"As for the rest of it, I don't think anyone who matters

gave it a second thought. Pretty much par for the course. We all work so damn much, we'd never find anyone otherwise. And like you were saying earlier, no one else would really understand it, the way we live. We're all insane in our own way."

I nodded. "Very much like the immortals. I admit, I did not even consider that it could be seen as strange because of the way the immortals are."

"You never were involved with any of them, though," he said, bringing us back to the original discussion of immortals and their love lives. "Except for Big Red." For some reason, the shifter insisted upon referring to Triton by this particular nickname.

"We were not involved," I said. "Like Hephaestus, he was my friend. *Is* my friend," I corrected. "And no, I never was involved with anyone. I was not supposed to be interested, so I tried not to be. It was really not all that difficult."

"Why not?" he asked quietly. "You just said yourself that no one else can quite understand what it's like to have lived as long as you have. That seems like it would probably be comforting."

I looked down at the tabletop, ran my fingers across the gap between the wooden slats. "I understand myself just fine without anyone else's help," I finally said. And then I looked up. "Besides, immortals tend to be rather full of themselves, and I find that tiresome."

He grinned. "It's a good thing I'm not cocky like that, huh?"

I rolled my eyes. "When you behave that way, I find it charming for some reason. Ridiculous male."

"Eunomia. Was that a compliment?"

"Do not let it go to your head."

He was about to say something else when Artemis called us in for our punishment… or supper, depending on how one chose to look at it. And again, I was unsure whether I was grateful or irritated by the interruption.

Honestly, it seemed like I was both, and that made no sense at all.

When we went inside, we walked into the kitchen to find Asclepius standing over the stove, stirring something in a large gray pot with a concerned expression on his face. Artemis was in the dining room setting out silverware, and the local jazz station played softly on the stereo in the living room.

Asclepius looked up and greeted me with a smile, his blue eyes twinkling happily. He still retained the snow white beard and long white hair he always had, but had traded the sky blue robes he'd always worn for jeans and a garish lime green polo shirt. "Guardian!" he said, stepping toward me.

"Asclepius. It is a pleasure to see you," I said, shaking the hand he'd offered.

"Very pleased to see you, as well. How is your back?" he asked, his tone taking on the warm, concerned note he used with all of those he healed. I reflexively flexed my shoulder blades, which, once upon a time, would have had my wings fluttering. "It gives me no pain," I finally said.

He studied me. "I am sorry I couldn't save them," he said softly.

"You did what you were able to. I remember one wing being completely chopped off in the fight. There would have been no way to save it anyway."

Asclepius furrowed his brow. "I tried. Sometimes, if you reattach the limb quickly enough, we can get it to fuse again. You were already fading…" he paused. "It was, honestly, save you or save the wing. So your Queen used her blood to keep you with us while I did what I had to do. At first, we tried doing both, her suffusing you with her blood while I tried to get the wing to take. It just didn't work."

"I did not know all of that," I said. I glanced at Brennan. "You did not tell me this part."

"I didn't know. I wasn't allowed in the room while they were trying to heal you," he said, throwing Asclepius an irritated glance.

"Yes, and that seems to have been a wise choice, considering your behavior over the bandage incident, son," Asclepius said mildly. Chastened, Brennan smiled and shook his head.

"You may have a point."

I shook my head and turned back to Asclepius. "Thank you for trying."

"Mollis was insistent that I try, until your condition just kept worsening despite her blood. I do not understand why her blood didn't work, though," he said, raising his eyebrows in a questioning manner.

"Most of my injuries were from Netherblades. The damage they inflict is horrific, for those souls we hunt, and for us as well," I explained, and Asclepius nodded slowly, as if lost in thought.

"If not for that influence then, we may have been able to save them," he murmured.

I shrugged. "There is no point in 'might haves.' I am alive, and I am grateful for that. I had not realized how truly grievous my injuries were, focused as I have been on the loss of my wings. So I thank you," I said to Asclepius.

He shook my hand again with a smile. "It is my role in this new world of ours. And it is a pleasure when I am able to save someone the world truly needs." He paused again, an uncomfortable look on his face. "This thing between you and your Queen... is there anything at all I can do? She likes me. I think," he added after a pause.

"She likes you," I assured him, taking a seat at the small dining room table when Artemis motioned for us to sit. Sean clambered into a chair next to where his grandmother would be sitting, and Brennan sat beside me. "But that matters little. She has every reason to be furious with me. I knew what I was risking." I disliked lying, especially to those few beings I actually liked, and it rankled me to have to do so with Asclepius.

"But you've always been by her side… since before we even knew who she was. I don't understand how she can just toss you aside like that," he said, no little frustration in his voice.

"She's a cold bitch at times," Artemis muttered, not loudly enough for Sean to hear, but Brennan heard. I waited for him to defend Mollis, but he did not.

"She is not cold. Never that. She often must do things she dislikes. And trust is very important to her. I broke that," I said. "Please do not insult her in front of me, or we may have a problem, Artemis."

Artemis stopped in the act of spooning some of the stew (at least I guessed that was what it was) onto Sean's plate.

"Was that a threat, Guardian?" she asked softly.

"I do not make threats. I make promises," I said mildly, keeping eye contact with her.

"All right now, let's not do this, hm?" Asclepius said, trying to lighten the mood.

"So she tosses you aside, bans you from setting foot anywhere near your former team and the Netherwoods, kicks him out," she said, gesturing to Brennan, "for the crime of being the one with you at the time, and you're just okay with that?"

"It is unfortunate that her ire extended to Brennan," I said, knowing, truly, that that was what had Artemis so irritated.

"She takes any opportunity she can to— "

"You do not want to finish that sentence," I said quietly.

She glared at me. Brennan and Asclepius showed more sense than I had originally credited them with by staying out of it.

"You and I have never had a problem, Guardian. I have always found you to be sensible. But this is completely asinine and the insult she has given to my family won't be forgotten," Artemis hissed.

"It wasn't an insult to your family, Grandma," Brennan finally said. "She's pissed at me because I went along with E and kept what was going on to myself. It's not the first time she's been pissed at me, and I don't think it'll be the last," he finished with a grin.

Artemis just grunted.

"Erm. About that," Asclepius said, looking uncomfortable again. "Word among our kind is that her ire over the situation is fueled by whatever it is that is going on between the two of you," he said, glancing between me and Brennan.

"Nothing is going on between us," we said in unison. Despite our earlier discussion, it seemed to be something we were protecting, something just for the two of us, both of us almost possessive of the fledgling relationship that was growing between us.

"Because you're both idiots," Artemis muttered as she tried to cajole Sean into taking a bite of something that may have been a potato.

"Whether there is or not, it is clear the two of you have gotten closer these past weeks," Asclepius said. He pushed some of the food around on his plate, trying not to grimace. Then he looked back up. "The first time I met you," he said, looking at Brennan, "I was there at the behest of Hades because you were gravely ill and Mollis begged him to help you somehow."

"Yes, and thanks," Brennan said. "But that feels like a lifetime ago, and she has everything she wanted back then. This has nothing to do with anything like that. She hates secrets, and she hates lying even more," Brennan said.

I could tell the conversation was starting to make him edgy. He disliked the charade just as much as I did, and neither of us felt comfortable hearing Mollis insulted.

"Do you want to take a walk?" I asked him, and he gave a terse nod. We got up, scraped our plates off into the garbage, loaded them into the dishwasher, and then left out the side door.

When we reached the end of the driveway, Brennan took my hand in his and we started walking down the tree-lined street he lived on. Small homes, almost identical in appearance, lined both sides. The streetlights that we passed gave everything a bluish glow, and I could hear, occasionally, a dog bark, or the sounds of television coming from the homes we passed.

"Are you working tonight?" I asked him, lacking anything better to say and far too distracted by how much I enjoyed being close to him.

He nodded. "I'm patrolling with the Grosse Pointe shifter alpha later."

"How is that working out?" I asked, and he gave my hand a gentle squeeze. The alpha of the Grosse Pointe shifter pack was not one of Brennan's favorite people, mainly because the man, the alpha, saw Brennan as a challenge to his authority. And, really, he was. Brennan had slowly but surely started to become recognized as a sort of alpha among alphas. He was the only one the shifter leaders would take orders from, most likely because they were able to sense that he out-powered them. Just as immortals do, shifters respect power even when they respect nothing else.

He shrugged. "It's all right. I can tell he wants to get yappy sometimes, but he has enough sense to just shut up and work."

I hid a smile. There was that arrogance, which, on any other male, I would have found distasteful. He did not state things to brag. He was honest. He recognized his strengths and had no problem with using them to his advantage.

"Is he still trying to set you up with his daughter?" I asked quietly, immediately wanting to kick myself for being pathetic enough to ask.

"Who told you about that?"

"Artemis," I said, breathing out an irritated breath. "I

think she was trying to goad me. She is angry with me over this entire thing."

"Which is stupid, but she's stubborn if nothing else," he said. "Yes, he's still trying to set me up with his daughter. I'm not interested and I told him so."

"Why not?"

He stopped walking and draw me into his arms, lowering his lips to mine, claiming my mouth as if he had every right to do so, as if the concept of me refusing to kiss him hadn't even entered his mind.

And he was right. I had no intention of refusing what I had been longing for the past several weeks. He held me tightly in his arms, and his lips on mine felt even more wonderful than I'd remembered. I was warm throughout my body, and when he traced his tongue over my lips, I opened, granting him the access I knew he wanted. After a few breathless, perfect moments that had my head spinning, he brushed his lips across mine one last time, and backed away.

We stood on a dark corner, and it almost looked as if his eyes glowed when he looked at me.

"Does that answer your question, Eunomia?" he asked, and I wet my lips, nervously running a hand through my hair.

"I thought…" I began, trailing off. Conversations like this one made me uncomfortable. In all honestly, I truly had not had to deal with anything quite like this before him.

"What, Tink? You thought that what happened in Japan was a fluke, that it wouldn't continue here?" I did not answer, and he stood, watching me as my mind went back to a flight we had shared together, the intensity of our first kiss once we landed. "You want it to, don't you?" he asked quietly, shaking me out of my memory.

"I do not know," I said.

"Yeah you do," he said, and even though I was looking down at my feet, I could hear the warmth in his voice, the smile there. "You're just freaked out by the fact that you want something that has nothing to do with duty or stabbing things."

"I only stab things as a matter of duty," I said, and he laughed, low, in a way that sent a pleasant tingle down my spine.

"Way to ignore the rest of it," he said quietly, and when I looked up at him, he was still smiling warmly. We had had this conversation before, of course, and it had mostly ended the same way.

"I am not ignoring it. What is it? Do you need so badly to hear me say the words?" I asked.

His face closed down, and I knew immediately that I had said the wrong thing.

"I did not mean it that way," I said softly, stepping closer to him. I rested my hands on his waist and leaned my head against his chest. He immediately wrapped me in his arms, and we stood that way. "You see what the issue is, yes? I have no idea how to do this."

He was silent for a few moments, and I continued talking. "This frustrates me. You confuse the Nether out of me, even though you try not to. I want things to be good between us. I want whatever this is to continue to grow, and I do not want it to end in such a way that we will be unable to even be in the same room together without it being awkward."

"You know, we haven't even really started anything and you're already thinking of how it's going to end," he said, squeezing me close to him. Held as I was, in his strong arms, pressed up against the firmness of his body, I could barely contain myself. Even breathing became complicated in his presence.

"I am very old. I am a master at planning ahead," I said wryly, and he laughed and started running his hand up my spine. I shivered at his touch, and when he reached the back of my neck, he gave my hair a gentle tug, a demanding movement that forced me to look up at him.

I should not have found that as alluring as I did.

"If I have my way, Eunomia, there won't be any kind of end for us."

I stared up at him, unable to even form words, unable to think of any to say in the first place.

"You said you like things to be spelled out for you. You are mine. I'm just waiting for you to realize it."

And with that, he let me go, took my hand, and started walking again.

I swallowed, and my face burned. We walked in silence for several minutes, and he turned toward the nearest main street. I could hear the traffic from where we were, and I could smell the aroma of food wafting from the restaurants there. "I'm starving," he said.

"Me too," I managed.

"Artemis's revenge," he said, looking down at me and grinning.

I gave a short laugh. "There is a burger place that way, yes?"

He nodded, and we went out to eat an awkward dinner together before he left for his patrol shift.

CHAPTER FOUR

When Brennan left to go to work, I rematerialized back to the apartment I was renting. It was a one bedroom unit, furnished simply, with a remarkable view of the city and the river beyond.

It is good to be friends with powerful people. In this case, the vampire queen of the Midwest region. Rayna. Not that she went easy on me, rent-wise, but I was happy to pay for the quiet location and private entrance. Word was that she'd kept a lover here for many years, but I was not sure how much truth there was to it. Rumors surround Rayna in the same way that honey draws flies.

I shrugged out of my coat and glanced at the clock. Brennan and I would be leaving in a few hours for our next mission to reclaim Mollis's lost souls. This time, we would be going to Denmark. In the past two weeks, we had been to Italy, India, and Pakistan. It was no longer merely an issue of tracking down my list of souls. Whoever was working against Mollis was taking newly-dead souls as well, before the crows even had a chance to claim them. And just when we began to think we figured out where they might be headquartered, they would start taking souls from a different part of the world.

They knew us too well. This is the problem with facing adversaries who have been among you and your kind for thousands of years.

I sat and rested my head against the back of the sofa as I thought. It was better not to think about Brennan but it was pointless not to. And while the things he'd said, that kiss, the feel of being in his arms were all definitely worth reliving, I worried that I already spent far too much time mooning over him. And there were other things that demanded my attention.

I felt tired. So much more tired than I should.

The act of going back and forth, rematerializing from city to city, tired me in a way it had not before the battle against my sisters. I was not fully myself yet. I did not know if that was due to the weapons they used against me still taking their toll, or emotional nonsense over my wings, over my sisters' existence and role in this new mess opposing Mollis. Likely, it was a bit of everything. Including the shifter who seemed determined to keep my life in turmoil.

It was all getting too muddied, too complicated. The fact that I was even beginning to feel as if I had some claim on the shifter was a giant warning sign that I could not afford to ignore any longer. I no longer believed, as I once had, that I needed to be emotionless. I was not, and trying to be something I was not only weakened me. But it did not change the fact that I have always been, at heart, a solitary creature. I was ruthless, unstoppable, focused. And I needed to be those things, especially in the current reality, especially with forces mounting against my Queen, forces that only I could fight against. I could not afford to be distracted, no matter how much I would have liked to let him distract me.

I grimaced and got up from the sofa and hastily packed the bag I would be taking with me to Denmark, then climbed into my bed, intending to get a few hours of sleep. I tossed and turned, my mind on overdrive. We were tracking the next soul on Mollis's list, along with claiming any souls in the area before Mollis's enemies could claim them first. We had three of my sisters in custody. But the fact that more souls were still coming up missing, the fact that the crows, myself, or my New Guardians were often too late to claim a soul, told us that it was very likely that at least one of my sisters was still in play. That, or there were enough undead about to make it nearly impossible to keep up with the new undead they were creating. Still, I wondered about my sisters.

How many still remained? Were all of them somewhere out there? Three were in Mollis's prison in the Netherwoods... if all those we thought were dead were still alive and well, that meant there were still nine of them left unaccounted for, despite all odds.

I did not believe they had all made it. Delo, when we had fought, had made it sound as if few remained, and I had been enough of a problem that they had ultimately come after me.

I would not be happy until every single one of them was either confirmed dead or captured. This was my own personal mission, in addition to the things I did for Mollis.

I finally dozed off, and woke in time to get myself cleaned up before heading back to Brennan's house to pick him up before we made the jump to Copenhagen. He greeted me with a nod, and I wordlessly took his hand, focused, and we fell away.

Copenhagen was not a place I knew very well. I had been there perhaps a handful of times during my existence. I had scouted ahead a week ago, finding a place where we could rematerialize without any mortals seeing us.

"There is a hotel this way," I said to Brennan, nodding my head to my right. We had appeared behind a store that I'd previously scouted and found to be closed for renovations. There were large dumpsters behind it, full of construction materials, and we had reappeared behind one of them.

Brennan nodded, keeping my hand in his as we turned out onto the street. Like many of the older European cities, this one was almost too narrow for modern traffic, and was flanked by tall stone and brick buildings. Black lampposts dotted the curb at regular intervals. The scent of bread wafting from a nearby bakery, combined with the scent of the sea air, filled the air. I felt myself relaxing, just a bit. I was still more comfortable in places like this, having spent most of my existence escorting souls from Europe. If anywhere other than Detroit could be considered "home," it was Europe. It really did not matter which city. They all had their differences, their own flavors and cultures, but I loved them all fairly equally.

We continued walking, turning a corner to the street where our hotel was located. "The New Guardians are here already. I brought them yesterday," I said quietly to Brennan. "They are scouting for any sign of lost souls, as well as doing their level best to beat whoever it is we're working against to any newly-dead souls."

"Are they keeping up?" he asked.

I shrugged. "They were able to get to two yesterday and held them until the crows showed up. They are doing their best."

"They can't do a whole lot other than hold them though, right?" he asked. "They can't actually claim them for Molly. They can't actually turn them over to her. They can't even de-power them the way you can with your Netherblade."

"No. They cannot."

He took a breath. "I know you don't want to take the chance, but— "

"You are right. I do not want to take the chance. I know you want me to fully train them. You want me to figure out how to get them Netherblades of their own. I am not comfortable with that. Not now."

"Are they Guardians or not?" he asked.

I glanced at him. "Gods, I hope not."

He shook his head. "You know, you can't predict how the future will turn out. And I get that you feel like you should be able to know everything, anticipate everything because of how much you've seen in your life, but you can't. Sometimes, you have to take a chance."

I arched an eyebrow at him. "Are we talking about my New Guardians now, or are we talking about us?"

"Both," he muttered. "But we'll have to take a backseat to the more pressing problem. You can't do it all alone. And I'm useless in dealing with the dead. And it pisses me off to have to admit that."

"If I teach them how to fight, and then put weapons in their hands, the types of weapons that can actually hurt me, and they betray me…" I shook my head. "I would rather just not sleep or rest and do it all myself."

"Tink."

"No. I cannot go through that again, Brennan, and I am really irritated that you cannot seem to understand that."

He stopped, pulling my hand to make me stop and face him. "I get it. Okay? I get it. But you can't do this yourself, Eunomia. And you try to hide it, but I know you're not a hundred percent yet, not after what happened in Japan." I tensed, and he continued. "And don't get all prickly with me over it. I don't know anyone else who would be out fighting and kicking ass two weeks after losing major body parts. This isn't a commentary on how strong or capable you are. It's common sense."

I looked away. "I am fine."

"Of course you are. It's the only way you know how to be," he said, frustration in his tone. "You don't think I notice the way you hold yourself sometimes, like your whole body is trying to curl in on itself to stop the pain? You don't think I see how, even when you're fighting, you're off balance and less sure? Your wings were part of your balance, your stance. I know it feels weird without them, and you're out here throwing yourself into this shit— "

"What else am I supposed to do, Brennan?" I demanded, finally losing my patience. He was the only one, it seemed, who was capable of making me lose it. "Am I supposed to lie around while Mollis's enemies work to weaken her further?'

"No— "

"Am I supposed to wait until I know perfectly well how well I can fight? Should I baby myself until— "

He held his hands up. "Okay. Stop."

I glared at him. People continued to walk past us, eyeing us usually with irritation as they did, since we were stopped in the middle of the sidewalk.

"I'm just saying, you're trying to do all of this alone and there's no need for it. And despite the fact that you'd wipe the floor with most beings, even with what you're going through now, I still want you to be careful. It was too close last time," he finished more quietly, eyes on mine. "It was too close, and I don't want to see you like that again."

"Careful is more likely to get me killed than anything else. You know this," I said, reaching up and resting my hand on his cheek, feeling the brush of his beard against my skin. He nuzzled into my hand, eyes still on mine.

"I know," he finally said. "Will you at least think about what I said about the New Guardians? The sooner you train them and work out the way your team functions, the better."

I sighed, pulling my hand away from his face. As I did, he took my wrist in his hand and brought my hand up to his lips, pressing a soft, warm kiss to my palm. That simple touch, the barest touch of his lips, had my body warming, shivers running up my spine. My mouth felt dry.

"I will give it some thought," I finally said.

He nodded, a small smile on his lips. "Thank you."

We checked into our hotel, then immediately headed out again. Brennan was meeting with his government counterpart in Copenhagen, trying to get any information about either strange, unexplained things, or, worse, word about any indication of undead activity. He planted a kiss on my lips before turning and walking away, his shoulders stiff, his entire posture radiating the fact that he disliked the fact that I was going off to do this without him, even though he well knew there was nothing he could do to help me.

There was a small theater where one of the lost souls, Anselm Fisker, had worked back in the day. He'd also stalked women from the audience, following them home, terrorizing them for weeks, and sometimes months on end, before finally killing them. He had never been caught, and those were the souls who always tended to be the most cocky, because they believed their luck would hold out forever.

They did not have me coming for them during their mortal lives.

I made my way to the theater. It was rarely used now, and mostly held the unmistakable scent of abandonment, that musty, stale odor that results when there are no doors opening and closing, no press of warm bodies moving in and out of a space. I supposed one could find places like that depressing. That was probably the appropriate response. I had always found them to be nearly sacred. There was something beautiful in a place, or even a person, that has lived out the course of its usefulness and rests in the final pulses of its natural life. This was one such place.

When I rematerialized inside, I found my New Guardians there waiting for me. Quinn stood, as he always seemed to. He was always watching, always ready, and I appreciated having someone like him helping me. He gave me a respectful nod when I appeared, and two of the women on my team, Claire and Erin, greeted me warmly. They genuinely seemed happy to see me, and I was happy to see them as well. We fought well together, barely needing words anymore for everyone to know what they wee supposed to be doing. They were an enormous help to me, ruthless and thorough.

I really hoped I could count on them not being betraying, backstabbing liars, the way almost all of the former Guardians had been.

Once we'd all greeted one another, I brought us back to the topic at hand. "We have two souls here in Copenhagen," I began.

"We got one already," Erin said, utter glee apparent in her voice.

I raised my eyebrow, looked around at my New Guardians. "Excuse me?"

"There was this guy, soul, kind of skulking around and we knew he didn't belong here, obviously," Erin continued. "So we kicked his ass and Cathleen is holding him."

I glanced at Quinn, who, stoic though he usually was, almost seemed unable to avoid smiling.

"Where?" I asked, and Claire took my hand, and the others joined hands with us as well. "There's a graveyard not far from here. Do you know it?" she asked me, and I nodded. "She's there," she added, and I focused, rematerializing all four of us to the old graveyard. Rows of weathered stones stretched all around us, along with several large marble monuments. At the base of one of them, I spotted Cathleen standing, holding the arm of a soul in her strong grasp.

I felt a smile spread across my face. This was indeed one of mine. Bors Larssen, who had been sure that God was telling him to rid the world of redheads. At least, that was what he had claimed when he'd tried to plead insanity for his crimes to the human courts. Mollis knew better, and so did I. It was a whole ridiculous backstory about his first girlfriend who was a redhead and his refusal to let go when his pride was hurt. Murderers, especially serial murderers like this one, always had one thing in common: they saw themselves as heroes. Even if they would never quite state it that way, they did. They believed their victims deserved it somehow, and that their world would be better for the deaths they caused.

"He was on the list," I said, and Erin and Cathleen smiled, obviously pleased. "Did he give you much trouble?"

Currently, the "he" in question was whimpering and trying to break free of Cathleen's grip. I casually pulled one of my Netherblades from its sheath and stuck it into his back. He stopped moving, but continued to whimper.

"He tried to run when he saw us, but he didn't get far," Quinn said. "He was followin' a pretty redhead around. We watched him follow her as she went to three different stores, and then he started following her to the bus and we grabbed him."

I shifted my gaze to Larssen. "You have not let it go yet, I see. One would think you would have possibly learned your lesson after spending all that time in prison."

He swore at me in Danish and I ignored him.

"So you just stumbled across him, then?" I asked Claire, and she nodded.

"We were near the theater, but we usually try to keep an eye out for any souls while we're waitin' for ye," she said. "And we spotted 'im and we knew we still had a few hours before you planned to arrive, so we figured at least it wouldna be wasted time if we tracked 'im for ye."

Larssen continued his verbal tirade as she spoke, glaring at me, still cursing.

"Oh, for fuck's sake," Quinn finally said, stepping forward and landing a hard punch to Larssen's face. Larssen crumpled to the ground. "I don't know what you were saying but it sounded disrespectful. Stay down," he added, kicking the soul when he tried to stand. Then Quinn turned to me. "So this was one of yer twenty-seven?"

I nodded. "He was a serial murderer. Of redheads," I added, and Quinn shook his head in disgust. I looked around at my New Guardians. "You did amazing work here today, and you have my thanks. Would it do any good at all to remind you to be careful?"

"We were careful," Erin said.

"You had Cathleen holding him by herself," I said, raising my eyebrows.

"She's fully capable of doing that," Quinn said. "When we spar, she comes close to besting me more often than not."

"Yeah, and someday I will," Cathleen warned, and Quinn grinned.

"If you say so," he told her, then he turned his gaze back to me. "I would not have had her guarding him if I thought otherwise."

I swallowed the response I was about to give, that he should have put a second guard on him, just in case. This was exactly what Brennan had been trying to tell me about needing to trust them. I was not there yet, but I could at least respect that Quinn knew the New Guardians better than I did at this point, and that he seemed to genuinely care about keeping them safe and having them in top fighting form.

"Thank you," I said instead. "I will escort him to the Netherwoods," I said. I had mentioned to my New Guardians that I had had a falling out with Mollis, because in the horrible event that one of them might be taken by the enemy, I needed it to look as if even my closest allies knew I was fighting with Mollis. They did not know any details, and that was probably for the best. As far as they knew, I just left them somewhere in the Netherwoods, and they were taken care of. It was all they needed to know, for now.

I glanced at our soul, who was lying silently on the ground, seething, Quinn and Cathleen ready to grab him if he tried anything stupid. "Our other soul here is Anselm Fisker. He was active near the docks, especially to the west." I thought back to what I knew of him. "He was not tall, perhaps only a few inches taller than I am. He had pale blond hair, a very angular, sharp look about him. He married women and then killed them. Usually he dumped their bodies there, and that was how he was found."

Erin made a sound of disgust.

"How many did he kill?" Claire asked.

"He wedded and murdered five wives," I said. "If you would start patrolling the west end docks, we can get a head start on finding him, hopefully. When I return from taking this one to his judgment, I will join you."

They all nodded, and Quinn met my eyes before turning and following the rest of them in the direction that would take them to the docks.

I watched them go, then pulled my phone from my pocket and sent a text to Mollis: "RWYA." Shortened code for "ready when you are," as in, if she was able to get away and meet me in the church, I could meet her there. I waited for a few minutes, and my phone finally dinged.

"NiF." Now is fine. I put my phone back in my pocket, hauled Larssen up to his feet, and focused on rematerializing in the abandoned church in Detroit.

I kept a hold on Larssen's arm and looked around. Shadows played across the graffitied walls, and a rat scurried where the pulpit had once stood.

Within moments, Mollis appeared a few feet away from me.

"Thanks, E," she said, pulling me into a hug.

One glance at her told me things were not right. It had been fewer than two days since I had captured my last soul, and even then, she had looked tired, tense. The goddess who stood before me now was even paler than usual, the bluish veins beneath her skin visible. She had the stretched, painful look of someone who had lost too much weight too quickly, and the dark circles under her eyes made her look much, much older than she actually was.

"Mollis," I whispered. She met my eyes, and for just a second, I thought she would cry. I thought she would let go of the control she holds so dearly.

Instead, she looked away, hunching her shoulders. "Let's get this over with," she said. Her voice was hollow, hard. I could just imagine how Nain was handling this drastic change in his mate, and I was immediately beset with guilt. I needed to work faster. I needed to do more.

"Fuck that mess, E," Mollis growled, and my gaze shot back to her face. She was glaring at me, a feral, angry expression replacing the exhausted one. "You're doing more than anyone. Do not do that. Do not beat yourself up. It pisses me off."

"I have the feeling everything pisses you off of late, demon girl," I said, trying to lighten her mood. It did not work.

"Everything does. Yeah," she said. Her gaze went to the soul, and his eyes widened and he started begging. "We're gonna get some answers today," she said, and the ice in her voice was enough to make even me feel like running. "The sooner you talk, the sooner the pain will stop," she told him. And then it began.

I was the only one who has ever seen my Queen this way, and I know I was likely the only one, including her mate, who could come away from it without being totally unsettled. It was in moments like these when she was every bit Hades' daughter, with the righteous rage of a Fury. His cold, calculating, frighteningly accurate punishments, along with the sheer strength that comes from being her mother's daughter. Her punishment was a scalpel when it needed to be, a bludgeon, a blade, fire and fear. She used it all, bringing her prey to the edge of ceasing to exist, and then pulling him back from the abyss only to begin again.

It was during moments like this when she was everything she usually tried to pretend she was not. This was when she fully became what she feared most about herself. All I could do was stand by and watch, and wait for her to ask for help. She usually did not.

Mollis broke into his mind, and, based on her infuriated muttering, found the same blank space the Furies have found in every recaptured soul, as well as in the minds of my sisters when we've managed to take them. Neither of us paid any attention to his screams as they eventually turned to sobs, then whimpers.

"I feel filthy just looking in here. Remind me to maim you as part of your punishment," Mollis hissed at Larssen, and he started crying again. "You are a sick little shit, you know that?"

He just cried, and Mollis exchanged a look with me and rolled her eyes. She had even less respect for the ones who cried. She grew disgusted eventually, frustrated, and she kicked him, hard, and he went silent.

She blew out a breath, put her hands on her hips, and paced back and forth, her humongous wings sweeping the thick dust on the stone floor. "There has to be some way to get around that," she muttered. "You can't hide things from me. I'm the motherfucking God of Death. Final judge and jury. This is…"

"This is something we will figure out," I said, trying to rein her back in. "Is it just blank, or do you feel something there?"

"It's blank," she said, still pacing. "But it's weird. I mean, I know how it's done. I've done it," she said, and I knew this was not something she was especially proud of. Before she knew what she could do, or who she was, she'd taken the memories of mortals who had crossed her path, because she did not want to be known or remembered.

That ship had very clearly sailed.

But it made sense for her then, and she had done it fairly often. It was something only Furies could do, which was why, unfortunately, her mother and aunt were our prime suspects.

"It all seems far too clean and easy to me," I said quietly, rubbing my hand over my shoulder.

"What do you mean?"

"Have you considered that your mother and aunt know very well that we know the memories are being erased, and that they are the only ones other than you who can do that?"

"Anyone who is stupid enough to betray me is likely to overlook a few things. Or think I'm stupid enough not to notice what's happening," she said, waving it off. "There is no other possibility. It's just a matter of trying to figure out which one it was. As you keep reminding me," she added.

"Yes. And there was no possibility for there to be souls you knew nothing about. There was no possibility that my sisters still lived," I pointed out, and she glared at me. It was a look that usually worked, because, to be honest, my Queen was an exceptionally intimidating being. It was not so much in her appearance, though there was a definite menace to her. It was in her power, which roared over whoever happened to be nearby, suffocating, dark and full of rage. Even those who do not know what she is could feel it. Mortals had a hard time being in her vicinity without becoming violent.

I, however, have known her since before she uncovered all of that power. I still remembered the young woman who doubted every move she made, who hated the violence she caused. And I knew, at heart, that is still who Mollis was. Her power did not frighten me. I just looked back at her and raised my eyebrows.

"Finished now?" I asked calmly. "Temper tantrums do not work on me, demon girl."

She snarled and turned away, pacing again.

"You know what I am saying, and you know it makes sense. You do not believe in your heart that they would do this to you."

"Meg might," Mollis said, still pacing. "My mother wouldn't. God, I hope my mother wouldn't," she added, a pleading tone in her voice. "I have my imps watching her when she's with my kids," she said, and now her voice was full of pain. "Do you know what that feels like, to not be able to trust one of the very few people you've truly come to rely on?"

"I do," I said quietly. She met my eyes, gave a small nod. "Perhaps you should tell your mother about all of this," I added.

"And if Tisiphone chooses Megaera's side over mine?" Mollis asked. Then she shook her head. "I hate this. I hate all of it."

"I know." I glanced back at the soul of Larssen on the ground, lying still and trying not to draw Mollis's attention. "This one's time is up anyway. See what more you are able to do," I said, and he started crying. Mollis met my gaze, and I nodded. "You might feel better," I added.

"We really need to find time to sit around and eat chocolate and watch Disney movies or something," she said. "That would make me feel better." She pulled the soul of Larssen back up. "So would getting laid, though."

"Well, I cannot help you with that one," I said wryly.

She huffed out a small laugh. "No, I guess not. Only demon love will do for that."

I scrunched up my face uncomfortably. "Is there a problem there?" I asked as she studied the soul.

She sighed. "No. He's trying to get me to actually sleep when we have a few minutes. He doesn't get that time with him, time spent in that way, does more for me than sleep ever will. He feels guilty all the time."

"What does he feel guilty about?" I asked.

"Everything," she muttered. "Everything. All of this. If he'd never let me kill Astaroth all those years ago, none of this immortal bullshit ever would've happened. And when you think about it all that way, it's pretty messed up, because he's right."

"Would you go back to that if you were able to?" I asked.

She shook her head. "No. I am what I was meant to be. I am my Father's daughter." She transferred her gaze to the soul. "And I'm gonna live up to his legacy." The next moment, she was breaking into his mind, and the screams started all over again.

After what could have been minutes or hours, Mollis let out an excited shout, and I shot up from where I was perched on a low stone bench, one of the few bits of adornment remaining in the church.

"What?" I asked.

She held up a finger, focusing on the soul. "Bors Larssen, you were absolute garbage in life, and continued to be garbage in death. You have suffered at my hands. And now, we've reached the end." She pulled the sword from the scabbard on her hip, and, the second her hand touched the pommel, black flames started to lick along the edges of the blade. The soul could do little more than whimper.

Mollis removed his head with one clean, long swipe of the blade. We both watched it fall to the ground, and the body slumped beside it. Within moments, both head and body had dissolved into nothing more than dust.

She shifted her gaze to me, a slight smile on her lips. "I still don't know who, or how. But I know those memories aren't erased the same way I would erase them."

I shook my head. "What does that even mean?"

"When we erase a memory, when we take one, it's gone. It's as if it never happened. The person has no idea something was taken from them, because they have no idea there was supposed to be something there in the first place. Are you following me?"

"A perfect erasure. As if it never existed at all," I said, and she nodded, still smiling. "All right. And?"

"And he knew something was taken from him. Even if he didn't realize it, the flash of a thought was there, that I was looking for something that was taken. He didn't know who took it, or when, or how or why. But he knew something was gone."

I watched her. "So not a Fury, then, maybe."

Her expression darkened a little. "It doesn't make them

free and clear, E. It was still someone who knew the Nether and how it and I work very, very well. It was someone who can manipulate someone mentally. There aren't many who can claim those things."

"All right. But that does at least give us the possibility that it was not your mother or aunt. This is all good," I said. "Though it does leave us with more questions than before."

She was studying me. "You don't want it to be Tisiphone," she said quietly.

"I like your mother, demon girl. She has my respect, and I would hate to have to face that I am such a poor judge of character." I paused. "I do not care either way about Megaera, though."

She laughed. "She has that endearing quality about her," she said.

I took in the pale complexion again, the tired eyes. "Mollis," I said.

"Hm?"

"You should take one of these hunting trips with me sometime. It would be very efficient. Capture, judge, destroy, and done."

She gave me a small smile. "We both know I can't do that, E. I'm needed where I am."

"A day or two, Mollis. You can get away. Hades sometimes disappeared for months at a time."

"That was Hades," she said. "And he didn't have the mess I have. Maybe after a few thousand years, I'll feel comfortable enough to take a day off." Her expression clouded. "I don't want to do this shit today. Thinking about spending millennia, spending the rest of my existence this way…" she trailed off, shaking her head. "I guess part of me does wish that none of this had ever happened," she added quietly, referring to our earlier conversation about her husband. "And that's selfish and whiny and you're the only one I feel even remotely comfortable confessing that to." She sat down beside me, and I took her hand in mine. She rested her head against mine, and we sat together in companionable silence for a few precious moments.

"It is fine to feel overwhelmed and afraid. It is even fine to feel like you are failing. It is evidence of how much you care, that you have these feelings. You have always been harder on yourself than anyone else," I told her. She was still, quiet, and I knew, because of all we have been through together, that I am one of the few she trusts to bring her back to herself. "If none of this had happened, you would never have known your father. Your mother. You would never have loved the shifter," I said, and it struck me that this could be a really odd conversation, considering my current status with the shifter in question. "And you know that loving him helped you learn more about yourself. You grew during your time with him, and when you had the chance to be with your mate again, you were strong enough, confident enough, to ensure that you were an equal partner to him." She squeezed my hand, and I continued. "You would never have found Zoe. You would never have given birth to young Hades. Your city, my friend, would have been over-run with demons and other nightmares, because even though you had no idea back then who you were, your father's enemies knew of you. You would have had no way to protect anyone, had you not stumbled into your powers after the night you destroyed Astaroth."

"We wouldn't have become friends," she said quietly.

"Probably not," I answered. "And perhaps it is selfish of me, but I am happy to have you in my life, demon girl. I would take the pain you suffer from you if I could, but I am glad you found your way to what you really are."

We were silent for a while. "I'm a mess, E," she finally said.

"You are fine," I said. "You are comparing yourself to your father and falling short. Yes?"

She nodded.

"I think perhaps you should talk to Persephone. She lived with your father for thousands of years. They were…" I trailed off. "He loved your mother, but he loved Persephone as well," I said, feeling awkward.

"I know he did. He was drawn to my mom because of the whole 'power wants power' thing. He wanted my mom the way Brennan wanted me. It was more instinct than anything else," she said. "But Persephone, he chose for himself, and she made him happy." She paused. "I think they would have ended up together again. Maybe it would have taken a few thousand years, maybe not. My parents loved each other, but it was infatuation more than anything else. I think that gets old, in time."

"Thank you for saving me from feeling like an imbecile for saying that," I said wryly, and she laughed. "Back to my point… your father did not have it all figured out. He was not always the stoic, hard man you knew. He had his moments of insecurity, though the rest of us rarely saw them. Persephone did, though. Perhaps she could shed some light on how he handled it all when things became impossible."

She sat up and looked at me. "That's a really good idea, E."

"Of course it is. I had it," I replied. She elbowed me, laughing.

"She's avoiding me, though. I have tried talking to her. She takes off the second she notices me coming toward her. And I don't want to be an insensitive asshole. I know it must hurt her to even look at me, considering everything I represent."

"I suppose I am not surprised. It may be worth trying harder, however. And she may find some therapeutic value in being of help as well."

We sat for a while longer together, and then she finally rose with a sigh. "Time to get back to it. I've been gone too long already." I stood, and she folded me in a strong hug. "Be careful, E," she murmured.

"You too." I gave her a quick squeeze, and then focused, leaving her behind as I returned to Denmark and whatever awaited me there.

CHAPTER FIVE

Brennan and I walked down a dark, rancid-smelling alleyway in Copenhagen. It was night, and we had been on the hunt for Anselm Fisker for hours. My New Guardians had found nothing at the docks, and I had assigned them the task of searching another area of the city Fisker was known to frequent in his lifetime.

I knew the shifter was getting frustrated. Of course, he disliked not being able to find what it was I was searching for. But he also could tell that I was even more tense than usual, and it seemed to wear on him, especially when I did not open up about what was bothering me. I did not want to talk to him about Mollis and the fact that I could far too easily see her going over the edge, breaking under the insane amount of pressure on her. She had trusted me with her vulnerability, and I was not going to betray that.

No matter what she said, it came down to one thing: I needed to find these souls faster.

"I think he has moved on," I finally said, turning to Brennan with a sigh. "We would have found him."

He nodded. "So he's not staying where he died," he said.

"Which very likely means he is working with our enemies. Yes."

"So what next?"

I scrubbed a hand over my face. "I do not know." He just watched me, waiting. "It feels like we are running around like ducks with their heads cut off."

"Chickens, Tink."

"Hm?"

"The phrase is 'running around like chickens with their heads cut off.'"

"Oh. Well I knew it was some kind of bird, anyway," I said, distracted. "We need to be more systematic about this." I took a breath. "From what Mollis said to me, since that last face-off against my sister, it seems as if the number of souls we're being beaten to has not slowed. In fact, it has gotten worse. That makes no sense. With fewer Guardians to steal the souls from me and the crows, it should be slowing." I shook my head.

"So how does that even make sense, then?" Brennan asked. Then he glanced around, taking in the damp, dark surroundings. "If we're not looking anymore, can we get out of this alley?"

I nodded, rematerialized us to my New Guardians to tell them to stop looking, and then I rematerialized Brennan back to our hotel room. Once we were there, he rifled through his bag and began devouring most of a bag of beef jerky. The man thought about food more than anyone I knew, I thought with some amusement as I watched him.

Of course, amusement turned to something else after he finished eating and started pulling his shirt off, revealing far too much toned muscle, it seemed, for my mind to handle. I looked down at my hands. I really should encourage him to keep his clothing on. Especially since we are not at the point of doing anything interesting when he has his clothing off.

"Okay. So explain that. We're losing souls, but the other side doesn't have your sisters anymore, or, at least, they have fewer of them. So how are they still messing with Molly?"

He lay on the bed, stretching out behind me as I sat on the edge of the bed. Do not turn around, do not turn around, do not turn around, I told myself.

Of course, I was incapable of listening to reason, even when it came from myself, where he was concerned. So of course I turned around, and of course, there he was, bare-chested, his arms folded under the back of his head, watching me. The only thing that would have made him look more perfect was if his hair had been loose instead of pulled back as it was. He did not even know he had that effect on me, at least, I did not think he knew. He was utterly comfortable in his body. I was not there yet, and when he was like that, I felt as virginal as I had been for most of my existence.

I looked away. "I believe they are simply taking matters into their own hands. Why wait for humans to die, when they can kill them, turn them, and add to their army all in one fell swoop?"

He was silent for a long while. "So it's not just a matter of tracking down those seventeen souls you have left anymore."

I shook my head.

"How do you kill the undead?" he asked.

"Usually decapitation works," I said. "Though the ones that were given the hearts of the immortals they abducted could very well come back from that in time. I am not certain, though. We never dealt with anything like this. Mollis destroyed the one we found in Japan," I added as an afterthought.

"There were two immortals they took the hearts from," he said quietly, and I nodded.

"I want to get the immortals more organized as well. We need an accounting of where everyone is. We need to know if anyone is missing." I took a breath. "I think that would be the type of task that you and Artemis would excel at."

"Trying to get rid of me again, Tink?" he asked, and I could hear the smile in his voice. Then, I felt his hand on my back, rubbing up and down my spine, gently, slowly. Even through the leather coat I was still wearing, I could feel the warmth of his hand.

"No," I murmured. "But this is not about us. Not now."

"Someday, it will be," he answered, his voice low, a promise. "And when we get to that point, there won't be any getting rid of me."

I turned and looked at him, meeting his blue-eyed gaze, feeling immediately as if I could stay there, just as we were, forever. "Someday may be a very long time from now, Cub."

"I'll wait. I want to see where this goes." He continued rubbing my back, and I nearly wanted to purr, despite the fact that unlike him, I am most certainly not a cat of any kind. "I have a sneaking suspicion it'll be worth the wait, Eunomia," he added after several long moments.

I swallowed, aware of how shallow my breaths had become, of the hot curl of desire forming deep inside of me. "I have the same suspicion."

He blew out a breath, and I knew he was at least as affected as I was. There was always this between us now, since Japan, this overwhelming need to touch, to feel. Every moment felt weighted with emotion. It was exhausting, exhilarating. It was something I had never felt before. I had some suspicions about what it meant on my end, but it was too soon to even consider expressing what it was I suspected I was feeling.

"So you want me and Artemis to start finding the immortals."

I nodded. "Can you get the time off work?"

He ran his hand along my side, over my hip, and rested it there. "I can. I don't think I'll need to, though. Artemis and I can work when it's night in Detroit. I want to keep an eye on things at work, see if I can get any reads on where things might be happening."

I nodded. "What about Sean?"

"Heph and Meaghan have offered to help with him if I need it, now that I can't take him to the loft. I'm pretty sure Meaghan is a saint," he added, and I laughed. "He likes it with them. He says Heph is fun and Gaia is scary but cool. I wonder how Gaia would feel about that description."

"She would likely be quite happy with it. It is accurate," I said, and he squeezed my hip gently. "We should get back to Detroit so you can work out the details of this with Artemis."

"In a while, Tink. We have this nice quiet room, and I need to sleep."

I shook my head, irritated with my own lack of consideration. He hadn't slept in over thirty hours, with us having left in early morning in Detroit. Even I was exhausted, but I was accustomed to working without sleep.

"Of course," I said.

"It's the middle of the night there anyway," he added.

I moved to get up so he could sleep, and he squeezed my hip again. "Stay with me," he murmured.

I turned to look at him, and he was watching me, his gaze even intense in his sleepiness.

I should get up, I told myself. I should say no, and go over to my own twin bed across the room. That would be the sensible, mature thing to do.

Instead, I shrugged my coat off, kicked off my boots, and crawled under the blankets that he'd flipped aside for me. I allowed him to gather me into his arms, and fell asleep with my face resting in the crook of his neck, my arms around him, curled into him as if he was the shelter I have been seeking my entire existence.

And I was coming to believe he was exactly that. And it was completely terrifying.

When I woke, the bed was empty. It took me a moment to shake loose the grogginess of sleep, but when I did, I heard the shower in the bathroom and let out a small groan. There was something I did not need to think about: Brennan, naked, mere feet away from me.

I got up and used the microwave to heat water, steep one of the bags of tea in our room. It was nothing like the delicious herbal teas Ada made, which I had grown accustomed to drinking at the loft. But there are some times when any tea will do, and this was one of them. I sipped some tea, and quickly changed while Brennan showered. When he came out, the scent of soap flowed into the room along with him. His hair was wet, but he'd slicked it back into what they refer to as a "man bun." It is a look that I did not often appreciate, but when Brennan wore it, it worked.

At least he was fully clothed now.

I gave him a small smile, then turned back to my phone. I was sitting at the small table in the corner of our room, tea and phone in hand. I could hear him shuffling around behind me, brewing one of those single-serving coffees I so often saw in hotel rooms now. The smell of coffee soon wafted through the room. The only text message waiting was a quick text from Hephaestus reminding me to be careful. I smiled to myself. I really did need to start spending more time with him, along with a certain other male in my life.

The "other male" in question took that moment to press his warm lips to the side of my neck, just below my ear. I jumped, surprised by the sudden sensation, and overwhelmed by the immediate sense of need I felt. His lips lingered, and I could feel his warm breath on my skin.

"Morning, Tink," he murmured just before pulling away.

I was of more than half a mind to pull him back to me.

I turned to him, and he was dressed in the dark suit he wore to work. Of course. We would be returning to Detroit around noon. He would go to work, and then go home to his son.

The sight of him in that suit never failed to make me feel a bit breathless.

"Good morning," I said, irritated by the breathy tone of my voice. He sat, coffee cup in hand, across the table from me.

"Thanks for that last night. I needed the sleep, and I knew that if I went back to Detroit, Sean would wake up and then he'd want to talk and then we'd both be cranky today."

I smiled. "Well, we can't have that."

"Did you sleep all right?" he asked, gulping his coffee.

"I slept better than I have in a very long time," I told him. He stilled, eyes on mine.

"Me too," he finally said. "Thanks for saying that," he added.

I nodded. I knew he needed to hear things like that. His ego was perfectly healthy, obviously, but where relationships were concerned, he was not all that secure with himself yet. Everything that had happened with Mollis had caused him to doubt himself. I wanted him to know how he made me feel, despite the fact that it went against everything I knew to be sensible. This, whatever this was between the two of us, had never been part of my life. All I could hope was that I was handling it well, and to me, that meant being honest with him.

He gulped back the last of his coffee, then stood up and put his shoes on. I tucked my phone into my pocket and pulled my coat on, then grabbed my small duffel bag off of the bed.

"Ready?" I asked him. He had his bag in his hand.

"Almost," he said.

"Almost?"

He stepped toward me, leaned down, resting a warm hand at the side of my neck and tilting my chin up with his thumb. He lowered his face to mine. "Almost," he murmured again. And then his lips met mine, warm, insistent, possessive, and I heard myself sigh contentedly into his mouth as I kissed him back. Everything, the feel of his lips against mine, his tongue dipping between my lips, that warm hand on my neck... all of it had me feeling, for just a moment, as if I was flying.

He swept his lips across mine a few more times, gently sucked my lower lip, then released it.

"Now, I'm ready," he said, his voice just a little hoarse.

"For what?" I asked.

He laughed, low, and it was perhaps the most alluring sound I have ever heard. "Don't tempt me, Tink."

I smiled up at him. His hand still rested on my neck, and his thumb traced my jawline. "We both already know you are more than tempted, Cub."

He grinned, bent and kissed me one more time, then moved his hand from my neck to lace his fingers with mine. "Let's get this mess straightened out so I can spend a hell of a lot more time being tempted then, hm?" I nodded, focused, and within seconds, we were back in Detroit, outside of his house. He turned to his car, opened the door, and tossed his bag in. Then he turned back to me. "Be careful," he said, as he always did.

"You too," I said. "Keep me updated."

"I will," he promised. "I'm going to look for patterns, anything at all today that can help with the undead thing you talked about. It would be murders, right? Or missing people?"

I nodded.

"Okay. Jamie and I will do some data gathering today then, assuming nothing stupid happens." "Stupid" was usually code for a supernatural causing trouble, which

Brennan and his department were responsible for officially taking care of. Most often, they did that in cooperation with either Nain's team or one of the shifter packs. More rarely, they did so working with Rayna's family, but, as always, the vampires were not trusted by most beings, supernatural or not, so they tended to withdraw from larger society.

"I will talk to you later," I said. He nodded, swept one more quick kiss across my lips, and then I watched him get into the car. Once he'd pulled out of the driveway and waved to me, I focused one more time, preparing to rematerialize. I'd moved my team to Detroit when I'd checked on them the night before, and they were supposed to be waiting in my apartment for me.

I just had to figure out where we would be going next.

CHAPTER SIX

"London," Brennan's voice said over the phone. "There have been thirty-eight reported missing persons, and thirteen murders in the last two weeks."

I held my hand up, indicating to my team to take a break. I had been showing them the most effective ways to use a Netherblade, in case they ever ended up using mine against a difficult soul. There was not really much space in my apartment of this type of thing, but it was better than nothing. Despite my doubts about showing them, I had to admit that the better they knew how to handle themselves, the less I would have to worry about them.

"Yes, that is quite the red flag," I said to Brennan.

"There have been a few scattered missing person reports elsewhere in Britain, but it seems focused in London. Specifically the East End."

I was about to say something, and clamped my mouth shut, then opened it again.

"Whitechapel?" I asked, taking a guess.

"Yeah. How'd you know?"

I groaned. "I should have thought of this."

I could hear a keyboard clicking, and could just picture him in his office, typing away, phone perched between his chin and his shoulder.

"Jack the Ripper?" he asked. Ah. So he was Googling.

"Yes."

"She was one of the ones who fought you when you tried to take her soul to the Nether," he said, remembering the night I'd shown him some of my better scars, including one from Jack the Ripper herself.

"She did. And she is on Mollis's list, and I should have gone to London sooner," I chided myself. "I only put it off because I was going by the countries and regions that had the most lost souls. She is the only one from there."

"You couldn't have known, Eunomia," he said. "And it might not even be her."

"Maybe," I said, though I did not feel it.

"So I guess you and the New Guardians are going to London next?" he asked.

"Yes."

"Artemis and I will be leaving in a bit for our first round of searching for immortals. Asclepius is coming too."

"That is good," I said with some relief. The more people with him, the better.

"She says that last she knew, they still mostly liked hanging out in the Mediterranean."

"Of course. So many temples built to them there," I said wryly, and he laughed.

"That's pretty much what Artemis said, too," he told me. "As soon as we're back, I'll let you know who we found."

"Thank you."

"Did you want a list of the London missing and murdered?" he asked.

"If you could send it, that would be helpful."

"I'll email it to you." He paused. "Be careful, Tink. I don't want to see any more scars on you."

I smiled, turning to hide it from Quinn and the others. "You have not even seen all of them yet."

"Yet," he said, and I let out a short laugh. "I'm serious though. Be careful, okay? I hate this."

"It will be fine. I will be careful, and I want you to be as well."

"Promise," he said.

"All right. I will talk to you soon, then," I said.

He told me to be careful yet again, and then finally hung up. And how ridiculous was it that I missed his voice the moment we were disconnected? I took a breath, and turned to my New Guardians.

"London," I said, and Quinn nodded.

"I heard you. Whitechapel." I nodded. "Well, this should be fun."

"I do not…oh. You are being sarcastic," I said.

He grinned. "I am. It's likely to be an absolute shitstorm."

I did not argue with him. Instead, I took his hand, and Claire's and together, we rematerialized to a quiet graveyard in London. It seemed appropriate somehow, to begin our mission in London among the dead.

London's East End had been known, back in the days of Jack the Ripper, as a slum. The murders and the mystery surrounding them had brought attention to the living conditions of the people of the Whitechapel district. It did not mean that they changed overmuch during that time period, but eventually, the slums became respectable. Part of the draw, of course, had been the morbid fascination with the area and what had occurred there. A murderer who had never been found, his grisly work left for all to see. Historically, the name of Jack the Ripper is one that lives on in infamy.

And those two things: drawing attention to her neighbors and gaining a certain level of fame, were the things that drove the woman who became known as "Jack the Ripper" to do the things she'd done. It was delicious irony, however, that history had appropriated her murders to a male. Jack the Ripper had been a woman, a prostitute from a poor family from Whitechapel by the name of Eveline Noonan. She'd been beautiful, buxom. A favorite among those who frequented the brothel where she worked. But she had wanted so much more from life. She had deemed herself worthy of fame, of remembrance. She had been a psychopath who, for whatever twisted reason, had decided that murder and mutilation was the way to gain that fame, and a witch who had used the blood and body parts she tore from her victims in some of her more sickening spells.

She had been power-hungry, devious, and full of rage in life. I had no reason to believe she was any better in death. In all likelihood, she was probably worse.

I stood before my team in the alley behind the building where she had once worked in Whitechapel. I unconsciously rubbed my hand along where I knew there remained a long, jagged pink scar on my arm from the last time I had seen her, which had been when I had arrived to claim her soul after death. She had put up a brutal fight, and, even then, had been stronger than I had expected a soul to be. She had taken me by surprise, wrestling with me when I'd tried to plunge my Netherblade into her, and she had ended up slicing my arm to the bone in some places before I had been able to get myself turned around and back in control. She was the only time, in my entire existence, that I had ever failed in a mission. She had gotten away, and managed to stay just out of reach for nearly a year before I finally caught up with her.

I remembered that as we stood in the rain. "She is dangerous," I said in a low voice. "She does not look it. She is beautiful. She is petite, and curvaceous, and the absolute picture of perfection. But she is evil to the core. She fights like a being possessed, and she is much stronger than she looks. She will not hesitate to fight you, and if she is doing what we suspect, she likely already has a corporeal form, as well as others she has turned undead aiding her."

"Um. Is this maybe one of those situations where it would be helpful to have another god or something with us?" Erin asked uncertainly.

"We've got this," Quinn told her, meeting my eyes.

I nodded. "Just be smart. Do not go off on your own. Do not split up. If she starts speaking, do not believe a word she says. If she seems calm or even afraid, it is a trap. Do not fall for it."

We started walking, and I focused on trying to pick up an energy trail. Hours later, we were still walking the streets of Whitechapel, having found nothing more than traces of other souls, souls who, very likely, she had since turned undead. Nothing but whispers, the barest sense of something that had once been there.

I knew Eveline, though. This was her home. She would not leave it, and she would not run. She very likely knew or at least suspected that I was there. She would want to face me eventually.

And I was more than happy to let her do so.

We made another circuit through the neighborhood, and this time, my New Guardians walked through buildings, scoping out interiors. A pair of Guardians on each side of the street, using their ability to simply walk through walls and other obstructions to their advantage. I stayed out on the street, eyes open, and, more importantly, senses focused, ready for even the slightest hint of a soul in the area.

As we neared a large factory, I was hit, hard, with the sense of a soul. A new soul.

"Come on," I said, just loudly enough for my team to hear me. They rejoined me, and we stalked toward the factory. I rematerialized inside, and they joined me.

It was dark. Pitch black, the hulking forms of the factory machines visible only thanks to the meager light shining in from the street lamps outside.

The sensation of death was stronger here, and I darted through the factory, around machinery, following the energy trail.

There was more. It came to me, that the person whose energy signature had brought me here was named Harold Swanson, age thirty-nine, murdered mere moments ago.

And I could already feel his energy signature moving away from me, along with another.

I reached the far end of the factory, where his energy signature had been the strongest. As I took a step, my foot kicked something soft, bulky.

"It's a body, boss," Quinn said gruffly.

"Yes, I figured."

A body. The body of Harold Swanson, and his energy signature was moving away at a fast clip. I closed my eyes, reopened them, letting the final vestige of my enchantment that kept me looking human drop. I heard Claire gasp, undoubtedly at the sight of my eyes glowing red in the darkness.

I ignored it. I looked down quickly at the body of Swanson, noting, as I'd feared, that he'd died thanks to a large cut to his chest area.

That, and the fact that I could see that his heart was missing though the gaping hole in his chest.

"Ah, fuck it all," Quinn groaned.

"My sentiments exactly. Let's go," I said.

We moved quickly now. I grabbed them, and they joined hands, and I rematerialized us several blocks north, which was the direction in which I'd felt his soul moving. This was it. This was what they did: murder a person, give its heart to a soul they were working on turning, and then steal the soul of the person they'd just murdered.

Not they. Not in this case. She. I could feel her energy signature, as well as Harold's and a soul I was able, after a few moments of focus, to identify as that of a woman who'd been murdered in an alley several blocks away. A woman on Brennan's list: Deirdre Ross.

We ran, drawing ever closer to them. My team simply ran through obstacles, and I rematerialized myself instantaneously on the other side of any fences or walls that stood in my path.

We were closing in. The feel of their energy signatures was so strong now. I rematerialized on the other side of a high wall surrounding a parking lot, heard a laugh I recognized from that night all those years ago.

And then the energy signatures vanished.

"What in the hell is going on?" Erin asked.

I gritted my teeth, stalked around the parking lot, then stopped and focused, trying to get a read on them.

They were gone. The trail ended, almost as if it had never existed.

I put my hands on my hips, pacing, trying to pick up anything at all.

"They're gone," Quinn said. I gave a terse nod.

"One of your kind?" Claire asked.

"It would seem so," I answered through my clenched jaw.

"Another one of your sisters, you think?" Quinn asked, joining me in my pacing as the others looked on. I could see in their postures that they were nearly as irritated, as angry as I was.

"Perhaps," I said. "We have reason to believe there is a higher immortal involved. All of the immortals can make that happen," I said, gesturing toward the area where I'd last felt the energy signatures.

"Well that makes our job a hell of lot harder then, doesn't it?" he asked. "Why, though?"

"Why, what?"

"Why are they here helping? We came across your sisters when they weren't expecting us."

"Except when they set that trap for us in Japan," I said quietly.

"You think that's what this is?" He asked, brow furrowed in concern. My New Guardians had not gotten off easily in that encounter, either. My sisters had used their Netherblades on them, incapacitating them, weakening them so they could not assist me. And they still, somewhere, had Mary, the soul they'd stolen from me. Her loss, and the fact that we had not yet uncovered any sign of her, wore on my team, especially Quinn, who had been her constant companion before they'd found me.

I shook my head. "I do not think so. I do not think they are in a hurry to face off against me again. Not yet, anyway."

"Cocky much?" he asked with a small grin.

I shook my head. "Just logical. They suffered losses last time, when they were sure they would be victorious. They underestimated me, and paid for it. They will be wary of doing so again."

"So what now?" he asked with a sigh. "Should we start circling the neighborhood again?"

"Let's go back to where the brothel was," I said. "We can rest there."

"You really think she'll come back there?"

I shrugged. "It was where I found her. It is where she knows I will return to check for her. If I am at all correct about her ego, she will want to face me again."

Quinn nodded, and I took his hand, then Claire's, and the rest of the team joined hands. I focused, and moments later, we were on the roof of the building that had once been an infamous brothel, the place Eveline, AKA Jack the Ripper, had called home for years. The place she'd eventually come to control, becoming a madame to some of the most well-paying clientele in all of the East End. While it had earned her a certain amount of power in her own little sphere, it had not brought her the attention or respect she desired so much. It did not improve the slums of Whitechapel. The wealthy men who enjoyed her services did not stay. They did not spend their money in the neighboring businesses, and being among Whitechapel's people had not made them see that something needed to be done. So when she'd been incapable of getting the attention of the wealthy via the favors she did for them, she turned to more grisly methods.

I mulled it all over as the team and I sat on the roof. The whole idea had been insane, of course, I reflected. Her mind had clearly been an interesting place, a place where logic held little sway. She had believed wholeheartedly in what she was doing. She had seen herself as a hero, as some kind of savior of the people of Whitechapel, when in reality, she'd been nothing but a nightmare, a grisly part of the history of the area, one that drew the more morbidly curious to visit.

No, she would return. Even if her orders were to avoid me, she would be unable to resist the idea of facing me again, undoubtedly stronger than she had been when I had collected her well over a century ago. Her ego would not allow the opportunity to pass her by.

I glanced around at my New Guardians. Cathleen and Erin snuggled together, Claire snored quietly several feet away, and Quinn, as always, remained at my side. Even he, for once, was resting, back leaning against the chimney beside me, arms crossed over his chest, eyes closed.

I took out my phone and checked the time. It was just after two in the morning where we were, which meant it was seven in Detroit.

I hesitated a moment, then typed a message to Brennan. "Are you home yet?"

I waited for only a moment, and there was a response. "We just got in. Was just about to text you."

I let out a breath I hadn't been aware I had been holding. "How did it go?"

He responded that they'd gone to Athens, and had found several lesser gods, as well as seven spirit daemons. The lesser gods had reported that they didn't know of anyone who was missing, which was a good sign.

"Good," I texted back.

"We're going to Crete tonight," he wrote.

And then my phone rang, and I saw that it was him.

"I hate texting. I want to hear your voice," he said when I picked up. I smiled.

"So is this better, then?" I asked.

"Much better," he answered. "How are things there?"

I filled him in on our chase through Whitechapel, the infuriating disappearance. I could hear him moving around on his end.

"You are not leaving for work now, are you?" I asked, interrupting myself.

"No. Just climbed into bed. I'm going to crash for a few hours and go in at ten."

"I should let you sleep then," I said.

"I'll sleep in a bit. Talk to me, Tink. So the trail just ended?"

I paused, and then gave in, telling him about how it had just ceased to be, which led me to conclude that one of my sisters or another immortal must have been in the area helping her.

He was silent for a moment. "I don't like it. If there's another immortal around, they could be setting you up again."

"I will be careful. I wish I had not made our presence known. We should have hung back more. If I had had more time, I may have been able to see who was helping them. Instead, they knew we were chasing them and they left in a hurry."

"Your job was to chase them down. Don't get annoyed with yourself for doing it," he said.

"I assume she will make a reappearance. We will wait around until she does so. While we are here I will look into

72

those murders you emailed me about. Though we did find one of the victims tonight, with her."

"And a missing heart, which means they're definitely making undead."

"Yes."

He let out a short, wry laugh. "You know there was a time when the biggest worry I had was whether the werewolves near Belle Isle were going to be a problem at the full moon or not."

"It is a whole new world," I agreed. "For us, as well. Life as an immortal was always fairly routine. Those like Zeus pretty much lived a life of luxury. Those of us in the Nether did our jobs, slept, and worked some more. It was rarely dramatic, and never as messy as it is now."

"Do you miss the old days?" he asked. His voice was sleepy, and I wished, for just a moment, that I was in his arms again.

"In some ways. Life was so much simpler," I said. "My life was straightforward, and I knew who had earned my trust and who had not. I was whole," I said, and for just moment, it felt as if my wings, wings that were no longer there, had flexed. That hurt most of all, that at times, I could almost believe they were still there, the sensations were so real.

"I can definitely understand that," he said quietly.

"But, in some ways, this is... not better, exactly. More, perhaps? I cannot say better, not with Hades gone," I finished quietly.

"Yeah. I think everyone's going to be feeling that loss for a long time," he said.

"At the same time, I would not have Mollis in my life if things were still the same," I said. "I would not have Shanti. We never had any time to bother with the living." I paused, debating whether to say what I wanted to say to him. As it happened, I was more of a coward than I would like to think. I let the moment pass.

"True," he said. "I wouldn't have Sean. I wouldn't know my grandmother, or anything about what I really am." I knew he felt odd about the whole god/immortal label for himself. He rarely, if ever, said the words, but I knew he thought about it, about what it meant for him and his son.

There was silence between us, words left unsaid.

"I should let you sleep," I finally said.

"I would sleep better if you were here with me," he murmured, and I felt my heart pound in response.

I took a breath. "That makes two of us."

"Be careful, Eunomia."

"Same to you, Cub. Good night."

"Night."

I hit the button, disconnecting our call. I looked at the phone for a moment, irritated with myself, then slid the phone into my coat pocket.

"You gonna tell that poor shifter you love him, or not?" Quinn said. I jumped a little, glared over at him.

"I thought you were asleep," I told him.

"I was. Until I wasn't," he said with a grin. "Seriously, though, boss. Three little words. You know he wants to hear 'em."

I watched him coolly. "You do not know that," I told him.

"Mmhmm. I have almost zero serious relationship experience, and even I can see it. Don't tell me you're that clueless."

"There are other things we need to be thinking about right now," I said.

He shook his head with a smile. "You are really good at avoiding shit you don't want to talk about."

"Yes. It is almost as if I am forced to prioritize where I can afford to spend my time and attention," I said.

He scratched his chin. "I know. I get that, boss. But consider that there's a reason yer fighting. There's a reason you want things to be safe, and it isn't all duty and honoring the role you were created for. Maybe it used to be, but that's not all there is now."

"Duly noted, thank you," I said, and he laughed. "We should move. I want to check out some of these locations throughout the city. I doubt we will be lucky enough to recover any souls for — " I stopped myself, remembering that as far as he knew, Mollis and I were enemies. "Recover any souls to send to the Netherwoods," I corrected myself, "but we must try."

He nodded, stood up, started gently shaking Claire's shoulder to wake her up. Once she was up, she and Quinn woke Cathleen and Erin.

Quinn glanced at me. "You didn't sleep," he said, as if just realizing it.

"I am not tired," I said with a shrug. The movement pulled at the area where my wings had been, and I immediately regretted it. I hated anything that reminded me of what I had lost.

Sleep was just another opportunity for me to have to remember.

Once everyone was awake and alert, I took their hands. "Several murders happened in the neighborhood around St. George Cathedral. We will poke around there first."

They nodded, and I focused, and then we were gone.

CHAPTER SEVEN

I watched as Cathleen stood, looking up at the impressive arched window above the doors of St. George Cathedral. She shook her head, then looked at me, as if she could sense me watching her.

"Once upon a time, I wanted to go into the Church," she said. "I would have, if I'd had my way about it."

I studied her as the team milled about, searching the immediate area. Erin stood nearby, listening. "And what happened to prevent it from being so?" I asked her.

"My father decided to marry me off," she said with a shrug. "It was not uncommon. I probably would not have done well in the Church in any kind of official way, anyway. But I also refused to marry, so I ran away, which was how I came to be at the inn where I was murdered." She gave me a wry smile. "It is ironic, isn't it? I ran so I would not die a slow death married to a man I didn't want, only to end up being murdered by another man I didn't want."

"Did you manage to do any living at all in the time after you ran away?" I asked

She nodded. "I did. I learned to read. Another girl who worked at the inn taught me," she finished, her voice and expression softening. "I danced. I worked. For a while, all was well. And then there came a point where all of my days stretched on, each exactly like the one before it. The same work, the same grubby hands trying to reach under my skirt, the same reprimands when I wasn't 'friendly' enough to the customers. The one who ended up killing me was merely the most insistent that he should have what he wanted." She took a breath. "And while I was angry that my life should be cut short by the likes of him, I was also happy to see it all finally come to an end."

I watched her, struck by her words. I had heard people say before, that they were glad to die. Usually, they were old, or had lived life in such horrid conditions that escape from the sphere of the living was a relief. I had not suspected the same of Cathleen. Murder victims rarely felt that way, at the very least holding onto the wish that they could make their murderer suffer.

She smiled at me. "Death was the first time in my entire life I was actually able to make my own decisions. Especially once I realized that the crows, that those like you, were not coming for me. It is freedom, and I am grateful for it all." She looked back at the church. "I still feel a deep love for the Church, though. The traditions, the peace of it all." She seemed lost in thought, or memory, and I nodded and stepped away. Erin approached her when I left, and held her hand.

I caught Quinn's eye. "This is one of the most concentrated areas of murders and missing people in the last month. I do not know if whoever is doing it has moved on already, but I want us to completely sweep this area. I can still feel the traces of energy signatures here, so I am hopeful. Perhaps we will find something of use here."

He nodded, and my team joined me as I started walking. The blocks around the cathedral were narrow; homes, apartment buildings, and storefronts giving each street we walked down a closed-in, almost claustrophobic feel.

It was not long before the trace of an energy signature I was tracking became stronger, and I moved more quickly, my team keeping pace with me.

Floyd Arthur. Murdered four days past. The information flooded my mind as a second energy signature flared to life. Genevieve Arthur. His wife, murdered at the same time.

I held my hands out to my sides, and my team knew by now that this meant to take my hands, to join hands. Once they had, I focused, rematerializing us several blocks ahead of where we had been.

A third energy signature now. Closer.

Not the one I expected. I nearly choked on the realization, glanced at Quinn.

"Mary is with them," I said quietly.

He shared a look with me, then I saw his face harden, and he continued running forward with them.

We came to an empty house. It looked as if it had been vacant for quite a while, the "for sale" sign on the patchy front lawn faded, the sign hanging askew from its bracket.

"They are in there," I said. My team nodded, Cathleen crossed herself with a look to the heavens, and we charged forward. They walked through the front wall, and I appeared inside.

The scene that met my eyes was not what I expected.

The souls of the Arthur couple, wavery, most definitely not corporeal at all yet, were fighting back against the onslaught of the third soul.

Mary.

She had a man, a live man with her. Badly beaten, whimpering, tied, gagged.

And it struck me that she had a fully corporeal form, if she'd managed to take a live human.

"Mary," I said.

She turned to me with a snarl and attacked, slashing out at me with the knife in her hand.

"Secure them," I said to my team, nodding toward the Arthurs, who stood watching in shock as Mary slashed out at me again.

"We don't want any trouble," the woman told Quinn, and I reached forward, trying to restrain Mary before she could do any more damage.

I remembered this look well, among those undead we had had to put down centuries before, when they'd first figured out how to regain a living form. That crazed hunger in the eyes, the feral expression, the desperation and strength in their movements. The undead were intelligent, even able to manage some semblance of acting like any other human, except when hunger hit them. As I looked at Mary, who was even then trying to slash or bite me, I had to wonder what exactly they had done to her to make her this way.

She was out of control, more animal, more beast, than the woman she had once been. Hungry, insane, and full of senseless rage. Mary was showing all of that now, and I had to push down the anger and guilt I felt, that she had been turned into this, undoubtedly, as a way to punish me. That one of the souls who had been helping me, who had been trying to do good in their death, and been turned into a raging, flesh-hungry monster… the knowledge and rage was a dead, searing hot weight within me.

"I do not want to hurt you, Mary," I said, and she snarled again. She was drooling, her mouth hanging open. I could smell her now, and she smelled like decay. "Surrender, and I will go easy on you," I pleaded with her, and she lunged, the blade of her small, razor-sharp knife slicing the side of my neck.

The Arthur woman gasped as my blood started flowing down my neck.

I shook my head, trying to convince myself that there was none of Mary left there, that the beast that she was now left little room for the woman she'd once been. Whatever they had done to her to cause this particularly vile version of undeath, she now knew only hunger. It had become her entire existence, and I knew now that she was responsible for leaving this particular path of death and destruction around St. George in her wake, never satisfied, always hungering the next taste of living flesh.

I swore to Hades in that moment that I would make whoever had done this unspeakable thing to her pay.

I swore this to myself as I pulled my Netherblade from its sheath under my jacket.

She noted the movement and flew at me, screaming wildly, the scent of my blood making her even more insane.

I stabbed my Netherblade into her stomach as she charged me, and, while it slowed her down, it did not stop her from striking forward, her teeth clamping onto my bloody neck.

"Boss?" Quinn asked, and his voice was tremulous. Shaken.

I gave a shake of my head, eased the other dagger out of my jacket, and plunged it into her back, even as my body screamed in agony at the sensation of her teeth gnawing, beginning to rip my flesh.

The second blade made her scream, releasing me. I gulped back a breath, took the thin chain from my pocket as Mary, or the thing that had once been Mary, writhed and screamed on the floor, her mouth and chin red with my blood. I wound the chain around her wrists as she flailed and wept.

My neck burned, and I tried to ignore it.

Once she was contained, I turned to my New Guardians, who had the Arthurs surrounded. Quinn held the male's arm, and Cathleen held the female. Erin's eyes were bright with tears, as were Claire's.

I pushed down my own emotions. Not now.

"Tell me what you know of this one," I said to the female. Genevieve.

"She murdered us," she said, staring at my still-bleeding throat. "She murdered us, and we watched as she ate our bodies." She clamped a delicate hand over her mouth, as if she was nauseous. I almost told her it was not possible for ghosts to actually vomit, but decided it was pointless. She was fairly newly-dead. She undoubtedly still felt alive, despite what she had seen.

Her husband picked up the story. "We saw her come in here, dragging that fellow there," he said, gesturing to the man on the floor, who was now watching me with a mix of horror and wonder. "We didn't know what we were even doing, but we knew we wanted to try to stop her from doing the same to him. So we followed her in here. I wasn't sure she'd be able to see us, but she did." He paused. "How is that possible?"

"She is also dead. She has done things, or had things done to her, that have resulted in what she is now," I said flatly, and both of the Arthurs looked down at Mary's still-writhing body. "This man owes you his life. He cannot see you, does not know you were here. Soon, he will not remember any of this," I said, realizing that Mollis would have to work her skills on him as well. "Thank you for what you have done. I hope you understand that this is where your time in the mortal realm ends."

Genevieve nodded. "We do. We have no intention of running. God, what if we became that?" she asked fearfully, looking at Mary again.

"Indeed," I said under my breath. I pulled my phone out of my pocket.

"Um. You're still bleeding," Genevieve said.

"It will stop," I said absentmindedly as I texted Mollis.

I got her signal to come to our place in the church. I glanced at the New Guardians. "You will come with me this time. We have a couple of added complications," I said, nodding toward the man tied up on the floor. I knew it would end my ploy of having separated from my Queen as far as my team was concerned, but it could not be helped. Quinn nodded his assent, still seeming dazed. He was able to look anywhere but at Mary. I hauled up the living male, then Mary, who screamed and thrashed. Cathleen took Mary's other arm, and I nodded my thanks. Quinn kept hold of the male Arthur, and Erin the female. We arranged ourselves so all of them had a hand on me, and I focused, taking us to Mollis.

"Oh, what the fuck, E?" the words were out of Mollis's mouth the second we rematerialized before her. She rushed over to me, tilting my head to examine my wounds.

"They will heal, Mollis," I said, even as she continued looking at them.

"Which of them bit you?" she asked, rage in her voice. She has a particular issue with biting, having been nearly drained by a vampire back in her vigilante days. It was one of those things that seemed to trigger her, though she usually managed to keep it hidden.

"Mary," I said quietly, nodding my head toward the still screeching undead I was holding.

Mollis studied her, then closed her eyes for a moment. When she looked at me again, she reached out and put a hand on my shoulder. "Those fucking bastards. This was your Mary."

I nodded, swallowing the lump that seemed to have formed in my throat. "This is my fault."

She shook her head. "Stop. No." She squeezed my shoulder and glanced at the human. "What's up with him?"

I glanced at my team, who were watching the two of us with a mixture of curiosity and confusion. I would have to try to explain all of this to them at some point. I was nervous about that. Could I trust them to keep this secret Mollis and I had been trying so hard to keep? I tore my eyes away from them and focused once again on Mollis.

I explained about how the Arthurs had seen Mary drag the human into the empty house, most likely as her next meal. "So they have been a great help. I think he will need his memories of this time taken, yes?"

She nodded. We both glanced at my New Guardians, all of whom (except for Cathleen, who was still holding onto Mary's arm) were kneeling on the dusty stone floor of the church, heads bowed.

"That's not necessary. Stand up," Mollis said, and they did.

She looked around. "Okay. I'll take his memories, knock him out, and then you can put him back near where you found him," she said to me, and I nodded. "Then we'll deal with the rest."

I watched as she untied and ungagged the human male. "I am sorry you got mixed up in this, but we are going to make sure you get home safe and sound, all right?" she said to him. He nodded, looking terrified, unsure. "All right." Things were silent for several moments, and I knew she was in his mind, likely looking for anything else he had seen at the time of his abduction, then erasing anything having to do with Mary, me, or her. He slumped, unconscious, and Mollis silently handed him off to me. I nodded, rematerialized to St. George's, and left him lying near the side of the cathedral. I gave him a final glance and made the jump back to Detroit.

When I reappeared, my head was swimming, dizzy. My neck was still on fire, though it seemed to have stopped bleeding.

I refused to let it show, that I felt weak. If I did, she would not let me continue working.

"All right," I said, and she nodded. The Arthurs were gone.

"She already sentenced and punished them. It was fast," Claire murmured to me as she came to stand at my side. "They seemed to be decent people."

I nodded. I did not want to watch what had to happen next. And I had the feeling it would not be good for my team to have to watch it, either.

"Do you want me to take you back?" I asked them. Mostly Quinn, who seemed as if he still could not make himself look at Mary. His throat worked, and his mouth was set in a hard line, his face a mask.

How stupid of me. I hadn't realized how close they had become in the time they had spent traveling together. I wondered to myself if he had loved her.

She reminds him of his sister. He feels like he's reliving it all over again, Mollis's voice came in my mind.

"We can stay," Quinn said after several long moments. "You need to heal anyway."

"You do not need to be here for this," I said gently.

"The fuck I don't," he growled. "This is the shit we're fighting against now. I want this moment burned into my memory to use against every one of these goddamned monsters we come up against."

He stood, glaring at me as if daring me to disagree. I met his gaze, held it, refused to look away.

Finally, he looked down. "I'm sorry," he said.

"We will stay," I said in response, and he gave an almost imperceptible nod. I looked at Mollis, who was watching the whole thing play out. She seemed somewhat better than she had seemed the last time I'd seen her, and that gave me hope. Nether knows there was little enough of that going around of late.

Mary was still shackled with the chain I had used to contain her. I walked over to her and pulled my Netherblades from her stomach and back. She bared her teeth, snapped her jaw toward me like a rabid dog. I did not flinch or jump. I watched her as she did it again, taking a small step back. Cathleen had one arm, and I took the other, keeping her still so that Mollis could work.

There was no asking, no questions. Mollis knew better than to try to get answers from Mary in her condition. She stood, and her eyes glazed over in that look she got when she was focusing particularly hard on breaking into someone's thoughts. Her eyes flashed, the bright light that usually came from them intensifying.

As I watched, Mollis's breathing became more labored, a slick sheen of sweat glistening across her forehead. It was absolutely silent, except for the occasional whisper or cry from Mary, who had long since stopped trying to fight any of us.

After what felt like an eternity, Mollis let out a gasp, took a step back, and seemed to come back to herself.

"I was trying to see if there was any way I could break what was done to her. I'm sorry," she said, mostly to Quinn, whose face softened.

"Thank you for trying," he told her quietly.

Mollis turned her gaze to me. "She was taken by your sister, which we already knew. It was Delo who gave her her first heart. She developed a type of bond to Delo as a result of that," she added.

"As a dog would to someone who feeds and cares for it," I said quietly. She nodded.

"When we took Delo, someone else took Mary under their wing."

"Let me guess. We don't know who," I said, and she nodded in irritation. "How did she turn out this way? This is abnormal, as far as I know."

Mollis nodded. "Whoever took her after Delo was gone made her suffer badly before her next two hearts. She was driven insane by hunger, by needing to complete the transition to undeath, and being kept, imprisoned, taunted with having to watch others devour the hearts she so badly needed. Once she was fully mad, they gave her the next two hearts. And then there is a blank spot in her mind again, and the next thing I can see is that the next thing she knew, she was in the area around St. George, and she was hungry," she finished, anger lacing her words.

"Stolen memories and new monstrosities," I said with a sigh.

"Same as before. But we do know now, at least, that Mary was the one responsible for the murders and disappearances from the St. George area. Whether she was just randomly set free there to cause chaos or whether there's more to it, I can't tell. If there was, she didn't know."

"If one of my sisters or anyone working with them took her under their wing, it is bigger than just setting her free," I said.

"Agreed. I know you're mostly focusing on the East End, and that's where I need you. This wasn't near there, was it?"

I shook my head. "I was becoming frustrated near Whitechapel, so we decided to move on for a bit and try to make some headway elsewhere. Brennan had a list of the missing and dead from London, and that was the next nearest area to where we were, so I went there. I will look around the St. George area for any other souls we may have missed."

She nodded. "Thanks, E."

I glanced over at Quinn who was silent, watching Mary.

"There is no point in punishing this one," Mollis said, gesturing toward Mary. "There is none of her old self in there. It's as if undeath took everything away from her."

"You will destroy her, then," I said quietly.

"It will be a mercy, for everyone," Mollis said, glancing toward Quinn. I nodded. Mollis stepped back and drew her sword from its scabbard, the black flames licking hungrily along its blade. She stopped, looked at Quinn. After a few moments, he met her eyes and gave a small nod, and then he turned away, facing the empty doorway, looking out into the deserted street beyond the church doors.

Go to him, E. This is one of those moments where your team needs to see what you are, Mollis said in my mind.

I gave her a nod, releasing Mary's arm and giving her a final look.

My fault. This was on me. "I am so sorry," I whispered to her, taking in her face. I would not forget.

I walked over to Quinn, who was still standing, facing away from us, his arms crossed over his chest, his head down. He glanced up in some surprise as I stood in front of him. We shared a look, and I took a deep breath and put my hands gently over his ears, and he closed his eyes and leaned his forehead against mine.

We stood there, and moments later, I heard the crackle of Mollis's sword, the swishing sound it made as it swung through the air.

A muffled thump of Mary's head falling to the floor.

A sob.

Quinn's breath hitched, and I saw tears spill from beneath his dark eyelashes.

"We will avenge her," I whispered to him. "I promise you."

He gave a small nod and opened his eyes, his gaze meeting mine. "Make this right, boss. Don't let this have been in vain."

"I will."

It is done. Her body has become dust, Mollis said telepathically.

I took my hands from Quinn's ears, then patted his arm gently before walking past him to go back to Mollis. She tilted my head to the side again, inspecting my wounds.

"You're going to have a scar from the knife wound," she finally said.

"One more for the collection, demon girl. It is not important."

"I think you and Brennan made a good call about London. Way more souls from there recently."

"Are any of them making it to you?" I asked.

"Some are. Not enough," she said. "Nain said Brennan and Artemis are tracking down the immortals?"

I nodded. "I wanted to know for certain if we are missing any more immortals, and to warn any we find about what is happening. I do not want them to be caught unaware as Winter and Autumn were."

"I agree," she said. "So far, so good?"

"So far, they have not heard about any missing," I said. "They are going to Crete next."

She stood silently. "I don't want this to go on much longer. We need our teams united again."

"We do," I agreed. "You should talk to your mother."

She gave a small smile. "You sound like Nain."

"Your husband is not the dumbest male I have ever met," I said, and she laughed.

"Give it time. I'm still seeing what I can learn when they're around. I really don't think it's my mom. Meg, though..." she trailed off, shrugging. "She's weird lately."

"Weird, how?"

"Irritated, angry. Snappish."

"Well, she does not have the world's most pleasant personality to begin with," I said, and she grinned.

"True. But even more so than usual. The other day, she was gone all day, no word she was leaving, nothing. And then when she got back, she said she needed some time away. Tell me that doesn't raise a few questions. She wouldn't tell me any more than that."

I did not answer.

"Yeah, that's what I thought," Mollis said with a small smile. "We'll figure it out. Just promise me you'll be by my side when I have to punish whoever betrayed me."

I smiled. "You know I will be."

She nodded, and then I took a step back and motioned for my team to join me. As they did, I gave Mollis a final nod and took us all back to London.

We had more hunting ahead of us, it seemed.

CHAPTER EIGHT

I rematerialized all of us back to London's East End. I had no desire to spend any more time near St. George's, and we ended up in the Spitalfields district. We had hunting to do, but I knew that now was not the time. My New Guardians had just been through something that had all of them, myself included, shaken. Seeing Mary that way, witnessing her end… no, there would be no hunting until we had time to talk. If there were grievances to be aired against me, I would rather it happen now than when I needed them to trust me.

And there rightly should have been grievances. Mary's capture, her forced transition to undeath, was my fault. There was no other way to see it.

I also had things to explain about my Queen, I thought with a sigh as my team looked around. I had made us appear near what was in this time, a brewery. When I had been in this place in Eveline's day, there had been more tall row houses where the brewery now stood. The tower of Christ Church rose high in the sky above us, just as it had back then, though now it was illuminated by floodlights from below. I would have rematerialized us in a more central location, or back to Whitechapel, but the pubs would be busy at this time of night, and I was too tired and heartsick to try to focus on not surprising any of the humans with our appearance. I still wore my blood, my coat crackling with it.

I turned away from the sight of the church tower looming over us, finally facing my team.

"Clearly, I am not fighting with my Queen," I said softly. They all watched me, and I tried to push away the overwhelming fear that one of them would betray me.

Betrayal. Oh, how the recent years of my existence had taught me to fear that very thing. It was not something I thought much about before the day I realized my sisters had worked with Hermes against Hades and his daughter. Now, it seemed that that word slithered its way through my existence and worries almost constantly.

"But pretty much everyone seems to think you are," Cathleen said. I sat, leaning back against the brick wall of the brewery, and my team sat with me. We formed a loose circle, Cathleen and Quinn on either side of me. Cathleen and Erin still held hands, as if they needed the comfort. Claire had her arms crossed over her body as if trying to keep herself warm. Quinn sat, stoic and silent for once, and I found myself wishing he would crack one of his ill-timed jokes.

I explained. I explained to my team about the betrayer in Mollis's realm, about the need to find them out before they did more damage. I explained what we were doing, and how we both hated it.

"You should have known all of this," I finished quietly. "That is another thing, perhaps, that I should be apologizing for this night. My only excuse is that I have come to see those around me in terms of who is most likely to betray us next, and I was too cowardly to trust you."

"And now you do?" Erin asked.

I gave a wry smile. "Now, I do not have much of a

choice. I could not have taken all of them to Mollis myself."

Erin and Cathleen each let out a short laugh. Claire shook her head.

"Considering how insane everything has become, it surprises me that you are willing to talk to anyone," Claire said with a smile. "You name yourself a coward. I do nae see that," she finished with a smile. "And our relationship is still new. You do not know us, not really," she paused, then smiled again. "Though it does strike me that you likely know me better than anyone knew me during my living years."

Erin and Cathleen nodded at this, and Quinn remained silent. I knew that of all of them, he had been affected most by what had happened with Mary.

"Still. You all vowed to help me. I should have been brave enough to be honest with you. Part of it was the fear that if you knew of it, others would be able to learn of our deception from you. Not through any malice on your part," I said quickly, aware that Erin was about to argue. She closed her mouth, and I continued. "Those we suspect are powerful telepaths. I need to keep you away from them, at the very least."

They all nodded, even Quinn.

"Can we hunt, boss?" Quinn asked quietly. "I feel like I need to do something. I can't just sit here right now."

I met his eyes for a moment, then nodded. He stood, held his hand out, and pulled me up after him.

"Some of Eveline's murders occurred in this area as well," I said, looking around us and trying to remember. "It is possible she would return here."

"A little walk down memory lane," Erin muttered, and I nodded.

"She always was a vain creature," I said. We walked out of the parking lot of the brewery, and started making a circuit of the immediate area, walking the twisting streets that formed the boundary of that particular little cluster of narrow streets and alleys, and then progressively making our circuits smaller, drawing us, eventually, to the area immediately surrounding the dealership. We were a block behind where we had begun, the church tower looming up even more prominent over us.

I felt something, and spun around. An energy signature.

A female soul was walking toward us. She was not the one I had been hunting, and she was not on any list I had. Her dress marked her as someone from a time long past, and her curly brown hair was in some manner of disarray. She stopped walking when she saw me.

By now, my New Guardians saw her as well, and stood around me, throwing questioning glances my way.

I had not known this soul upon her appearance, but as we stood there studying one another, details filtered into my conscience. I recognized this for what it was: she was another soul overlooked by both the crows and my kind, a soul that the God or Goddess of Death knew nothing about.

Another potential New Guardian.

And one that had, in her time, fallen victim to Jack the Ripper, or, as we knew her, Eveline Noonan.

Her name had been Annie Chapman.

She stood, staring, and I let her. My team were all studying her closely.

"You can see me?" she asked quietly, surprise in her tone, a bit of a tremble to an otherwise rich voice.

"I can."

"You are one of them though. The dark angels who take the dead."

I watched her closely. "We are called Guardians. We are not angels. We are hunters for the God of Death, Annie Chapman."

She looked at me with some surprise. "Are you finally here to collect me? I have been passed over for years."

It hurt, the pain in those final words.

I slowly walked toward her, and though she tensed, she

92

allowed me to take her hands in mine. "I do not doubt that it looks that way. The others of my kind, as well as the crows that do our job now, could not see you."

"Why not? Is this some kind of purgatory for the kind of life I lived?"

"No. Never that. You were meant for something more," I said quietly, keeping my eyes on hers. Her eyes were a lovely shade of green, with hints of gold.

"Something more?" she asked with a snort.

"I can see you. That means that you are meant for more than an eternity of aimless wandering. It means that you are meant for more, even, than your final judgment and punishment by My Lady, the Queen of the Dead." She still had that look of disbelief on her face, and it did not surprise me. This woman had lived a difficult human life, as a prostitute in the East End, and then had been tormented and murdered by Eveline.

"Those standing behind me," I said to her, nodding toward my New Guardians. "The others of my kind passed them over as well. They now work with me, hunting the souls of the dead, and sometimes, even more dangerous things. If you were left behind, it was because you still have a role to play here."

She tore her gaze away from my New Guardians, and looked at me again.

"We are here hunting she who murdered you and so many others," I said softly, and she looked at me in shock.

"She's here?" she asked fearfully, pulling her hands out of mine.

"She escaped, with the help of someone who tries to undermine my Queen. We are here to take her and bring her back." I paused. "You have not seen her, have you?"

Annie shook her head, looking as if she might fall over from the shock. "I hide. There is a cellar over there that no one ever goes in, and I feel safe there. I only came out because I felt… something," she said, looking confused.

"You felt something different from the souls of other

dead you have seen," I said, and she nodded.

"Yes. That was you?"

I nodded.

"Wait. You were killed by Jack the Ripper?" Claire asked, and the rest of my team approached. Annie nodded uncertainly.

"Annie Chapman, please meet Quinn Connoly, Erin Finnegan, Cathleen Boyle, and Claire Magee. I am Eunomia." Each of my team nodded in turn as I introduced them, and there were handshakes and quiet greetings.

"They help you hunt the dead?" Annie asked, and we all nodded.

"Would you like to help?"

She looked uncertain. "I am not really a fighter." She let out a low laugh. "Though I wish, all these years later, that I had been."

I smiled.

"I was not a fighter, either," Claire said with a smile. "Eunomia has taught us so much. More than anything else, though, it's beautiful not to be invisible anymore."

At this a look of such longing crossed Annie's face that I felt the urge to hug her. I did not, of course, but I wanted to.

"I started hiding in the cellar because the solitude was easier without people and dark angels walking past all the time. Not being seen…" she trailed off with a shake of her head.

"I can see you. They can see you," I said, nodding toward my team.

She gave a timid smile. "I still can't believe it," she said.

"Well," Quinn said with one of his disarming smiles. "If you plan on joinin' up, let's hear it: we all tell our death stories. And since we're hunting the monster who killed you, I'm even more interested in hearing yours."

She shook her head and sat on the curb. I sat beside her, Quinn on my other side, and the rest of my team on his other side.

She took a deep breath. "The view from this spot hasn't changed overmuch," she began. "I looked up at that damned church tower as I died." She paused. "There used to be a house here," she said, nodding toward where the parking area for the brewery began. "I was walking down Hanbury after finishing work," she said.

"What kind of work?" Erin asked, and I hid a grimace.

"The work a woman does on her back," Annie explained in a bland tone.

"Oh. Oh!" Erin said, and Quinn met my glance, gave a small roll of his eyes.

"I was walking back toward the rooming house I hoped to rent a bed in with the wages I'd earned. It was summer, and I could have well slept outdoors, but I had already done that recently enough and I wanted some escape from the stench."

I nodded. I remembered the malodorous air in Whitechapel during the times I had come to collect the souls in this area, that month during which I had originally hunted for Eveline's soul. The thick, oppressive odor of unwashed bodies, horse manure, and human waste was only made worse by the summer heat. Too many people crowded into too small of a space, and no means by which to move on. It had smelled of desperation and decay, back then. I had come there often, even before "Jack the Ripper" commanded so much of the world's attention. Humans had died here from fights, abuse, starvation, infection… I had collected them all.

I tore my mind away from the memories, and focused once again on Annie, who had continued speaking.

"I remember that the yard of the house was surrounded by a low brick wall. There was a gate at one end, the led to the alleyway behind," she said, lost now in memory. None of us interrupted, knowing by now how much it meant to finally tell the story of how one met his or her end. "I walked, and trailed my fingers over the brick. Ahead of me, a woman stepped out of the alley. She was dressed plainly, nothing much out of the ordinary. But she was beautiful," she said. "I remember envying her her youth and beauty, and thinking she was one of the lucky ones. When I made to walk past her, she stopped me, and asked if I might like a drink. I said no, not wanting anything from this woman who clearly had everything I did not," she said.

There were a few moments of silence. "And when she didn't convince me with a drink, she mentioned that her brother was looking for someone with my skills," she said quietly. "And I was tired, but the prospect of a bit more to get by on, maybe the ability to buy a pint to dull everything for a while," she shrugged. "It was too good to pass up. So I let her lead me into the alley, though the gate, and into the yard. We neared the back door. She was behind me, and we had been chatting about the heat. All of a sudden, she grabbed my hair. I didn't realize what was happening until I felt the blade slicing my throat open."

We were all silent. Annie's hands were shaking, and I reached over and gently took one in my hand. She gave me a grateful look, one that spoke to how little kindness this woman must have received during her existence.

"She sliced my throat, and then she sliced it again, just above the first cut," she continued. "I just remember feeling like I was drowning. I couldn't get any air, and I struggled. I remember putting my hands to my throat," she said, putting the hand that was not clasped with mine to her throat in memory. "I don't know if I thought I could stop the bleeding, but all I could think was that I had to keep pressure on it," she said, shaking her head.

"I fell down, and I was vaguely aware of her stripping my skirt back, cutting my bloomers off." She closed her eyes. "I thought it couldn't get any worse. I knew I would die there. And then she knelt next to me, and she plunged her knife into my abdomen. I could feel everything. Every slice, and I gurgled and tried to move away, but my body had already given up. I died looking up at that cursed church tower, and I didn't bother praying, because I knew for damn sure that no one was coming to save me."

We sat in silence for several long moments, Erin's sniffles the only sound in the night. I held Annie's hand in mine, and Quinn had seemed to edge himself closer to me, as if offering me... what, I did not know. Support? Warmth? I sorely needed it. It was not so much her story. After all of this time, I was well aware of the horrors of death. It was her tone. That hopelessness, the loneliness.

"I am sorry for what was done to you," I said softly, meeting Annie's eyes. "All of my team," I said, tilting my head in Quinn and the others' direction, "all of them died under violent circumstances. It seems to be something my New Guardians have in common. Perhaps the violence is what creates you. I do not know," I said. "But I do know that none of them are alone now. We are a team, and a family, and they have found a purpose in death. If you want it, I offer you the same."

She gave a small smile. "I am yours, then. I felt your presence a few days ago, and I felt like I needed to get to you. I was afraid, though," she said, and then a look of concern crossed her face. "I don't know how much good I'll be for you."

"You are enough," I said softly. "Welcome to the New Guardians. We have much hunting to do here."

After two days of almost ceaseless hunting, my New Guardians and I had brought twelve wandering souls to Mollis and come across three more in the very earliest stage of undeath. Mollis had destroyed the undead, judged, tried, and released the dead to the Everafter. Annie was slowly but surely becoming acclimated to life among those who could see her, and I was noting a strange thing about my team: when we passed the living on the street, it seemed as if they could see not just me, but Quinn and the others as well. I made a note of it, realizing that we would have to be more careful about how we moved. They could still, somehow, walk through walls and other obstacles, which would have certainly drawn the attention of any mortals who happened to be looking at them.

I had predicted this happening, and had thought it had happened when we'd hunted in Germany, before the face-off with my sisters in Japan. At the time, they had merely been more solid to me, but the mortals could not see them, nor could any Aether immortals. Now, the humans clearly saw them, and I made a note to get them more modern clothing. Their period dresses certainly did not make us more inconspicuous. It seemed to have happened the night we had all watched Mollis destroy the being who had once been Mary. Whether it was because they had become more bound to me with that experience, or because they'd become more devoted to their roles and what we fought against, they were now much more. Anyone looking at them would think they were just as alive as I was and, truly, they were.

They were Guardians.

My team had become unstoppable after witnessing what had become of Mary. I still could not let go of the guilt I felt over Mary's demise. It was not what I had promised her, and, had I been smarter and not left her vulnerable, it never would have happened.

They did not seem to share that opinion. Instead, they had become like hardened steel. Unbreakable, unstoppable. Quinn had not smiled or joked since the day we'd discovered Mary, and the pale complexions of every member of my team let on how tired, how tense they truly were.

And still, we hunted.

We finally stopped once we were positive the area round St. George was clear. I had checked nearly half of the names off of the list Brennan had put together for me. Brennan and his grandmother were still working their way through the Mediterranean, though I had not had much of a chance to talk to him other than quick updates.

"Back to Whitechapel, then," I said to my team.

"You should eat something. And sleep," Claire said.

"I am fine," I said.

"We've been going nonstop since Mary," she argued. "You can take a couple of hours."

I was about to argue, but stopped myself. Undoubtedly, they needed time as well. "As long as you rest, too," I said, and they nodded. We settled into the empty house in which we'd found Mary and the Arthurs, Erin and Cathleen together in one of the upstairs rooms, Claire and Annie, who had become fast friends, in one corner of the large living room. Quinn stretched out a few feet away from me, his hands resting on his stomach, and closed his eyes.

I looked around. I did not feel safe with us all asleep.

"Go to sleep, boss. I'm awake," Quinn said.

"You are tired as well."

He sighed. "I'm not gonna sleep. Every time I close my eyes, there she is…"

"I am sorry for your loss. You two were close," I said, deciding to keep what Mollis had told me to myself.

"She was nice. She reminded me of my sister. Really, that…" he shook his head. "She had the same laugh as Abbie. Exact same– that rich, deep belly laugh. Now it feels like I failed my sister twice." He glanced at me. "I know it makes no sense."

"Guilt often makes no sense," I said softly.

"You have nothing to feel guilty about, either," he told me.

"She was there because of me. I should have taken her with me. There are so many things I could have done differently."

He watched me. "You gave Mary the gift of bringing her tormentor to justice. I traveled with her for a long time, and every time the woman slept, she had nightmares about him. All she ever asked of you was the chance to do that. She never would have blamed you for what happened after."

"Perhaps," I said softly, not quite believing.

We sat in silence. "Your Queen is a good woman," he said after a while. "I guess she's my Queen as well, hm?"

"She is."

He nodded. "Honorable. Scary, maybe, but honorable. I can see why you two are close. There's all of that in you, too."

I gave him a small smile. "Thank you."

His gaze locked with mine for just a moment, and then he looked away. "I'll keep watch. You need the sleep more than I do," he said, and when I raised my eyebrow at him, he gave a wry smile. "I'm dead. Doesn't make a difference to me either way. Sleep just gives us a break from the endless reality of life. We don't need it the way you do."

I wanted to ask him what he thought of his endless reality, but to be honest, I had had far too much emotion to deal with in the past few days. I simply nodded, settled myself on my side, using my arm as a pillow, and closed my eyes.

I stood in a lonely field, and I knew I was in the Nether. Not the new Netherwoods, but the original Nether. My homeland, the place I had always returned to through centuries of fulfilling my duty. I stood, and the amethyst sky with its abundant shining white stars stretched endlessly overhead. The wind blew, and the tall grasses around me rustled. The longer I stood there, the harder the wind blew, until my hair was blowing into my eyes and I was holding my hands out as if trying to shield myself from its fury. Thunder rolled through the sky, and when I called out, I was utterly alone.

The wind died down, and as it did, I heard him calling for me. Across the field, I could just make out his blond hair, the strong slope of his shoulders under a white t-shirt. It was only after a moment that I realized the shirt was streaked with blood, and a dark shape behind him was ready to pounce.

I ran.

I ran toward him, shouting, urging him to look behind him, to run, to do anything but stand where he was, with that thing closing in on him.

I was not fast enough. It felt as if I moved through mud, my legs an absolute failure at taking me where I needed to go.

I leapt up, flapping my wings, rising into the air. I would swoop in, and save Brennan, and everything would be fine as long as I could just get to him.

But of course, I had no wings, and I fell face-first into the hard soil of the Nether. His voice roused me, and I forced myself to stand, glancing back only to see that my back was bloody and there was nothing but bare bone where my wings had once been.

I ran to him, and I screamed his name, and I watched in horror as a blade came from the thing behind him and his head fell to the ground.

"Hey. Hey, boss," I heard Quinn's voice, felt a large hand shaking my shoulder. My eyes shot open, and he was crouched beside me. I was panting, my body slick with sweat, the lingering terror from my dream still with me, even in the light of day, sunlight shining through the windows of the empty house we were in.

I glanced around. The other members of the team were awake as well, all of them watching me. Claire looked as if she was about to cry, and Cathleen and Erin both looked stricken. Annie stood behind them, hands clenching and unclenching the fabric of her skirt, a worried expression on her face.

I sat up. My head ached, and my throat felt raw. My wings... no. Not my wings. The memory of my wings, my phantom limbs or whatever the human doctors called the phenomenon, hurt. "Please tell me I did not scream," I said to Quinn.

He shook his head. "No screaming. Just lots of thrashing about and whimpering."

I nodded, then rested my face in my hands. I stood up,

shook my head, trying to get rid of the sick, uneasy feeling the nightmare had left me with.

"We will go to Whitechapel," I said. I glanced at my phone. Six thirty, which meant it was nearly noon in Detroit. I only hesitated for a moment, then I started typing.

Just wanted to check in. Is everything okay?

I waited a few moments that felt like an absolute eternity, and nearly cried with relief when my phone vibrated.

Good here. Artemis and I are taking a couple of nights off to give Heph and Meg a break. Most of the immortals seem to be moving here now.

Oh?

They feel safer I guess.

After a pause, my phone vibrated again.

I miss you.

My heart gave a little leap, and it felt hard to breathe. Stupid tears stung my eyes, and I wanted to smack myself for how ridiculously emotional I was being.

Instead, I typed back.

I miss you too. Please be careful, Cub.

Come back soon, okay? How are you supposed to corrupt me if you're not even here?

I allowed myself a smile. That "corruption" joke had come after our first lost soul mission together, when I informed him that the lady in charge of the inn we were staying in seemed to think I had corrupted him somehow into spending time with me.

I think maybe you are corrupting me. But it could be fun to corrupt you as well. I hit "send" before I could second-guess myself.

A couple of seconds passed.

Don't make me jump on a plane, Tink. I'll do it.

Don't do that. I will see you soon. I hope. I will talk to you later. We have to get moving.

Okay. Be careful.

You too.

With that, I shoved my phone in my pocket, picked up the small duffel bag I always traveled with, and turned to face my team. My uneasiness over the stupid nightmare continued. I shook my head again. "Come. We have a nightmare to find." I held my hands out, and we reappeared moments later on the brothel roof in Whitechapel.

"We are not stopping until we find her," I said. "If we want this mess to end, if we want to be able to point to a definitive success from this particular mission, we need to find her and turn her over to my Queen. We find her, and I believe we will find answers."

During the day, Whitechapel was a bustling place, and I tried to look inconspicuous as I walked through the streets. My New Guardians fanned out around me, we moved through the neighborhood, sometimes by foot, sometimes via rematerializing. She had been here again. I could feel the traces of her energy signature.

Three days later, we were still looking, and my team was becoming restless, snapping at one another. Tempers were running short, as was patience. We had taken two new souls, along with three more who were beginning the path to undeath. It felt as if for every soul we took in, four more took their place.

The humans were starting to notice that something was very wrong. Not only in London, but, to a lesser extent, in Tokyo, Athens, and Paris as well. Humans were going missing at an alarming rate, and the media was picking up on the story. Every newsstand we passed in our hunts was plastered with the news, the number dead or missing overnight. The screaming, large type asking what could be done to stop it.

They had begun to call for answers from the immortal

the entire world now knew about: Mollis Eth-Hades, the goddess of death.

I was not entirely surprised when I received a text message from Mollis. "Come home, E. We need to make a move here."

My team and I were back in Detroit in seconds. I left them in my apartment, texted Mollis to meet me in our place, and within minutes, I was standing there with a very tired-looking death goddess.

"This is a motherfucking mess," she growled in greeting. "It's getting worse. You're doing everything you can. You're bringing me souls and undead at a crazy rate. When's the last time you slept?"

"Recently. Kind of," I added with a shrug. "You know sleep is not as necessary for me."

"No. But everyone needs a break and you have been going non-stop and I can't fucking rest either with this mess. We can't just let them keep on doing this. We can't keep up. It needs to stop."

I nodded in agreement. "So? What is the plan?"

"I have spoken to my mother. It's not her."

"I am glad, demon girl," I said, and she gave a wan smile.

"She doesn't believe it's Aunt Meg, either. We disagree about that part."

I nodded.

"It seems to me that maybe we need to force their hand. Maybe we need to make it very clear that there are sides to be chosen. We both started this little farce thinking the betrayer would come to you. Maybe they need a little more encouragement."

I studied her.

"We should fight. Publicly. Make damn sure everyone knows we can't stand one another. If anything's going to draw them out, that would do it. They've been working with your sisters. They wouldn't let a powerful possible ally like you go to waste. Especially one that knows me as well as you do," she added.

I thought, considering it. "And if it doesn't work?"

She shrugged. "Then if nothing else we can finally drop the act and at least that part of our lives can get back to normal. But I think we should try it. The sooner I know who the betrayer is, the sooner one part of this mess is wrapped up."

"You could just ask Megaera," I said.

"I did. She denied everything, and I can't get into her mind. Not without fighting her, and if she's innocent, I really don't want to have my aunt's destruction on my conscience if she pushes too hard. You know how we are. Neither one of us would give up if we got pissed off enough. I don't trust myself in my current mindset," she added quietly.

I studied her, feeling as if she was not telling me everything. "Did something happen, Mollis?"

She met my gaze, then turned away. "You've seen the news lately. They want answers I can't give them."

"I know," I said.

"Every day has been more insane. I feel like I'm ready to crawl out of my skin, with all of these souls, more every day, on the loose. Nether is…" she shook her head. "She is not trying to be difficult. She's very affected by my mental and emotional state, and it's not good."

I nodded. Mollis and Nether were a deadly combination. An out-of-control combination, because Nether lacked care for anything but herself and maybe Mollis, and both beings were full of rage and destruction. Should Nether gain the upper hand, in Mollis's weakened state, it was not likely that Mollis would be able to gain control again.

"I attacked Nain," she said, in a voice so quiet I was sure I had heard her wrong.

"What?" I asked.

She turned back to me. Her enormous wings trailed despondently behind her, her shoulders slumped. "I attacked my mate. The love of my life, because he startled me. It was instinct, automatic. I set him on fire, without a thought," she finished.

I closed my eyes and knew this was destroying her. He was the person, along with her children, that she loved and treasured most in this world or any other. She had hurt him, and now had another reason to fear herself. What if it was one of the children next? Or another team member, not as strong or resilient as the demon?

The weight of the chaos was getting to her. She fought. Still, she fought, because she is Mollis and she will fight until there is nothing left to fight for, until life itself ceases to be.

But no one, no matter how powerful they are, can bear the weight of so much responsibility alone. We needed to resolve at least some of this. Figuring out who the betrayer was, taking them, would likely lead us to anyone else involved and stop the flow of undead into our world.

"We will fight," I said. "I will say many things indicating that you are not among my favorite people."

I could see her worry, even as she nodded in agreement.

"It will be like sparring. We beat the Nether out of one another when we spar, demon girl. This will be no different."

"We haven't sparred since all of this," she pointed out, second-guessing her plan already.

I put my hands on my hips. "I trust you to keep control of yourself and Nether, my Queen. You are not some weak, undisciplined child. Remember who you are, Mollis Eth-Hades," I demanded, knowing she needed a bit of a pep talk. I did not know if I really knew how to give one or not, but I was the only one there.

Her shoulders straightened, and she seemed to draw herself taller. "I will remember, E. I promise."

"Good." Then she looked as if something had come to her. "Wait here a sec. I have something for you."

Before I could respond, she was gone.

When she left, much of the anxiety left as well. It was not her fault, but I welcomed the respite, short though it would likely be.

I crossed my arms, glancing around at the empty church. Mortal worship ceremonies held a certain fascination for me, and old churches like this one, even dilapidated and empty as it was, held the power that came with faith. I could feel it even now. It did not matter whether the faith had been the mortals believing in us or some other god. In the end, it was all the same, anyway. It was the same whether I stood in a Christian church, a Jewish temple, a temple built to one of my own kind, or the standing stones scattered throughout Britain. The sense of faith, of power, of the hope and belief in something more, imbued them all. In that way, I could understand what Cathleen had said about the soothing nature of the Church she had loved. There was comfort in that feeling, in the remnants of faith that remained even after those who had worshipped were gone.

I paced, and let myself be surrounded by it.

Mollis reappeared moments later with a "pop," something held behind her back. I raised an eyebrow at her, and she brought it out, a somewhat shy look on her face, and in that moment she reminded me of a child presenting something of great importance to someone she loved. I smiled at her, and then my eyes lit on what she was holding out to me.

"That is Hades'," I said softly.

"I want you to have it." She held it out more, insisting that I take it. I could not move, surprised by the emotions that overwhelmed me. She was holding Hades' sword, the very same one he had wielded for thousands of years, the one he held in the enormous monument Hephaestus had created. Its black blade gleamed, and the power of the Nether, the old Nether, radiated from it. The pommel held a deep black gem, and the crosspiece ended in deadly-looking points.

I raised my eyes to Mollis's. "I cannot accept this."

"E. He respected you. He trusted you, when he trusted very few. And I love and trust you, and I know he would have wanted you to have this." I hesitated a while longer, and she pushed it toward me again. "Take the damn sword, E."

"You do not want me to use this against you later," I said, my gaze going back to the blade, even as a new ache in mourning for the god I had so revered washed over me.

"No. But I still want you to have it," she said softly, reading my emotions as she always did. "In my grief, and my mom's grief, I never once thought about how much losing Hades affected you. And I'm sorry for that. He cared for you. I hope you know that."

I nodded, and slowly reached out and grasped the handle of the sword. It felt cold, as it should, being a creation of the Nether.

"It should work against souls and undead, right?" Molly asked.

Without taking my eyes from the sword, I gave another small nod.

She gave a small laugh. "Then use it well. He would have loved seeing the damage you could cause with that."

"I do not feel deserving of wielding this blade, demon girl. Someday, perhaps I will."

"Then on that day, take it up and make your enemies pay. But keep it now, anyway. He would have wanted it that way."

"Very well. There are no adequate words of thanks for this, my friend," I said, meeting her eyes.

"Just try not to hurt me too badly later, okay?" she said, and I rolled my eyes. She gave me a small, tired grin then. "After school, by the twisty slide. You and me, Guardian."

I lifted my hands in a "what in the Nether are you talking about?" gesture. She confused me. Often.

She shook her head and gave a snort of a laugh. "Never

mind. You didn't have the public school experience, clearly."

"Obviously." Then I smiled at her. "This evening, I will come to the Netherwoods and you will be enraged to find me there. Words will be exchanged, and we will fight. I will leave it to you and your imps to ensure that as many immortals are present as possible. Particularly Megaera, but any others you can get there as well."

She nodded. "We'll take care of it. I'll see you later then, E."

"All right." I began to close my eyes, preparing to rematerialize back to my apartment.

"Hey, E."

"Hm?" I asked, opening my eyes again.

"Just so you know when we're kicking one another's asses later, I love you."

I smiled. "I know you do. And I love you too, demon girl." With that, I closed my eyes again and focused on my apartment. I needed a shower, and a nap. And then I needed to prepare.

What does one wear when fighting her best friend?

CHAPTER NINE

I walked into the Netherwoods, which felt strange after so long away. I stalked along the black gravel path, the castle where the Goddess of Death ruled looming, dark and menacing, ahead of me. In the distance was the monument to Hades. As usual, Persephone was beside it, kneeling, head bowed, a tiny figure dwarfed even more by the sheer size of Hades' memorial. Demons patrolled around the castle, and I could see several immortals, including Mollis, sitting in the courtyard where we had held Hades' funeral what felt like mere moments ago.

"Hey, you're not supposed to be here," a hulking greenish-gray demon called upon seeing me. I just sneered at him, determined to stay in character. I was a former friend, coming to confront the woman who I believed had wronged me. I kept walking, and soon other demon guards were heading toward me. Out of the corner of my eye, I saw the assembled gods looking my way. Many were there. Mollis had done a good job of gathering them all. Hephaestus and Meaghan, Gaia, Demeter, Asclepius, Hestia, Megaera, Tisiphone, and even a few lesser gods were now looking at me. Nain stood beside Mollis.

Mollis said something, holding her hand out as if telling them all to say put. I strode toward where she was, drawing closer to the palace. She waved her hand at the demon guards who were surrounding me, and they fell back. Not far, but far enough to give us room.

"I told you before," Mollis said as she stalked forward, "you are unwelcome here. I don't have any room for liars in my life." Her voice was cold, harsh, and it made me glad I was not actually on her bad side.

"So you say. I never had my say, my Queen," I said derisively. "And I have no time for the temper tantrums of the likes of you."

She crossed her arms. "I'm giving you three seconds to get the hell out of here, Guardian."

"I would suggest something you can do with your three seconds, child," I hissed, and she launched herself at me then, hitting out.

Sparring. We are sparring, I reminded myself.

I ducked away from her, kicked out, and she danced out of the way, then came back almost impossibly fast with another punch aimed at my stomach. I pivoted, and landed a decent punch to her right side. I heard an "oof" of breath escape her, and then she was kicking me. I fell back, then sprung up quickly again.

Behind her, I could see some of the gods coming forward toward us.

"Stay the fuck back," Mollis snarled at them before launching herself at me again.

I made a mental note to myself: do not ever actually anger Mollis. When she hits, she hits with the power and rage of two powerful immortals. And I knew she was holding back.

I ducked another hit, kicked her, hard, in the stomach, and she fell back. I did not waste the opportunity, leaping on top of her. We grappled, the two of us wrestling on the sharp gravel of the path, each of us trying to gain the upper hand.

I got a knee up, connecting hard with Mollis's stomach. It was enough to get out from under her. I sprang up, drew my dagger.

"Eunomia, no!" I heard Hephaestus shout.

Mollis just laughed and drew her sword from its scabbard. Instantly, black flames began licking their way along the blade.

"You do not deserve that sword," I snarled. "Foolish godling. You have no idea what to do with the power you have. You turn away those you should be embracing, because of your own stupid pride."

"So says the betraying bitch," Mollis hissed.

She got into a stance as if she was about to strike, and I used that moment to throw my dagger, hard and fast, at her sword hand. It hit her just right, the handle striking her knuckles in such a way that her hand flexed, and the sword fell from her stunned grip, its flames sizzling then flickering out.

"Like I said: you do not deserve that weapon," I said, and then she launched herself at me.

"Betraying, lying, backstabbing Guardian," she shouted. She landed a decent hit to my stomach.

I'm sorry. She said in my thoughts, and I had to suppress a laugh.

"You're just angry with me for that time I fucked your husband," I taunted, and she snarled, growled, and hit me again, this time a punch to the kidneys, though I could see that she was biting her lip as if trying not to laugh.

Ooh, that was a good one. You are very good at this bitchy thing, she said in my mind.

I punched then.

"Yeah, and then you started up with Brennan. What is up with that, anyway? You like my leftovers?" she said aloud. *Actually, you just have really good fucking taste,* she added in my mind, and then it was my turn to bite back a laugh.

"Perhaps if you did not leave so many leftovers behind," I said aloud. "Are you going to continue sleeping your way through Nain's team, or are you done now?" She fell against me. It looked like we were grappling, when in truth she was smothering her laughter against my shoulder.

Such a bitch, she said admiringly in my mind. *We're gonna wrap this up. I'm gong to hit you. Stay down, like I hurt you. Then I'm going to tell you to go.*

I grunted, which I hoped she would take as my assent.

She kicked out, catching me hard in the stomach, and then she punched, giving my jaw a fairly brutal uppercut.

I fell back, groaning.

I stayed down.

She retrieved her sword, held it, its flames flickering above me.

"I should end you," she sneered. "The only thing saving you is the history we had together. Get the fuck out of my realm and do not ever come back. You won't get another chance to walk away."

With that, she stalked away.

I pulled myself up slowly, wiping blood away from my mouth where I'd bitten my lip. Four demons surrounded me, ready to escort me out. I could see the immortals watching.

I bent and picked up my dagger, sheathed it.

"I can find my own way out, thanks," I said to the demons. And then I focused and reappeared in my apartment.

"What the hell happened to you?" Quinn asked in greeting. I glanced toward the small table and chairs near the window in my living room. Quinn, Erin, and Cathleen were there, playing cards in hand.

"It is not important," I said, waving him off. "Are you rested up?"

"We are," he answered.

"Good. We have souls and undead to track." I headed into the bathroom to change and get myself cleaned up. My phone was in my pocket, and it buzzed.

As I guessed, it was Brennan. I sighed before hitting the button to answer. Word spread fast, apparently.

"What the hell is this I hear about Molly fighting you?" he demanded. "Are you okay?"

"I am fine. Be silent and listen." I told him in a low voice out what had happened, about our ploy, as I changed and wiped my face with a washcloth.

Once I was finished, there were a few moments of silence from his end. "Well, I'm glad you're okay," he said, and I was relieved that he had the sense to remember himself, just in case anyone was listening on his end. "I'm on patrol duty tonight. Can I see you soon? Tomorrow night? Dinner?"

"I should work," I began to argue. He hung up on me, and I stared at my phone in disbelief. Then it vibrated in my hand, showing a message from Brennan.

You just got back. She called you back here for a reason. You can't be approached by whoever it is if you take off right away.

He had made a good choice in going with text rather than speaking the words out loud. It would have been annoying to have gone through being Mollis's punching bag only to have someone overhear us discussing the farce.

I grimaced. He was right. In my desire to go after more souls, I had forgotten that I still had a part to play in Detroit. Another message appeared.

It's easiest to do that if you get out in public some. Get seen, so whoever it is knows you're around.

I shook my head and typed in a response. *You are willing to use just about anything to your advantage, aren't you?*

After a moment, his answer appeared. *Absolutely. I'll be there at eight tomorrow. Want to try out that new fancy restaurant Rayna opened?*

I sighed. Typed again: *Lovely. See you then.*

I shook my head and put my phone on the counter. I shrugged out of my jacket.

In spite of myself, I was more than a little excited to see him again. It had been too long, and the prospect of touching him, kissing him again was too tempting to ignore. And while I fully intended to do nothing more than sleep, within moments I had another text, this time from Rayna, asking me to meet her for dinner. With a sigh, I accepted, then headed into my bedroom to change.

This whole "being seen" thing was causing me to be more sociable than I usually liked.

* * *

I leaned back in my seat, waiting for Rayna to arrive. Why I had allowed this ridiculous outing was beyond me.

That wasn't the entire truth, I thought to myself. The fact was, I quite liked the woman who was the leader of the region's vampires. Shanti looked up to her, and in the time I had gotten to know her, I could see that the amount of respect she received had definitely been earned. And yes. Brennan had had a point: I would have to be seen if I wanted to be approached by our betrayer.

As I sat, I looked around. I was sitting at a small table on a patio outside a sushi restaurant in Grosse Pointe. Soft jazz music filtered from the speakers mounted on the outer wall of the small brick building, and the tables around mine were all packed, conversation and laughter surrounding me. My mind wandered and I had to keep pulling it back every time it wandered to a certain shifter I was trying not to think about.

"Are you waiting for anyone?" a familiar voice asked to my left. I looked up into the achingly beautiful face of Persephone, her long curtain of fiery hair still visible beneath the black veil she continued to wear.

"Persephone," I said in greeting. "I am, but she seems to be running late. Would you like to sit?"

She nodded, and sat in the wrought-iron chair opposite me. The water came to take her order, and she waved him off.

"You were the last person I expected to see here," I said to her after a few awkward moments. Persephone, despite all the hundreds of years she'd spent as Hades' wife, was not ever anyone that I had much contact with. She chose to keep to herself, so, while she was always at Hades' side, it mostly felt as if the other beings of the Nether weren't even there, invisible to her, somehow.

"I was out wandering. That flower shop down the block is quite nice, actually," she said. Then she gave a wry smile. "You expected me to be at my husb— at Hades' monument," she said, correcting herself in mid sentence.

"It is where you usually seem to be. I have considered coming to speak with you, but I do not want to intrude."

She gave a small nod. "Thank you for that." She took a breath. "We each have our own way of working through things. This is mine."

I stirred my drink listlessly. "How are you holding up?"

She shrugged, a move that, when she made it, looked elegant and refined. It was very easy to see how the god of death had fallen for this woman, despite the love he had for Tisiphone.

"Well enough. I never truly realized before all of this how horrible I am at letting go of things."

I did not know how to respond to that. She was watching me, then gave a tiny nod. "Even as isolated as I am from the rest of you, I have heard whispers that you and Hades' daughter have parted ways. And that fight earlier today was... honestly you are lucky you walked away from that alive, Guardian."

I shrugged. "She has a temper, and a great dislike for lying."

She nodded again. "You know, as does everyone, that I do not have much love for Mollis. Perhaps I am petty. Either way, I have to say that she seems like a complete fool for cutting ties to you over this. You did your job, a much harder job than anyone could have guessed, from what my mother has said. How you can put up with Mollis and her high horse is beyond me."

"Well, I am not currently putting up with her at all," I said with a shrug.

"But if she called today, even after what happened earlier, you would come. It is in your nature," she said, watching me appraisingly.

I, for one, was really beginning to tire of the assumption that because I am a Guardian, I am also essentially the equivalent of a well-trained and very loyal guard dog.

"We have all changed much since being cut off from the Aether and Nether. And the Guardians were never entirely what everyone believed us to be."

She sat, still watching me, an impassive look on her face. And then she smiled, just a little. "You always were the least conforming of your kind."

"You are just noticing this?" I asked, raising my eyebrow.

She laughed, and at the sound, which was rich and warm and full of an underlying seductiveness, made men at other tables turned to look at her. She had that effect on people. "No. I have always known it. Hades noticed it long ago. He could never tell any of the Guardians apart, except for you. I daresay he liked that about you, if for no other reason than that he enjoyed knowing which of you he was speaking to when you talked."

I smiled, remembering the few, but always interesting, discussions I had had with the Lord of the Nether over the millennia.

I noticed that she had what appeared to be a black piece of paper in her hand. She held her hand out, apparently aware that I had observed it. It was not paper, but a single black flower petal, dried, almost shriveled.

"Is that from the Netherwoods?" I asked her, and she nodded.

"Did you know that my mother and Gaia each created a variety of flower that only grows at the base of Hades' monument?" she asked quietly, eyes on the petal.

"I had heard that," I answered.

"They said I should do the same, that it would help me heal." As she spoke, I felt the prickling sensation of immortal power, and, as I watched, the shriveled petal swelled, becoming glossy, with a deep luster that reminded me of dark satin. And, more, over the span of a few seconds, an entire pitch-black bloom, complete with silver-thorned stem, formed in her hand.

I looked up at her, and her eyes were on the flower. "I always have one of those stupid petals with me lately, when I am not there," she said quietly.

"Why?"

She tore her eyes away from the blossom, meeting my eyes. "After thousands of years living with death, I had forgotten that what I am, more than anything, is the embodiment of life eternal. I have the power to create," she said, and then I watched as the flower shriveled and fell apart in her hand, until only a few petals remained in her hand, the rest having fallen to dust. "Just as much as I have the power to destroy." She glanced up at me again. "I lost my way. I forgot how magical life can be."

I did not know what to say. She did not seem like someone who was particularly cherishing the joy of life. However, I knew that each of us mourns and heals in our own way. Perhaps if she said it enough, she would, one day, come to believe it again.

"I think perhaps you should consider creating something for the monument," I finally said. "Maybe your mother is right?"

"Perhaps. I have some ideas," she answered. "I should go. I want to get back to say my goodnights before Tisiphone shows up there."

I watched her rise, and give me a curt nod, and then she was gone. I stared at where she had been, feeling an ache inside. Her sadness, her sense of loss, was all-encompassing. And I was beginning to realize what that could feel like.

It was not something I particularly wanted to feel. Ever.

"Well you look like someone just stole your lollipop or something," Rayna's wry voice said. I glanced up, and she was standing beside the table.

"Just thinking," I said, shaking my head.

She sat, chuckling softly. "Yeah. I can guess what you were thinking about."

"There is one topic I do not want to discuss this evening. Can we do that?" I asked her.

She grinned. "Fine with me." A waiter arrived and we ordered, and then Rayna leaned back in her seat, looking around.

"Does it tempt you at all?" I asked, glancing at the humans, the Normals, as the superpowered beings in the city called them, seated around us.

Rayna shook her head. "I am old enough that I really only need to feed every week or two."

"And how do you do that, then? Do you just find a random person?" I had had very little contact with the bloodborn in general. They had always been rather out of our sphere of interest, and, until Shanti, I had never actually spoken to one. But I realized that like any other group of people, each of them was different and chose to use their powers in their own way.

Bloodborn. I had become aware, in the past few weeks, that the vampires rarely ever used the label "vampire" when referring to themselves. "Bloodborn" was the term they used, and I was attempting to break my habit of thinking of them by any name other than the one they preferred.

Rayna sipped her water, and continued. "We have two humans on staff. One, a woman Ronan insisted on hiring, is off-limits because we freak her out."

"Yet she works for the bloodborn?" I asked, raising my eyebrow.

She shrugged. "We pay very well. She is a genius at handling all of the day to day details of our home and dealing with the other humans. Besides her, we have a male butler and driver. He also manages the landscapers and oversees the property in general. He enjoys the bonuses he receives when he lets us feed from him."

I nodded. "Do you have to be careful about feeding from him too often?"

"Oh, of course. Too much will weaken him, and that's the last thing we want. Luckily, other than Zero, all of us are old enough to have control of our blood lust."

"And how is Zero?" I asked, crossing my legs. Zero was Shanti's boyfriend, turned just before I had left for a while a couple of years ago. I nodded a thanks to the waiter when he set a plate of sushi before each of us, along with small cups of sake.

"He mostly handles it," she said, picking up her chopsticks and selecting a bite. "At this point, it is more his fear of losing control holding him back than anything else. I am astounded by how disciplined he has been. All of us: me, Ronan, Shanti, Sam... we all messed up early on and went too far. It is one of the dangers of being what we are, and not having someone strong watching over us. Even without us, Zero would be fine. He is going to be a formidable warrior for us once he masters his fear."

"And are warriors much needed in your territory, Queen Rayna?" I asked. They were a very secretive group, and even Mollis was not privy to all that happened in their family.

She took another bite, then smiled. "There is one topic I do not want to discuss this evening. Can we do that?" she asked, throwing my own words back at me.

I raised my eyebrow at her, partially in irritation, and partially in amusement. "Fine. It is only fair."

She laughed, and we shared our meal, and she talked about an exhibit of Frida Kahlo and Diego Rivera's artworks that she had attended at the Detroit Institute of Arts. Over tea, she shared a few of the more amusing stories from what I knew to be her and Ronan's rather difficult past. By the time we were finished, I had laughed more than I had expected to and found that the rather intimidating (for a non-god, at any rate) bloodborn queen was really quite amusing when she wanted to be.

We stood up and started walking down the street. The cool late fall night air was laced with the scent of fallen leaves and smoke from fireplaces in the neighborhood.

"As fun as this was, and as much as I enjoy sitting and staring at you," Rayna began. I rolled my eyes and she laughed. She continued, "I do actually have something I wanted to ask you about. Work-related," she added.

"What is it?"

She wrinkled her brow. "Shanti came across a couple of dead bodies. One, unfortunately was one of ours. The other was..." she shrugged, trailing off. "It smells wrong."

I nodded. I knew that the bloodborn had very acute senses. "Wrong, how?"

"I'm not sure. Just not normal. We were planning to dispose of both bodies, but I wanted one of your kind to have a look at them first. It's not anything I'm familiar with, but you all might be."

"Are they at your home?"

She nodded.

"Have you rematerialized before?"

"No. But I have always wondered what that felt like."

"Are vampires prone to vomiting?"

She let out a short laugh. "Not this one, E."

"We shall see," I murmured, holding my hand out for her to take. She put her cool hand in mine with a smirk. "What?"

"You could have just told me how badly you wanted to hold hands, babe."

I rolled my eyes. "Please. We both know you've wanted to have your hands on me all evening."

She laughed. "Not even gonna bother denying that," she answered with a wink. I shook my head and laughed, and then I closed my eyes and focused on rematerializing into the foyer of the large home the queen and her family lived in in the Indian Village neighborhood.

When we reappeared in the large foyer at her home, we were met with a scream and the sound of something breaking. I looked to our left, where a human female was standing, mouth hanging open, a tray and what looked as if they had been coffee cups shattered on the wood floor around her.

"I'm sorry we startled you, Rebecca," Rayna said. I glanced at her. Not a sign of nausea, I noted with some respect. "Immortals and their weird travel methods," she joked, trying to help the shaken human relax.

"Oh. Of course," the woman said, bowing her head in my direction a little. "I am sorry about the dishes," she said to Rayna. "You can take them out of my pay if you wish."

"Not a chance. That was my fault. Well, really, it was her fault," she said, pointing at me. "I'll have her pay me."

I rolled my eyes and made a subtle rude gesture in her direction, and Rayna laughed. My gaze went back to the human. She was quite pretty. Shapely, voluptuous, with a mass of dark brown curls flowing over her shoulders and down her back. She was dressed in a skirt, knee-length brown boots and a black top that showed just a bit of enviable cleavage.

"Sorry again about the surprise," Rayna told her. "Are you all right?"

The woman laughed. "I'm fine. Really, you think I'd be used to insanity by now," she said wryly, and Rayna laughed.

Rayna tuned to me. "This way, E. They're in the cellar." I nodded, and we started walking, leaving the poor human behind.

"Well I can see why Ronan insisted on hiring her," I said under my breath.

Rayna chuckled. "Everyone except him seems to see it for what it is. You should see him around her. He becomes an absolute fool."

I laughed, finding it impossible to envision the taciturn bloodborn warrior acting foolishly, but knowing, at the same time, that we all have sides to our personality that only come out around the right people.

Rayna led me through the large kitchen, into a back hallway, and then down a rather steep flight of stairs into the basement level of the home.

"Those are our sleeping quarters on that half of the basement," she said, gesturing toward a row of identical steel doors. "The bodies are in here." She opened a steel door on the other side of the cellar, and gestured for me to go in.

Two bodies were laid out on a surgical-looking steel table. I raised an eyebrow questioningly.

"Sam and the other healing crew sometimes need to stitch us up. We heal quickly, but a deep enough gash needs help with healing," she explained. "Hell, Sam has attached entire limbs in this room. After living in our first house and having things like that occur in our kitchen, I decided we would never live in a place without a dedicated hospital area again."

"That would put a damper on morning coffee," I murmured, my attention turning to the pale bodies on the table.

One male, one female. Both pale, with the waxen look the newly-dead so often have. The female was young, possibly in her early twenties. Her mouth was open, as if in an endless scream, and I could see two fangs behind her lips.

"So she was yours?" I asked Rayna.

She nodded. "Tracy. She was a badass. She and Shanti were becoming friends," she finished. Then she pulled the sheet back from Tracy's body, and I could immediately see why this vampire, this immortal creature, had died: her chest was brutally ripped open, a gaping hole. A glance inside showed that her heart had been ripped from her.

My gaze shifted to the other one. The body that felt "wrong" to the vampire queen. And I immediately knew why as my Guardian knowledge flared. This was Fisker, a man who'd died in Copenhagen, and escaped from his prison on the Nether with twenty-seven other souls. He was the one Brennan and I had been unable to locate during our time in Denmark. Fisker had been a serial murderer in life and, in death, he had become something nearly as horrid.

Undead.

He had a body. A full, corporeal form, despite the fact that I still recognized him as a soul that belonged to my Queen. I looked him over. Two small puncture wounds in his neck suggested that Tracy had tried to feed from him. I pointed them out to Rayna, and she nodded.

"I noticed that too. What the hell is this thing, E? And did it do this to Tracy?"

"My guess is, yes. Damn it," I muttered.

She looked at me questioningly.

"We have had a problem... Mollis and her family have had this problem. Several souls escaped from their prison in the old Nether when her father still ruled there. Well, escaped with the aid of someone else," I added, and she nodded. "I have been tracking them down to bring them back where they belong."

"It's what you're meant to do, right?" she asked, and I was reminded that as little as I understood of the bloodborn, she understood just as little about our kind.

I nodded. "That is my one and only role, yes. I began tracking them down, and what I found was that some of them were gaining corporeal, solid forms. In that form, they can manipulate objects. They can harm the living." I took a breath, trying to decide how much to tell her. "It does not happen without aid. And some of our kind… some of my sisters were aiding them. They become this," I said, gesturing to the male body, "which we refer to as undead, by eating the still-beating heart of a human three times."

"Okay," she said slowly, her brow furrowed, her arms crossed. "And?"

"They are ridiculously strong. Cunning. Endlessly hungry for living flesh. The heart, of course, is their favorite part, but they will feed on other parts as well," I said, pointing to the chunks of flesh missing from Tracy's throat and arm.

"Stronger than one of us, though?" Rayna asked dubiously.

"Usually not," I said, looking at the bodies again. "But it looks as if Tracy fed from him. Perhaps his blood did not agree with her. And once she was distracted or weak or whatever the issue was, he was able to do the rest of this," I said, gesturing to Tracy's chest.

"But he's dead, too. So what happened?"

"My guess is that we now know what happens when an undead tries to feed from one of the bloodborn," I said, chewing my lip as I thought. "Or his own blood flowing through her heart hurt him when he ate it. I can only guess at this point. We have never come across a situation like this." I transferred my gaze to Rayna. "I am sorry for your loss."

"Thank you," she said quietly. "I did not know her well. Is it cold of me that at this point, it only bothers me because one of mine was taken from me?"

I shook my head. "You are old enough to understand certain things my kind know well. You know that life is ever-fleeting."

She nodded.

"And if you are cold, that makes me just as cold. My only concern when I look at this situation is that things just got a whole lot worse."

She looked at me questioningly. "How so?"

"The undead threat has arrived in Detroit. It is spreading. It was contained to certain areas in Europe and Asia. I thought we had more time before we would have to deal with it here."

Rayna's gaze went to the body of the undead again. "Well, count us in if you all need help containing this shit. I don't want to lose any more of my people."

CHAPTER TEN

Rayna and I left her home shortly after, and ended up walking through a neighborhood on the city's Southwest side. This time of night, some of the bars in the area were a tempting place for less scrupulous vampires to cause trouble, and Rayna confirmed what I had already heard from Nain's team: there had been a surge in violence in the area of late. We strolled casually, though I knew Rayna was constantly listening for any signs of trouble, though it soon became clear that all was quiet, in this part of the city, at least.

"Shanti was on duty here last night," Rayna said. "It is likely any troublemakers have been scared off."

I nodded. This had been Shanti's neighborhood during her human life, and she still had mortal family in the area. I knew she had taken responsibility for keeping the Southwest side safe because of them.

We were on a busy street; bars, restaurants, and shops on each side of the wide, multi-laned road. The sounds of laughter and music flowed from the buildings as doors opened and closed, and traffic roared past, carrying with it the scent of exhaust. Ahead, I saw a familiar sign: large black letters that said "Punch, Inc" over a red boxing glove. This was the martial arts studio Shanti's boyfriend, Zero, owned with a friend of his.

And it occurred to me that I had a new sword and very little practice using one. I glanced over at Rayna.

"I do not suppose you would be interested in sparring with me, then?" I asked, nodding my head toward Zero's studio. The lights were on, and I had a feeling we might find Shanti there, since it was her night off and Zero would undoubtedly want to check in on his business and the friend he ran it with. "I have heard numerous times how deadly you are with a sword."

She smiled. "Haven't you had enough fighting for a while?"

At that moment, Megaera appeared, turning a corner barely ten feet in front of me.

"Hey. I was looking for you," she said, walking toward me. My stomach turned. I had hoped, very much, that we had been wrong about Megaera. Meg never sought me out. We were not one another's favorite people. I generally made her uncomfortable and she made me tense.

"What can I do for you, Megaera?" I asked, trying to keep my tone neutral. Rayna and I stopped walking, and Megaera approached us, stopping inches from me, ignoring Rayna completely.

"That little tussle you had with my niece was cute," she snarled. "You really think you're some kind of a badass, don't you?"

"With thousands of years of evidence to support the belief. Yes," I said, crossing my arms over my chest. "And you are not supposed to be talking to me."

"I'll talk to who I want to talk to." She finally seemed to notice that Rayna was present. "Excuse us," she said, taking my arm roughly and pulling me a few feet away. I glanced back at Rayna to see her watching us with a concerned expression on her face. I held my hand up, urging her to stay out of it, and she gave a small nod.

"All right. What do you want?" I asked, shaking her hand off of me.

"You come into our realm and start a fight with Mollis. I don't even know what you're thinking anymore," she hissed.

"Well, technically, it is my realm as well. And there were things I wanted to say."

"Such as?"

"Those things are for her ears, not yours, Fury."

"Yeah? Well here's the thing, Guardian. My niece has no shortage of enemies. She has earned every single one of them."

"Indeed she has," I said mildly.

"She is not an enemy you want. And neither am I. Because make no mistake about it, if you continue to add more problems to everything else she is already dealing with, I will show you why it is that I am the Fury most known for being an absolutely spiteful bitch."

"I— what?" I asked, thrown off guard. This was the last thing I had expected to hear from her.

"Do not mess with my family, Guardian. I'm not her mother, but she's the closest thing I have to a child of my own, and I will not hesitate to punish those who cause her grief. Don't make me have to come after you again." She paused, and a cold smile crossed her lips. "Or do. It has been a while since my sword has been bathed in the blood of my enemies." In the next instant she was gone, and Rayna walked up to me.

"Well, she was pissed," she said.

I nodded.

"And also hot as fuck," she said breathlessly. "Damn."

"She just threatened my life," I pointed out.

"Like I said. Hot," she repeated, and I rolled my eyes. "Does she like girls?"

"Megaera does not like anybody," I said, and we started walking again.

She shook her head. "Anyway," she finally said. "Like we were saying. I think you said something about wanting to fight?" she laughed. "Her timing was perfect."

"She is the perfect example. The fighting never ends."

"Maybe you should stop pissing so many people off," she said, and I shook my head.

"I have been called an ice queen. That one? She can freeze you with nothing but a look. I have never seen her show any regard for anyone other than Mollis. And sometimes Tisiphone."

I felt immeasurably better about Megaera now. Of course, we still did not know who the betrayer was, but I was more than happy to still have to figure it out as long as I could tell Mollis that it did not appear to be her aunt. I typed out a quick text to Mollis updating her, noted that Brennan had sent a message telling me he was looking forward to the next night, and tried not to be too giddy over the prospect.

"You immortals are no fun. You need to lighten up a little."

I looked at her in disbelief and shoved my phone back into my pocket. "Rayna, I am Death's hunter. I am an immortal of the Nether. I do not lighten up."

She laughed, and I sunk back into my morose state, the temporary relief over Megaera having passed. "And I think you are at least a little familiar with what that is like."

We walked in silence for a few moments. "Yeah, I am. Like you can't breathe sometimes. Like you feel like an asshole every time you take a break, because you know that the second you let your guard down, some jackass is going to take advantage of it."

"Yes."

"Like every bad thing that happens on your watch is your own personal failing."

"That, too," I said.

"And sometimes the only thing that makes any sense is the way it feels when you're fighting."

"Fighting, I understand. It is clear-cut. If someone is attacking me or someone I care for, they get destroyed," I said. "All of this," I said, waving my hand, indicating everything and nothing. "This maneuvering and backstabbing and betrayal and revenge… it is all so pointless. You would think that after eons of existence, my kind would get over this desire for power or revenge or whatever reason it is this time that trouble is stirring."

"And you're sure it's your kind doing this?"

I nodded. "It is the only thing I am absolutely sure of. And this world is suffering again. We thought things were bad with the various immortals who were going after Mollis, facing off against her. At least that is a threat that can be fought in a straightforward way. This, what is happening now? It is a whole new level of insanity. The human realm would be much better off without my kind in it at all."

We continued walking. "Well. I am glad you're here," she said. "I mean, the fact is, you always have been, right?"

I nodded. "But we did not usually live here among you. Not most of us, at any rate."

"It's a period of change for your people. There's bound to be turmoil. The troublemakers will have their asses handed to them by you or Molly or the other immortals who are trying to keep things calm. It'll all work itself out eventually."

I gave her a small smile. "You have a lot more faith than I do."

She grinned. "Old enough to know better, young enough to still hope. It's a nice place to be. So do you want to spar, or what?" she asked, nodding toward Zero's studio.

I nodded, and she opened the front door and waved me inside.

The studio was exactly what one would expect from two military men, I mused as I glanced around. The front wall of the building was mostly taken up by the plate-glass windows that looked out onto the street. The walls were painted a deep warm brown, and the wood floors gleamed. Punching bags stood in two of the corners, and one wall held a row of steel lockers.

Toward the rear of the building, there was a doorway into what I supposed was some kind of office or storage area, and it was through there that Shanti, Zero, and another male I had not yet met came out to see who had entered.

"E!" Shanti said, rushing to me and hugging me. I hugged her back, laughing a bit as she gave me a squeeze. "It's good to see you."

"Are you sure she's supposed to be here?" Zero asked quietly, eyes on me. Shanti sent a glare over her shoulder at him, and he met it calmly. "She's fighting with Molly, right?" he asked.

Shanti turned back to me, rolling her eyes. "Well, Molly is not here right now, is she? And honestly," she said this part to me, still holding me in her arms, "the whole thing is stupid. I get that you lied."

I nodded.

"And that was wrong" she chided, even as she continued to smile, her dimples deepening as she did so, "but I also know you enough to know that if you did that, you had your damn reasons. And if Molly gets mad at me for hanging out with you, I am fine with telling her that."

I smiled at Shanti. "Thank you. How have you been?" She looked fabulous. She still wore her customary sleek bob, her black hair shining under the lights of the studio. Her dark eyes sparkled, and I noticed with a smile that she now wore a diamond ring, the gem sparkling beautifully against her skin.

"Perfect," she said happily, another glance in Zero's direction. This one, however, elicited an adoring look from the male she had selected as her mate. "What are you doing here?" She finally released me.

"I seem to be in possession of a new sword, and my skills with that weapon are a bit rusty. Rayna and I were out tonight, and I saw this place and remembered that she has quite the reputation with a blade."

Shanti nodded. "She does. I can help you practice, too. And Parker's not half bad, either," she added, gesturing toward the male I did not know.

I glanced his way. He was likely the same age as Zero, somewhere in his late twenties or early thirties. And I cursed Brennan for insisting that I watch the Thor superhero movies, because when I looked at him all I could see was the actor who played the role of Heimdall.

"Oh, right. You two haven't met," Shanti said. "Parker Rowland, this is Eunomia."

"She's not a vampire," he said, studying me.

"No. She's a god," Shanti said, and, after a moment, Parker nodded.

"Nice to meet you," he said, and I found myself smiling. He was clearly not a Normal who had had much experience dealing with supernaturals. I knew he was Zero's best friend, and I realized it was likely that his knowledge of non-humans had begun the day Zero told him what he was.

"Likewise," I said.

"So, are we going to stand her talking all night, or are we going to spar?" Rayna asked.

Zero shook his head and went over to one of the locked storage lockers, returning moments later with two swords.

"Yours is similar in style to this, yes?" Rayna asked me.

I nodded. "It was why I asked you, specifically. The blade you use is very similar to the one I will be using."

"Perfect," she said. We each had a blade, and stood in the center of the studio while Parker, Zero, and Shanti sat on one of the benches near the wall. Rayna smirked at me. "I assume I don't need to tell you how to hold it, at least."

"I think I can manage that much. Shall we?" I asked, and she grinned, and then she was on me with a flash of steel and speed.

I spent the next several hours fending off the deadly sword arm of the bloodborn queen, and it was exactly what I needed.

The next day passed in a flurry of gathering as many souls from Detroit and the surrounding area as we were able to in an attempt to head off the creation of any more undead. When we were not doing that, I spent time training my team. After all we had been through, I now had little fear of them betraying me, and I recognized that Brennan had been right about the benefits of training them. When I finally made my way back to my apartment after turning more souls over to Mollis in our meeting place, I did so with my stomach twisting, my nervousness growing as the minutes ticked by.

I was that much closer to seeing him again, and I had never felt so nervous in my entire life.

My team teased me ceaselessly, and I finally tore myself away from their bawdy jokes with a half-hearted rude gesture before I ducked into my bedroom, their laughter following me.

I rifled through the minimal items in my closet. There was a long-sleeved black dress I had bought for an event I had gone to during the time I had spent in New York during my travels. It fell to just above my knees. It fit me well, and covered all of my scars, which I liked. I did not enjoy the humans staring at them. I pulled it on, as well as my usual black boots. I tucked a Netherblade into each boot, did my makeup, and messed around with my hair until it fell in a way I was satisfied with. When I went back out into the living room, Quinn whistled.

"So I'm guessin' not to wait up for ye, eh?" Claire asked with a grin.

I shook my head. "Enjoy the night off. We will be leaving when I return."

There was a knock at the door, and I waved to them, leaving their laughs behind.

I opened the door.

"You are stunning," Brennan said in greeting. I looked at him appraisingly. He was still dressed in the suit he'd likely worn to work, though his hair was down and he had splashed on cologne. I smiled to myself at the realization that he had put effort into this as well.

"Same to you. You are a manipulative male. You know this, yes?" I answered.

He grinned. "Did it get me what I wanted?"

I raised my eyebrow at him, and he placed his hand at the base of my spine, drawing me further into the hallway and out of my apartment. I closed the door behind me, locking it. "I suppose."

"Just admit that you wanted to see me, Tink," he said, leaning down and nuzzling the side of my neck. My breath hitched at the contact, and my heart pounded.

"Maybe," I breathed, and he laughed, low, against my neck.

"Soon, Eunomia. Soon I'm going to make sure you can't keep up this cool and collected act around me."

I swallowed, wondering if he knew how close he was to succeeding that already.

"Well, you can try," I said.

He raised his face, met my eyes. "I believe you just issued a challenge. I enjoy those." He smiled. "And I think you probably will, too."

I walked right into that one, I thought to myself as I let him pull me toward the elevator.

The drive to the restaurant was more comforting than I had expected it to be. I usually did not enjoy being in automobiles, and I particularly disliked being in an automobile that Brennan was driving. His tendency to dive in and out of traffic, to accelerate, to brake hard, often made me want to hurt him, at least a little bit. I knew I could not die, but somehow it did not make the experience any less stressful. He made an effort to drive more slowly when I was with him, and I appreciated it.

As we drove, he talked about work, and about Sean, and I filled him in on what we had accomplished in London.

"So she keeps just slipping away when you get anywhere near her?" he asked.

"Yes. It is extremely frustrating. She was difficult to apprehend in the first place. She knows more now. And I have no doubt that she is getting help. Too much is happening in London."

"I think you're right. But why her? What makes her so important, that she gets extra help from whoever is running this mess?" he asked.

"The only thing I can think of now is that she impressed whoever it is with her sheer will to be a nuisance. I can't help thinking that chaos is a huge part of what we are dealing with. Chaos, fear. And now that the humans are noticing, it is only becoming more chaotic."

"Is it just me, or do you get the feeling they're in a holding pattern or something? Like they're waiting, and then shit's going to get bad."

My stomach sank. He had voiced precisely the worries I had been harboring since our fruitless search in Whitechapel. I nodded. " I do. Which is why we need to stop this. I need the betrayer to reveal themselves. I do not think it will solve all of our problems, but it will halt the creation of more chaos."

He pulled up to the doors in front of a large, limestone building with a sign in the front window that said "Rayna's" in a gold flourish of letters. A valet opened my door, and I exited, then stood and waited as Brennan came around after giving his keys to another valet.

He took my hand in his. "Okay. So we have fun. We get seen. And when this is all over, we're going to spend days on end doing nothing but lying around bingewatching the Golden Girls."

I felt a smile forming, even as I shook my head and rolled my eyes. "You are not going to let me live that down, are you?"

He laughed and squeezed my hand. "It's one of the things I love about you, Tink."

Once we were inside the restaurant, I made a note to myself to make sure I told Rayna how impressed I was. The interior of the restaurant had a 1920s feel to it, a very authentic sense of the period, which made sense. I had been there, after all, and so had she, though she had been a child at the time. The walls were painted a deep red, which was, perhaps, a nod to Rayna's bloodborn status. In the waiting area, there were two long rows of white velvet upholstered art deco settees. Beyond, in the dining area, I could see a long mahogany bar, a row of matching stools. The tables were all set with white linens, period-inspired arrangements of blood red roses in the center of each one. Enormous chandeliers hung from the ceiling at regular intervals, dripping with hundreds of crystals that twinkled as they caught the light. A man in a tuxedo played a grand piano on a stage in one corner. Overall, it had a dramatic, opulent feel.

"It's very Rayna, isn't it?" Brennan murmured to me after speaking with the *maître d'*. I nodded, and he put his arm around me, resting his hand on my hip. Once we were seated, we sat in awkward silence for a few moments.

"Can we do something, Cub?" I finally asked.

He started to smile, and I knew he was about to make some type of flirty remark, but he thought better of it. "Sure. What do you want to do?" he said instead.

I particularly loved it when he dropped the flirty act with me. I loved it when he flirted, but I enjoyed our time together even more when he was simply himself.

"Can we not talk about work tonight? At all?"

He smiled and nodded. "That sounds like something we both sorely need."

"It seems like it is all we talk about."

"I know. Not tonight, though," he said, and I smiled.

After a few more moments of silence, both of us sipping our drinks and fiddling with our napkins for a lack of anything else to do, he finally laughed. "We are so bad at this, Eunomia."

"I suspected as much," I said in agreement. Workaholics, both of us, defined almost entirely by the things we did in service of our friends and family and those unfortunate enough to have to deal with us. I opened the small handbag I had brought with me and pulled out a piece of paper I'd ripped from a steno notebook in my apartment.

"What is that?" he asked with a laugh.

"A list."

"A list of what?"

"Questions to ask you."

"This feels very formal, Tink," he said with a smile.

"I am new at this," I said wryly, and he reached across the table and took one of my hands in his.

"I am too. Ask away. Just promise me you'll answer some questions about yourself, too."

I nodded, aware that I was blushing yet again. How did he manage to do that so easily?

"All right. First question: when were you born and what were your parents' names?"

He squeezed my hand again, then sat back and we both waited as the waiter set an appetizer of shrimp cocktail in front of us.

"I was born on October 4th, 1975. Shifter women usually have home births, because the pain of labor tends to make it hard for them to control the shift, and we definitely do not want to have to answer questions at at time like that."

I nodded, and he continued. "So I was born in the bedroom of my grandmother's house in Hamtramck. We were part of the Hamtramck pack back then, though our alliance ended when my parents started working more with Nain."

"Why?" I asked.

"The packs have a weird relationship with Nain. We appreciate that he does good things. But shifters are almost notoriously obsessed with privacy, with taking care of their own problems. It was always a source of embarrassment when things among any of the shifter packs got so back that Nain had to step in. My parents believed in what he was doing, though. It was a bit easier to make that decision after my dad's mother, my grandmother, died, which was shortly after I was born, I guess. No more family ties to the pack," he explained, and I nodded.

"My mother's name was Rhiannon Matthews. My father's name was Sean."

I tilted my head. "You have your mother's last name."

He nodded, and smiled, as if remembering. "My father took her name and gave up his own. I didn't realize why that might have been until I found out what it is, exactly, that I am."

I nodded. Of course, his father would have recognized how much more powerful Brennan's mother, who, herself, was also a direct descendent of Artemis, would have been.

"Can you tell me about them?"

He gave a small laugh. "Why?"

I shrugged. "Perhaps I want to understand you. You are often a mystery to me, Cub. Maybe if I know more about the people who raised you, I will have some understanding of you."

"If either of us is a mystery, it's you, Eunomia," he said, taking my hand again. The warmth in his gaze, that small smile on his lips. In that moment, he was my entire world, and I had never, ever felt that before. I had never felt so completely overcome by anyone in my entire existence. I would have suspected some kind of sorcery, but I am old enough to have seen it all.

There was no spell, no enchantment, that could match what I was feeling when I looked at him.

"There is nothing mysterious about me," I managed in a quiet voice.

"So you say," he answered. "I want to know it all, eventually."

I blushed, and gave a small nod. "Your parents?" I reminded him.

He tangled his fingers with mine, and began rubbing his thumb along the side of my hand as he spoke. "My dad was a lot like Nain, I guess. It makes sense that they were good friends. Really gruff, not a man of many words, but when he said something, everyone listened. I look a lot like him." He paused. "I can show you a picture of them sometime."

"That would be nice," I said.

"Except for my eyes, I think. My mom's eyes were the same color as mine. My dad was a workaholic. He was with Nain during the '67 riots, and I think it changed him. Made him more focused. That's when he met my mom, actually."

"Oh?"

"She was on Nain's team. She was really close to Ada," he stopped and smiled. "Actually, Ada was with my mom when she gave birth to me."

I found myself smiling back. "No wonder she has so much love for you."

He nodded. "She was always around when I was a kid. And after my parents died, and I went to live with Nain, Ada was the only mother figure I had. And she is everything I could have asked for, beyond having my own mom back."

Our food arrived, and I missed his hand in mine almost immediately. I glanced down at my food. I had ordered a steak, as had Brennan, and my stomach rumbled just a bit as the peppery, rich smell of it wafted toward me.

"This looks amazing," I said, and Brennan nodded. We ate in silence for a few moments.

"So you've told me about your father. Tell me about your mother," I finally said, taking another bite of steak.

He nodded. "My mom was… she was living magic. She was loud, and opinionated. She did not take any crap, you know?"

I nodded again, watched him as he chewed a bite of his steak.

"She lived fully. Everything she did, she did fully. If she fought, it was almost a given that whoever's ass she was kicking would come away bruised and limping. When she looked at my dad, you could practically feel the love. And when she hugged you, she hugged you so hard, so completely, that it was impossible to feel anything but warm and loved."

He paused, and for not the first time, I wished I had known Rhiannon Matthews. Brennan clearly had no idea how much of his mother lived on in him.

"You could say the same for yourself, Brennan," I said.

He shook his head. "Only sometimes, maybe. Too often, I'm more like my dad. Which would be fine. A lot of the time, I'm not like either of them. A lot of the time, I'm more like some kind of robot that just does things in the order it's supposed to to finish a task."

I set down my utensils. He was not saying anything I had not already noticed.

"But when you are yourself, you are everything you admired in both of your parents. It is only when you forget who you are that you go into robot mode."

"At least in robot mode, I don't screw up." I wanted to fold him into my arms at the flat tone of his voice. He had made so many mistakes, with Mollis and everyone else. He had spent the past few years trying to make amends and rebuild the trust he had ruined among some on Nain's team, and with Mollis, especially.

"Making mistakes is not something to be ashamed of. It is how we learn. It is how we become better," I told him softly.

"You say 'we' as if you think it applies to you, too," he said.

"Because it does. If anyone is intimately familiar with living life in robot mode, it is me. I spent thousands of years in it."

"What made you change?"

"It did not happen all at once. I was ever devoted to serving Hermes and then Hades. Once command of the Guardians had been given to Hades, it felt like everything changed. Hermes truly saw us as machines of some kind, no more noticeable than a table, or a hammer. Required to perform, but beneath notice, really, beyond that. Of course, that was how we were meant to be seen. We are soldiers. Servants. Lesser gods," I said with a wry smile. "Hades treated us with more respect. It seemed to make no difference to my sisters. They carried on as they always had. But something changed in me the longer I worked for Hades. I began to see myself as more. I was still loyal to my duties, but, more so, I was loyal to Hades. It was the first time I realized there was something very wrong with me. We are supposed to feel loyalty for no one."

Brennan sat silently, listening.

"I came to know the Furies. Tisiphone, especially, treated me with kindness, which is very out of character for a Fury. I had a sense that we were two oddballs. She was perhaps the first being I considered a friend. That was the second indication that something was wrong with me. Emotion. We were not supposed to have them, especially not ones like that. Anger, rage, determination. Those are all right. Genuinely liking someone? I did not even know what it was I was feeling for a long time. I hid my defects well," I said with a smile. "And then I came to know

Hephaestus after his return to the Aether, and he was a friend to me in a way that not even Tisiphone had been. He was the only one I confided my fears about myself to. I knew all of his secrets, and he knew all of mine. Two defective beings surrounded by perfection."

"Or the only two really sane ones surrounded by immortal jerks," he said. I laughed.

"Perhaps," I said in agreement.

I took a breath. I knew he had questions about another immortal, and if I wanted this man in my life, which I was beginning to suspect I did, he needed to understand. "Triton changed things even more," I said.

I could see him trying to keep an impassive expression on his face. I knew he realized there was something more there, and his behavior in general toward Triton was reserved, and, while not rude, not exactly friendly, either.

"The first time I saw Triton, he was standing on one of the cliffs in Greece. I was there, searching for a soul. Anyway. I walked around a large outcropping, and there he was. Muscles and fiery hair and the way my body reacted to him scared the Nether out of me." I kept my eyes on his, holding contact. "I had never felt lust before. Never felt what it felt like to want something. It threw my entire world into chaos."

"Wanting him messed you up that much?" he asked, confused.

"I had never wanted *anything* before, Brennan," I said, trying to explain. "Not a thing. I did not know 'want.' And lust is a more overwhelming sense of wanting. It was terrifying, the way my stomach flipped, the way my body warmed, the way it felt as if I would suffocate, because it seemed like I could not remember how to breathe when he was around."

I knew he needed to hear something, so I smiled at him. "It is still terrifying, every time I look at you."

His gaze focused, intensified. "Me?"

I nodded.

His shoulders relaxed, and it looked as if the tension all fell away at once. "Same to you, Tink."

I smiled. "We became friends, and I believe he was completely unsuspecting of what I felt for him. I kept it hidden well, mostly. I think later, he knew. The feelings I had for him led to the first time I ever behaved badly. It marked the day my life changed completely."

"Tell me," he said softly.

We had finished our meal, and cups of steaming coffee and plates of rich chocolate tarts sat before us. I ran the tines of my fork through the dollop of whipped cream on my plate, trying to gather the courage to give words to something that had so shamed me at the time.

"I had been harboring all of those intense, terrifying feelings for him. Keeping them hidden from him. He did not know," I emphasized, trying to make Brennan understand it, and he nodded. "We had agreed to meet at a particular beach once my duties were finished for the day. I finished, and arrived there earlier than he expected me. I found him and a sea nymph together. I remember feeling frozen, numb. And then she cried out with pleasure, and I snapped out of it and rematerialized to a cave where I knew no one would come looking for me. I had never felt pain like that. Physical pain was something I understood, something I even welcomed because there is pride in besting a worthy opponent. But this kind of pain… it felt like something inside of me was dying a slow, agonizing death. Everything hurt, and I hated myself for it. I felt weak and foolish." I paused, and met his eyes.

"It was on that day that I realized that the danger in loving is in giving someone the ability to destroy you. Because you cannot truly love without giving up some of yourself, and it is a leap of faith to hope that the person you give it to cares enough for it that you keep yourself all in one piece. I came apart. I neglected my duties, and refused to heed Hades' call. I left, and I stayed gone for a very long time."

"What happened?" he asked.

"Hades finally came to get me. And he told me that now I truly understood what it was to be alive. I became his most trusted Guardian after that, and I worked for him as I now work for Mollis." I paused. "I suspect that was why I was sent to Detroit in the first place. He knew his daughter was here somewhere."

CHAPTER ELEVEN

After we left the restaurant, rather than having his car pulled around so we could leave, Brennan and I strolled down Jefferson Avenue, past the GM Building and ended up at the Riverwalk. The night air was cool bordering on cold; an early December preview of a winter to come. It did not bother me, of course, and Brennan did not seem overly bothered by it either. We walked, my hand held tightly, warmly in his, his thumb caressing the underside of my wrist.

We walked, and we talked. Mostly, I talked, and he listened. I told him about living as a Guardian, about Hermes, about my sisters. I told him about the first time I had tasted chocolate, and he laughed at the wonder in my voice.

"You threw a few names at me that night we talked about your scars," he said, sitting on a bench overlooking the Detroit River. I settled myself beside him, the side of my body pressed tightly to the side of his, and he put his arm around me. "Jack the Ripper, Genghis Khan, Al Capone. I'm still finding it all a little crazy. The concept of what you've seen in your lifetime is almost too much to comprehend." He smiled. "What does it feel like?"

"Immortality, you mean?" I asked softly, knowing it was something he thought about more often, since I had suggested that he likely had an unnaturally (for a shifter) long life ahead of him.

He nodded.

I took a breath, thinking. "It feels like you belong everywhere and nowhere. As if you can call any city on Earth home, because you know them all so well, yet, at the same time, finding a place that actually makes you feel centered and comfortable is nearly impossible." I put my hand on his thigh. I wondered to myself if his penchant for maintaining physical contact with those he cared for was not beginning to wear off on me as well. I enjoyed touching him, the feel of his warm skin against mine, the contours of his muscled body beneath my hands. "It is easy to become jaded. At some point, it begins to feel as if you have seen everything, and you tire of seeing humanity make the same mistakes over and over and over again. The first time you watch an empire fall, you will feel sure it will be impossible for anything like to happen again. And then you watch it happen countless times thereafter, and the impermanence of empires becomes commonplace. The space of a human life becomes fleeting. You realize this, and it makes you sure that getting to know any particular human is a waste of time, because they will be dust before you know it."

His head was bowed, listening to me, his hand rubbing up and down my arm. I smiled. "And then you realize how foolish you have been. The impermanence of life is what makes it beautiful, something to cherish. Each human is here for such a short time… they live more in sixty years than many immortals do in a thousand. We can learn so much from them, once we realize that everlasting life is nothing more than an excuse to avoid having to truly learn anything about ourselves or anyone else."

We sat in silence, his hand still running up and down my arm. The scent of him surrounded me, clean, wild, and comforting. I rested my head against his shoulder. "Your grandmother wants me to remind you that we are not positive you are immortal and you need to start being more careful, by the way," I said. "She messaged me this morning because she knew you would be seeing me." He chuckled.

"I know. She said the same thing to me. She's not letting it go since I got shot. You know what, though?"

"What?"

"I saw a picture of myself from when Molly first joined our team, and then I saw a photo Sean took of me when he was messing around with my phone. It's been almost seven years, and I look younger now than I did then."

I patted his thigh. "You have had Asclepius's healing and some of Mollis's blood. It makes sense that those things would take a few years of age off of you."

"I'm stronger than I was," he pressed.

"Same reasons for that, Cub." He was about to speak, and I held my hand up. "I believe you are immortal. But that tiny possibility that you might not be terrifies me. Please do not test it," I said, raising my face to his and meeting his eyes. "I would miss you if you were gone."

Hie gaze warmed, and he slowly lowered his lips to mine. I was caught up immediately, as always, in the feelings he raised within me. The things I had told him about Triton, the emotions Triton had made me feel, paled in comparison to the things I felt every time I looked at Brennan. If only I was brave enough to tell him so.

His kisses, first soft and sensual, became hungrier, more demanding. He kissed me, sucked and nibbled on my lower lip, and when his tongue lazily caressed mine, I gently bit it, and he groaned. His arms around me were like iron, and I tangled my fingers into his hair, keeping him close to me as we devoured one another.

Gods, he made me feel insane. Undone. Reckless and inexperienced and as if, for just a moment, I could still fly.

When I finally made myself pull away, I was breathless, my hands trembling from the sheer raw emotion his touch inspired. He had a wild look in his eyes, his hair disheveled from the way I'd tangled my fingers into it.

"Come home with me, Eunomia," he said, his voice rough, hoarse.

I managed a smile. "We both know I am not ready for that, Cub." I said it gently, regretfully, because as much as my body wanted him, I knew my heart was not ready. I knew he was not a distraction I could manage with everything else going on, and, oh how I wanted him to distract me. I reached out and gently ran my fingertips through his beard, and he nuzzled into my palm. "Can you be patient with me?" I whispered.

He turned his head, laying a kiss on my palm. "You know I'm not going anywhere."

I smiled, still shaken by everything he made me feel. "Someday. When everything settles down and the world is not falling down around us."

He smiled and kissed my palm again. "The way things are going, it should be a few hundred years or so."

"Hm. Good thing you are likely immortal, then," I said, and he laughed, and some of the tension between us cooled. Not entirely. That strange energy between us was always there, but it had calmed enough to at least make it so that I was able to think straight. "I hope you know…" I trailed off, biting my lip, unsure and regretting the words already because I was, at heart, a coward.

"Know what, Tink?"

I looked into his eyes, and it felt like leaping from the highest cliff with no wings to rely on to save me. "I hope you know how much I care about you," I said softly, and it felt as if I could barely breathe. "I hope you know that I want this, whatever this is between us, to stay as good as it is right now."

"And I hope you know that I feel the same," he said in a low voice. And then he grinned. "I didn't expect to hear anything like that from you tonight. Especially since you were so prickly when I asked you out."

I laughed. "I do stupid things when you kiss me like that," I said, raising an eyebrow at him.

"I'll have to kiss you that way more often, then."

"It seems unfair. You seem perfectly calm."

He choked a little, then looked away, a bit of a blush staining his cheeks.

"What?" I asked, laughing.

"Oh, honey. I am feeling anything but calm right now," he said, looking toward me again. "Really I'm just trying not to embarrass myself too much."

Now it was my turn to blush. "Oh."

"Mmhmm," he murmured, leaning in and kissing his way along my jawline. His hand traced up my hip, my side and rested just below my breast, spanning my ribcage. I was sure he must have been able to feel my heart pounding.

"Eunomia," he murmured.

"Yes," I whispered, hoping he understood.

He did. He gently cupped my breast in his hand, and I gasped. He continued to kiss my jawline, my neck, that sensitive place where my neck meets my shoulder, and he gently squeezed me, rubbed his thumb over my breast in a way that had me pushing my body closer to his hand.

After a few amazing, torturous moments, he pulled away, giving my breast one final caress before sitting back.

"You are trying to kill me," he groaned, sitting back and looking up at the night sky. A glance down at his lap was all the proof I needed that I did, indeed, affect him at least as much as he affected me.

"You would not be any good to me dead," I said, and he laughed. He was about to say something else when first his phone, then mine, rang.

We glanced at one another.

"Well, this probably isn't gonna be good," he said, digging his phone out of his pocket. I pulled my phone out of my bag. Mollis's number.

"Demon girl?" I asked, bringing the phone to my ear.

"It's me," Nain's voice said. He sounded strange, hollow. In the background, I could hear screams.

"What in the Nether is happening?" I asked, jumping up from my seat.

"E, you gotta come. Our son is gone."

My mouth dropped open and I turned to glance at Brennan, who, at that moment, roared in rage into the night. He started pulling clothing off, and I took his phone when he handed it wordlessly to me.

"Sean is missing," he said.

"So is Hades," I said. He stared at me.

"Go to Molly. I'm going after my son."

And with that, man became enormous black panther, and then he was gone.

Nain was still on the line.

"You heard that?" I asked him.

"Yeah. And Heph just got here. Michael's gone, too." The rage and panic in his voice chilled me, and those screams in the background continued, and I knew there was only one being who could scream with that much rage.

"I am on my way."

I picked up Brennan's suit and other clothing, not thinking, distracted, and then focused on rematerializing in the Nether.

I was met by the sound of enraged screams.

Everything in the Nether was chaos. Demons ran everywhere, searching the woods and beyond for Mollis and Nain's son. Many of the immortals had converged as well upon hearing the news that not one, but all three immortal children had been taken. I made my way to the palace, taking note of which immortals and other beings I saw on the way. None of the demons bothered saying anything to me, and I wondered if Mollis had told them I had been summoned.

This ended our charade, apparently.

Inside Mollis's palace, there was just as much chaos as there had been outside. Demons, imps, and the occasional lesser god brushed past me as I made my way through the corridors. It was eerily quiet, despite all of the activity. No one seemed to be in the mood to make conversation.

I went through a large set of wooden doors that led into Mollis's living quarters, the part of her palace that was where the family truly made their home. Meaghan was in the living room area, sitting between Gaia and Demeter, who were talking to her in low voices, trying to soothe her. She was pale, trembling. Her eyes were red and there was a blank expression on her face. Demeter looked up at me in surprise as I walked toward them. Mollis's screams punctuated the insanity, and my stomach twisted at the enraged sound of it. I leaned down to Gaia.

"Meaghan is going into shock. She needs blankets and a quiet place. Sleep would be a good thing, at least for a little while," I said quietly in her ear.

She nodded, and patted my hand, and she and Demeter pulled Meaghan up.

"Find him, E," Meaghan said. I patted her shoulder, not knowing what else to do.

I followed the screams.

In Mollis's office, I found her, the demon, Tisiphone, Megaera, Hephaestus, and Athena.

"Brennan's son is missing, too?" Hephaestus said upon seeing me. I nodded.

"He is out searching. I assume Artemis is as well."

Hephaestus nodded, and I went to him. I could see how hard he was trying to hold it together. I hugged him, hard, and he hugged me back.

"We will find him," I said softly. "I swear it."

He stepped back, his face stone.

"We have people out looking, yes?" I asked, glancing to where Nain was holding Mollis, trying to talk her down. I could only imagine that in addition to the terror of finding her son gone, Nether was likely acting up as well, which was the only thing that would have her there, and not out looking for baby Hades.

Hephaestus nodded. "Asclepius, Triton, Hestia, a bunch of demons. Shanti and Zero are out looking, too, as are Rayna and her brother."

"Have the shifter packs been informed? They are skilled trackers," I said.

"They have," Tisiphone said, looking stricken. "They have each taken a section of the city. They knew Sean's scent, but we had the imps bring them items of Michael's and Hades' to help them with the scent."

"How did it happen? How did you find them missing?" I asked Hephaestus.

"We were all asleep. And you know how it is with us, there's that feeling of another of your kind nearby, or not. I think everyone in my household felt it the instant Michael was gone. There were no doors opened, no windows. None of use felt or saw a fuckin' thing," he growled, and I knew he blamed himself.

"Was it the same here?" I asked Tisiphone, and she nodded.

"We were all asleep, except for Megaera, who was on duty tonight in the prisons," Tisiphone said. "As Hephaestus said, we all pretty much felt it when Hades was taken. His presence was missing."

"Artemis said the same thing happened with Sean. She and Asclepius wee asleep, and then she felt Sean missing. From what we can guess, all three were taken at pretty much the same moment," Hephaestus said. "You know what this fuckin' means," he snarled.

"Immortals," I said.

"Fuckin' immortals. And I have had it with immortals and their bullshit," he said, and his voice rose to a shout.

Mollis was inconsolable in Nain's arms, screaming every once in a while, out of control. I went to her, gently pushed Nain away, and took her in my arms.

The screams turned to sobs, and she clutched my body to hers.

"E… I need to look for him, E," she said.

"Nether?" I asked, and Mollis gave an almost painful-looking nod.

"Nether," I said. "Calm down, goddess. You are responding to Mollis's anguish. Help her calm down," I murmured as Mollis trembled. "You care for her. I know you do. Hear me, and focus, and bring yourself under control, for her sake."

Mollis continued to tremble, and the demon stood off to the side, watching me, on edge, waiting to jump back in to comfort his mate.

"She needs you to help her now, Nether," I said softly. "You are power incarnate. You were among the first beings in existence. I know you can grant this gift to your Prison." I knew, from what Mollis had told me, that "My Prison," was Nether's endearment for Mollis. She needed Mollis, and she, in her more sane moments, understood what Mollis risked by allowing her sanctuary in her soul.

I watched as Mollis's trembling subsided, as the look of pain on her face turned to one I much preferred to see there: rage.

"Thanks, Nether," I heard Mollis whisper. "Thank you, goddess." Then she hugged me harder. "Thank you, E. What in the fuck would I do without you?"

"You'll never have to know. We have babies to find," I said.

"And we will find them. And whoever took them is going to suffer things they could not have even imagined."

"Yes. Yes, they will. They could be anywhere, if we are dealing with an immortal. Where do you want me?" I glanced around. "We need to find out who is neglecting to show up. Persephone and Eros, to begin with, should be here."

"Persephone checked in with Demeter a while ago. She's going to catch up with Asclepius and work with them. I do not expect her to go after my son," she said with a resigned look. "At least she can help find Michael or Sean." She gripped my hand. "Where's Bren?"

"Looking for his son. He took off in panther form. He has a better chance of finding him that way."

She nodded.

"Demon girl, I can't help but think that it is all connected. Perhaps we are getting to close to figuring out who your betrayer is. Perhaps this is a desperate ploy to keep us distracted. When we find whoever has the children, I believe we will find the betrayer."

"Three betrayers," Mollis said, and I met her eyes. After a moment, I nodded in resignation. Three children, taken at almost the exact moment, by beings who were able to get in and away without a sound. Beings who knew not only where the children slept, but also at what point during the night it would be likely that all three would be alone, asleep in their rooms.

I could see Nain working it out as well, likely thinking the same thoughts I was.

"Were you here, or in the loft?" I asked Mollis.

"The loft," she said quietly. "I won't make that mistake again."

"Where is Zoe?" Mollis's adopted daughter had not been mentioned.

"She's with Ada and Stone in her room here, surrounded by about a dozen demons," she said.

"They wanted immortal children," I murmured. "Everyone who knows you knows how much you treasure Zoe. If this had merely been an attack to hurt you, they would have taken her as well."

"Maybe it's just because she was sleeping in a different room," Nain said.

Mollis shook her head. "No, I think she's right. They could have grabbed them both and really fucked me up. They took the kids with immortal heritage."

I blew out a breath. "Someone needs to be checking London. I will go."

I could see the desperation in Mollis's eyes, and then she tried to pull herself together. "You're right," she said instead, nodding.

"They know we're looking there, right?" Nain asked. "Even if it's all related, which, sorry, I think is stretching, E... even if they're the ones who did it, they'd have to be really fucking stupid to take the kids back there now."

"Unless they figure we'll all be running around here looking in a panic right now," Mollis said.

I thought, and made a decision. "I can send my New Guardians," I said. "They are skilled trackers. They know the energy signature of the one we seek there. If she is involved in this, and if somehow the children show up in London, they would pick up the trail. And then at least we know that situation is being looked at, and I can remain here if you need me." It was not the searching part that Mollis needed me for. For whatever reason, Nether had listened to me when neither Mollis nor her mate had been able to reason with her. Mollis was under extreme stress, and I knew she feared Nether trying again, and me not being there to help calm her down.

"You trust them with something like that?" Nain asked, doubt in his tone.

I nodded. "I do. You have trained and managed teams. You know there is always a point at which you must let go and trust them to do everything you have trained them for. My team has done that in small ways over the past weeks. It is time to give them free rein and see what they come up with."

"Please do that, E," Mollis said. "I'm going out to look and break into a few minds. Find me when you get back from getting them settled, okay?"

I took her hand in mine. "I will, demon girl. We will find him," I told her in a firm voice, and she gave a shaky looking nod, and then she and the demon disappeared, likely heading out into the city to see if they could find any kind of a trail to lead them to their son.

I looked at Tisiphone. "We still have no word on Eros."

"I know."

"That is a loose end that needs to be tied up. I do not especially trust him after that incident with Meaghan and Hephaestus."

"Same. I will spread word that we are keeping an eye out for him as well. If he has nothing to fear, then he will come of his own free will to let us know it wasn't him. If he doesn't and we have to hunt him down..." she trailed off. At that moment she reminded me of some kind of feral, wild animal, full of rage and a hunger for violence. She pulled herself back together, then looked at me. "I am glad you are here, Guardian. And I am glad you and my daughter have been there for one another." She paused. "I am glad you are not like your sisters," she finished quietly.

I put a hand on her arm. "Never that. Mollis and I went through that charade out of desperation. I only wish it had worked the way we had hoped it would." I paused, shaking my head in frustration. Now we had a whole new mess to deal with. "I will return as soon as I possibly can. We will find him," I said to Tisiphone, as I had said to Mollis. I rematerialized back to my apartment, thinking how odd it was that I was the one comforting people. It was not exactly what my kind were known for.

When I arrived in my apartment, it was to find my team asleep, sprawled out on sofas or, in Quinn's case, on the floor. I turned on a lamp, and bent down, shaking Quinn awake.

"Hm? What's up boss?" he asked, looking up at me blearily. "Didn't expect you home tonight."

"We have a situation," I said, and my team, who were all slowly but surely waking up, seemed to come fully awake at the words.

"What is it?" Annie asked.

I quickly explained about the missing immortal children, and the way they were taken, and our suspicion about it all being connected.

"Since we have seen so much activity there, and because we know it is becoming a hub for the creation of undead— "

"You want us to go back to Whitechapel," Annie finished for me, and I nodded.

"I must remain here. My queen needs me, and there is hardly a guarantee that it is all connected. But I have a hunch and I have gotten good at not ignoring those."

Quinn nodded. "It makes sense. Take the kids, distract you all, throw you off their scent to give them a chance to make more undead to fuck with your Queen."

"Exactly," I said. "As I said, I am needed here. I want to take you to Whitechapel, and I want you to scour the city. I know it is frustrating. I know we have been over it countless times already."

"But the only reason we keep going over it is because we keep picking up her energy signature there," Annie said. "We know the worthless bitch is there. It's just a matter of catching up with her."

"Will you do this for me?" I asked, meeting first Quinn's eyes, then Kathleen's, Erin's , Claire's, and, finally, Annie's.

"You even need to ask?" Quinn asked gruffly. "Point us in the right direction. I'm ready to get this shit wrapped up." The rest of my team nodded in agreement.

I hesitated for only a moment, and then I pulled my Netherblades out of each of my boots. I handed one to Quinn, and the other to Claire. "I wish I had more of them. It is the best I can offer you."

"Thank you," Claire murmured. "Annie is better with a knife than I am, though." She smiled at Annie. "And I think she wants this particular target more than the rest of us do."

Annie took the dagger with a nod. Then she looked at me. "If she's there, we'll find her. I swear it on... eh. Can you swear something on your own grave?"

I let out a short laugh. "Why not?"

I held my hands out, and my team joined hands with one another, and with me, and seconds later, we were standing on a dark corner near the former brothel in Whitechapel.

"Contact me if you come across anything," I said. "If you are unsure, if there are more people working together than you expected, call me before you confront them. Understand?"

They nodded, and I reminded them again to call me as soon as they found anything, and then I focused again, taking myself back to Detroit.

CHAPTER TWELVE

We searched for three days without stopping once I had made my way back to Detroit. The first two days, I searched at Mollis and Nain's sides. Detroit, the Netherwoods, the surrounding areas, the Packard Plant, the woods on Belle Isle. We searched it all. The rest of Nain's team, as well as the shifters and bloodborn, along with any immortals in the city, searched the rest of the area. A group of other lesser gods had been sent to check out different locations around the world. Aided by Mollis's imps and Netherhounds, immortals chased leads in Greece, Italy, Germany, Australia, Mexico, and Kenya. In every case, the Netherhounds scented baby Hades in those places and communicated that to Mollis in their way. Each lead led us to nothing.

By the time we had returned yet again, empty-handed, to Mollis's home, everyone was at the end of their patience. Mollis and Nain were snapping at one another, and even the imps were in a foul humor. Shanti and Zero, who had searched with the rest of us since sunset, barely spoke. And while I was certainly frustrated and upset that we had not found Hades yet, I was also feeling more and more guilty over the fact that I had left Brennan alone so long. He needed support as well, and I felt like a failure for not having been at his side when he needed me. I fought an internal battle over staying with Mollis and going to Brennan while I watched Shanti and Zero pace. Both of them seemed like they wanted to be doing something, but we were at a loss.

"You two can go see where Rayna needs you," Mollis said to Shanti and Zero, tension and exhaustion evident in her voice. "I have nothing until we get another lead to chase down."

Shanti nodded, went to Mollis, and hugged her. They stood together like that for a bit, Shanti speaking in a low voice to Mollis. When they released one another, Shanti was blinking back tears, and Mollis thanked both her and Zero once again and sent them on their way. With a hug for me and then one for the demon, Shanti left. Zero went with her, and I knew that while he certainly liked Mollis, he was really only there because it meant so much to Shanti.

That left Mollis and her mate, the Furies, and myself, and I was about to tell Mollis I was going to check on Brennan when Mollis's tired gaze landed on her aunt.

"You know what I'd like to know?" she said to Megaera.

"What, Molly?" Megaera asked.

"I want to know where you keep disappearing to lately. I want to know why you, the only one of us who was awake that night, somehow didn't feel anything."

"Mollis!" I said, and she ignored me.

"I want to know why you keep refusing to let me into your mind. What are you hiding from me, Aunt Meg?"

Megaera stared at Mollis in disbelief. "You think I had something to do with this?" she asked, and the pain in her voice was clear.

"All I can go by is what I can see. And from what I see, there are a whole lot of questions where you're concerned."

Megaera stared at Mollis, and then briefly met my eyes. I wanted to comfort her. I believed, as I had the night she had confronted me, that she was not guilty of any wrongdoing.

"I know that you are terrified for your son, so I am trying not to take that personally," Megaera said to Mollis. "But I also know that I do not have to stand here and take this nonsense from you. I am going to search with the bloodborn queen's team."

"All you have to do is let me into your mind," Mollis said, some uncertainty in her tone now.

"And all you have to do is trust me. My mind is my own, niece." With that, Megaera was gone. After a moment, Mollis turned wordlessly and headed toward the living quarters of her palace, and her mate followed.

I asked an imp to tell me where to find Brennan. He nodded and took me to one of the many empty neighborhoods in the city, and there was Brennan, in panther form, nose to the ground. Artemis, in her panther form, was in the distance, and I could also see Asclepius not too far away. I approached Brennan, and he stopped, raising his head when he caught my scent. I went and knelt in front of him and put my hand on his head, and then gently scratched the sides of his neck. I looked into his eyes, and, after a moment, he shifted. For once, I was undistracted by his nakedness. I pulled him into my arms and he held me tightly.

"I am sorry I left you alone with this so long, my love," I murmured against his ear as he held me. "I wanted to be with you."

"Molly needed you to help control Nether. Dahael was here that first night helping, and she told me what happened when you went to see Molly that night."

I nodded, and held him tighter as we knelt on the cold ground together. "You picked up a scent here?" I asked.

"A faint one," he said. "He's definitely not here anymore, but we're following it, hoping it'll lead us to some kind of clue or point us in which direction to look next."

I kissed the side of his neck. "Let us get back to tracking then. I can fill you in on what else we know while you follow the trail."

He squeezed me, hard, as if he did not want to let go. I knew it was a hard thing for him. This was one of those times, when he was tense and afraid, when my touch was what he needed to help deal with it, yet he could not allow himself even that small comfort, because he had to keep moving.

He shifted, and began moving again, and I walked beside him. I kept reaching out to rest my hand on his back as we walked, as he tracked. I felt a helplessness I had never experienced before, that this was one person I never wanted to fail, and I could do so little to help him. It also struck me that this helplessness was part of what love was, the sense that I would do anything to make our life better, and there was nothing of significance I could do until we tracked his son.

He began circling back, picked up the scent again, and then continued on. Whether he was aware of it or not, he kept rubbing his flank against my legs as he walked. It was another sign that he needed contact with me but would not stop the search for his son for something like that.

"Stop a moment," I said, and he glanced up at me, those blue eyes the exact ones that looked at me after he kissed me, or when he held me in his arms. I only hesitated for a moment before I lifted my leg and swung it over his strong, wide back, mounting him.

"Is this insulting? Or does it make you feel better?" I asked him.

In response, he began moving, quickening his pace and following the trail in a more focused way than he'd been before. As he tracked, I sat on his back and ran my fingers through the dense fur at the back of his neck, and I talked, filling him in on what was going on with the search elsewhere. I told him about my New Guardians, and about Mollis and Nain, and about how we still had not been able to track Eros down. I told him about the way we had travelled around the world, chasing the trail the Netherhounds had followed, to no avail. "We will find him," I promised, a phrase that felt emptier and emptier with every hour that passed, knowing we were dealing with immortals who had taken the children practically from right under our noses.

We searched through night and into the next day. The trail led us eventually to the Detroit River. Brennan sniffed along its banks, and, once there, circled around several times, seeming to grow more frustrated as time went on. Finally, he released a frustrated, anguished roar, which Artemis echoed. I slid off of his back and watched as he stumbled making another pass. Artemis shifted back, and shrugged into the dress Asclepius handed to her.

I looked at her questioningly.

"The trail ends here. This spot was the last place he was. It just ends."

"So they went by water, or, more likely, he was rematerialized elsewhere," I said.

She nodded.

"We still should not leave the possibility of having gone by boat to chance," I said, and she agreed. I pulled my phone out of my pocket and dialed. Brennan continued sniffing, stumbling. He was exhausted and we had reached a dead end.

Triton picked up on the first ring.

"Hey! Did you find anything?" he asked.

"No. We came up against a dead end. What about you?" I knew he was searching with Hephaestus, Athena, and a few of the other immortals for Michael.

"No luck yet," he said, a dejected tone in his voice, and I realized he had hoped I had been calling with some good news. "The imps said they thought they saw him in Scotland, so we all went there and searched for a day and a half, and it came to nothing. The Netherhound that was with us definitely picked up a scent, but it ended. My father is searching the seas nearby now," he finished in a low tone, and I knew it meant they feared the child had been discarded.

"I do not think they would go to all that trouble to just toss him away," I said.

"Who knows what these asses are thinking?" he said back with a sigh.

"I was wondering if you could give us some aid here. We have been tracking Brennan's son, and they had his scent until they reached the river. Would you mind coming and checking it out for us?"

"I'm on my way." He got our location from me, and moments later, he stood beside me. He gathered me into his arms, and the comforting scent of sea and sunlight enveloped me.

"Thank you for coming," I said.

"Of course, little ghost," he murmured, keeping an arm around me. Brennan was still in panther form, though he had finally stopped moving. His grandmother crouched before him, talking quietly as Asclepius looked on. "He's exhausted," Triton said. "Has he stopped at all?"

I shook my head.

"Even Hephaestus gave in and let Meaghan talk him into resting with her for a while," Triton said.

"Brennan is a very stubborn male," I murmured. "And there is nothing he hates more than a problem he cannot solve. This is killing him."

Triton looked at me, and a look of understanding crossed his features. He gave my shoulder a squeeze, and then released me and stepped away a bit. I looked at him questioningly. He smiled. "He is stressed out enough. The last thing he needs is another male putting his hands on you. Shifters," he added with a good-natured shrug.

I smiled. "You are a good man, Triton. Very much like your father."

He looked a bit uncomfortable about the comment, and looked down, but his shoulders straightened a bit, and he held himself taller. I knew he was not overly comfortable with compliments, but I wanted to let him know I appreciated his help.

"I'll search the river. There are several types of fish and the animals in these waters that are intelligent enough to pay attention to their surroundings. If they have seen anything at all, I will know about it."

I nodded. "Thank you. I am going to try to get him to rest for a while. Please call if there is any word at all."

"I will." He gave me a nod, and then he walked into the water, and, once it was deep enough, disappeared beneath the surface. He was in his element now, and if there was any sign of Sean or any of the other children there, he would find it.

I sent a silent hope that he would find nothing but a trail to Brennan's son, then turned and went to where Artemis was still trying to cajole Brennan into resting. He sat mutely, rigid, exhausted, in his panther form. I put my hand on Artemis's shoulder, and she stood. Her eyes were bright with angry, frustrated tears. I squeezed her shoulder once, then knelt before Brennan.

"My love," I murmured to him. "There is no more you can do tonight. If there is some trail in the river, Triton will pick it up and report back. You will be no good to him, exhausted as you are, if we finally track him down and have to fight for him. You know that is likely how this will play out. We will not get any of these children back without a fight. Do you really want to find him, only to lose him again because you can barely stand up straight, let alone fight an immortal?"

He bowed his head, and started shifting back. As soon as he had, I pulled him into my arms and rematerialized him back to my apartment, where I had left his phone and clothing, and where he could rest.

With me.

He held me tightly, and I wrapped my arms around his body, and we just stood there for several minutes, not a word between us.

Finally, I ran my hands up his back, patted him gently. "Go have a shower. And then you need to eat something, and then we need to sleep."

"I need to get back out there, Eunomia," he said against the side of my neck.

"You do. And we will. But you can take a few hours to get yourself back into fighting form. You know this is necessary." He nodded, then squeezed me one more time and headed toward my bathroom. He grabbed the pants he'd been wearing from the pile where I had dumped them when I had come for my New Guardians, then closed the bathroom door behind him.

Once I heard the shower start up, I quickly changed into some comfortable pajama pants and a t-shirt, then scoured my kitchen cabinets for anything to feed him. I had plenty of tea and hot chocolate mix, microwave popcorn. In the end, I ended up frying eggs for both myself and Brennan. I was just finishing buttering the toast when he came out of the bathroom, steam following him out, the scent of my shampoo clinging to him.

He met my eyes, and took the plate I was holding out to him. He lowered his face to mine, and kissed me, slowly, gently, a silent thanks. He devoured the eggs on his plate and I gave him mine as well. I was not hungry. Mollis had insisted on making me eat when I was searching with her.

He ate, sitting in one of the chairs in my small dining room. I handed him a cup of tea, then led him into my bedroom, to the large, comfortable chair in the corner. He sat down, and I grabbed a comb and climbed onto the chair behind him.

He sat and drank his tea, and I went to work sorting out the tangles in his hair, focusing on not pulling too much, on being gentle, on showing him, through this simple act, how much he meant to me.

"I have wanted to do this for a long time," I murmured as I worked at his tangles. "Your hair is enviable, Cub."

He answered by resting a hand on my calf and giving it a gentle squeeze. We sat in silence, him obediently drinking the tea I'd given him, and me working my way, section by section, through his thick blond mane. When I was finished, I set the comb down on the table beside the chair and wrapped my arms around his waist. I rested my cheek against his back. He put his hands on mine, covering them, keeping my arms around him.

"You are exhausted," I said, kissing his back. "Rest with me."

"I should get out there— "

"We have been over this. You know I am right. Until we pick up his trail again, there is nothing you can do. So the best use of your time is to regain your strength and be ready to kick the ass of whoever has your son," I said sharply.

He stood up, then turned and picked me up, hefting me as if I weighed nothing.

"As long as you come with me," he said, looking into my eyes.

"I am pretty sure I would do whatever it took to stay by your side, Brennan," I said softly.

He stilled, staring down at me as he held me in his arms. We were almost at my bed. "Well. That makes two of us, then," he finally said.

"I am glad to hear it," I told him. "And thank you for letting me take care of you."

A small smile crossed his exhausted, haggard features. "Thank you for wanting to take care of me."

He set me down on my bed, and I pulled back the bedspread and sheet, and he climbed in beside me. Without a word, without needing any words, I settled into his arms, holding his body tight against mine. There was no space between us, pressed so tightly together it felt as if we were one. And I knew I wanted it to be this way for the rest of my existence.

"Sleep. Rest. He could turn up at any moment."

He nodded, face buried against my neck, and I knew he would not vocalize the thing he feared most, that his son would not be alive when we finally found him.

"You would know, Brennan. You would feel it if his life ended," I whispered. "There is a bond between those of immortal blood and their children. I do not believe whoever it is went through all of this trouble merely to destroy them," I said, and he held me tighter. He lay awake for a long time, unable to let himself relax. Finally, I heard the first soft snores, and felt his shoulders slump a bit in sleep, and I closed my eyes and drifted off beside him.

I was awakened what felt like minutes later by my phone ringing on the nightstand beside the bed. I looked at it with a combination of loathing and fear.

"Tink?" Brennan murmured sleepily beside me, his arms still warm around my body. I patted his behind gently and turned, reaching for my phone.

"Boss?"

"Quinn?" I said, sitting up, suddenly wide awake. "What is wrong?"

"That Hephaestus guy's kid? He's about six months old, wearing blue pajamas, yeah? Otherwise we took some other guy's brat."

CHAPTER THIRTEEN

Brennan and I threw on whichever articles of clothing were closest as I kept Quinn on the phone. "Where are you?" I tossed a t-shirt at Brennan, then let him zip me into my coat.

"Remember that farm where you found me in Ireland?"

"You are there?" I met Brennan's eyes as he listened to my side of the conversation.

"Yeah."

"And the rest of the New Guardians?"

"We're all here. Uh. This kid seems hungry and he stinks like the devil's armpit. Are you coming or what?"

"We are coming," I said. I hung up and took Brennan's hand, focused, and moments later we were standing outside of the decrepit, abandoned house that had once been Quinn's home. It was mid-morning there, and the sun shone weakly from an overcast sky. A light breeze brushed past me, carrying with it the high-pitched cries of a baby, Quinn's deep voice trying to make soothing noises. I looked toward the house, at its crumbling porch, at its empty windows. This was where Quinn had died, where he had remained for all of the long years of his time as a soul before I had come upon him and Mary. He had come to this place when he had needed a safe place. I wondered if he recognized the irony in that reasoning.

Brennan and I exchanged a look, and we headed up the rickety porch stairs and ducked inside. We had put off calling Hephaestus and Meaghan in case my New Guardians had, in fact, taken some other poor person's baby.

We walked into the dimly-lit living room, the weak daylight barely illuminating our surroundings. The scent of dust, animal droppings, and a disgustingly full diaper reached my nose.

"Is it him? All babies look alike to me," I said to Brennan, who had gone to Quinn and the child.

"It's him," Brennan said, and for the first time in a long time I heard hope in his voice. "Hey, buddy," Brennan said softly, holding Michael against his chest and bouncing, just a little. "It's him. Call Heph. He needs to know right away."

I took my phone out and hit Hephaestus's number. Meaghan answered on the first ring.

"E?" Meaghan asked.

"We have him, Meaghan. He is well."

The news was met by sobs, and then Hephaestus was on the phone and I told him the news and where we were, trying to describe how to get to us as clearly as possible. He hung up, and we waited, Brennan murmuring and bouncing Michael in his arms, my New Guardians looking exhausted but proud, standing in one corner of the living room.

Within minutes, Hephaestus and his mate had found us, and Meaghan took her son in her arms. After weeping over him for a few moments, she started checking him over. Gaia and Demeter arrived as well, both of them teary-eyed and cooing over the boy.

"All right. So how in the Nether did you manage this?" I asked my team as we stood a bit away from the others.

Brennan stood beside me, listening. And I knew he was happy for his friends, but also wishing it was his son.

"We were hunting souls in Whitechapel, right?" Quinn began, "and we chased one of them pretty far. I hate it when the bastards run. Anyway, we're chasing it, and it turns, and then Erin grabs it and stabs it."

"Lovely," I said softly, and Erin gave me a shy smile.

"And just as we're getting ready to call you, Claire's looking down the street and she says, "'isn't that that loud bearded fella's son?' And I have no idea because who the hell even looks at babies?" He paused, and Claire met my gaze and rolled her eyes. I hid a smile. "But they were all sure since we saw those pictures so many times that time Hephaestus hunted with us a while back, so we started chasing it. It was some lass with long black hair. Kinda looked like your Queen."

At that, Brennan and I exchanged a glance. My heart sank. I knew he was thinking what I was: Megaera.

"Anyway, so we kept trailing her, and then we got lucky and she had to answer her phone. And she seemed not to know how to handle a baby and a phone, so he set him down on a bench."

"And then what?" I asked.

"I snatched him and then ran back to them and we rematerialized," Quinn said, grinning.

"You did?" I asked in surprise. I had not yet trained them in how to travel that way, though I fully intended to.

"I wasn't sure it would work. But I watched you enough and I figured I generally got the gist. At first I didn't think we were goin' anywhere but then I felt like I was gonna puke my guts out, so I knew something was happening." He paused, and we laughed, well knowing Quinn's usual reaction to rematerializing. "But we didn't get far that first time. For some reason, we only made it a little way down the street, and she saw us and followed us."

"She stabbed him," Annie said, clearly shaken despite the general levity surrounding us.

I took Quinn's arm and turned him around while he grumbled that it was nothing. I inspected him and saw that the back of his shirt was soaked with blood.

"We need to get you looked at," I chided him. "Are you feeling all right?"

"It hurts like a bitch. And I haven't been this tired since Tokyo," he said, and I knew what he meant. Tokyo, where I had lost my wings and where my New Guardians had been gravely injured by my sisters earning their first taste of the danger their new lives entailed.

He took a breath. "All I kept thinking was that if I didn't get us out of there, we were fucked. It wasn't just me or even the kid. I knew the witch who had him would hurt them, too," he said, glancing toward the other New Guardians. "So I focused hard again and told everyone to hold on to me, and Annie's stabbing out at the chick the whole time," he said, grinning at Annie, who blushed and shook her head. "And then we ended up here and I may have pissed myself a little, boss." With that, he held my daggers out to me, and I took them, even more grateful now that I sent them with my team. I took them and tucked them into my boots. "I may have screamed like a little girl, too," Quinn added.

I laughed, even as I stared at him in awe. "Well done," I said softly, smiling at him and then at each member of my team, who beamed at me in return. I took Quinn's hand in mine, gave it a squeeze. "Thank the gods it was the right baby."

"That would have been awkward," Claire agreed with a laugh.

Brennan shook Quinn's hand, then the rest of the team's, and then Hephaestus came over and hugged me, then each member of my team in turn, telling them with varying levels of enthusiastic profanity how amazing they were. Asclepius showed up and quickly saw to Quinn's wounds, even as Hephaestus and Meaghan chatted gratefully with the New Guardians, and then there was another round of hugs. By the time Hephaestus had hugged them all, he was practically shouting in happiness and relief. He glanced at Brennan and sobered.

"This is a good sign for your boy, Matthews," Hephaestus said, clamping a hand on Brennan's shoulder. "We'll find him, man."

Brennan nodded. "Go home and hug your kid, Heph," he said, and Heph grinned and patted his shoulder one more time. Meaghan hugged me, still weeping with relief, then we watched the family disappear. Asclepius was finishing up checking over Quinn and the others. I could hear his low voice talking to Quinn.

"You need to rest, understand? Sleep. You hear me?" Asclepius asked, and Quinn gave a noncommittal response. Sleep was not his favorite thing, and I could understand why, especially after what had happened with Mary. He was still living with the haunting memories of not just his sister's death, but his nephews', as well as his own. And now, Mary's final death. Sleep was not a happy state when all it brought was nightmares of all you had lost. Asclepius checked him over once more, and Quinn withstood it patiently, though I could tell he disliked the fuss being made over him.

I turned to the rest of my team to say something, and practically jumped out of my skin at the sight of the silvery, nearly transparent goddess of the winds, Lethe. I had not even noticed the winds kicking up, absorbed as I had been in the excitement over Hephaestus's son. However, now that I was aware of her presence, I was also aware of the wind moaning, howling outside the rickety farmhouse, of the house itself creaking under the onslaught of the winds she brought with her.

She stood there, silently, her clear eyes on me.

"Lethe. Can I help you?" I asked respectfully. The goddess of the winds was flighty, easily distracted, and sensitive. One wrong word, one wrong look, could result in her taking off. And if she had left her beloved cliffs to seek me out, there had to be a good reason.

"Certainly not. It is my help I am giving to you this time, Guardian."

"Oh? Do you know something, Lethe?" I asked. Brennan stood beside me, and I took his hand.

A tepid smile crossed her white lips. "I know many things, Guardian. I know the wind, and I know the clouds, and I know that yesterday in France, a certain baker burned a batch of chocolate cakes. The wind carries it all, and I know all." She breathed in deeply. "Love and lust and death and which variety of blossom blooms in southern India. The wind shares it all with me."

Brennan and I exchanged another quick look.

"And what else does the wind tell you, Lethe?" I asked, hoping to keep her lucid and talking before she went off on one of her dazed tangents.

Her gaze focused. "I know that a certain Fury has the child of the one that stands beside you, and they wait on the beaches below my cliffs for another. It is as if they cared not that I was there!" she said, full of indignation. "As if I did not exist!"

I did not answer. Many of the higher gods paid little to no mind to the lesser gods, and perhaps even less so to the nature gods, which was what Lethe was.

"May we go to your cliffs now?" I asked.

A wide smile lit her face. "Of course." I glanced back at my team. "Asclepius, will you take them back to Detroit, please? They need to rest." Asclepius nodded, and I watched as he and my New Guardians disappeared.

Brennan joined hands with me and Lethe, and in the next instant we were standing in a rocky cave beneath the outcropping where Lethe usually sat to create and listen to the winds. She gave a nod toward something on the beach, and Brennan and I looked in the direction of her gaze.

A Fury. And not at all the one I expected to see.

Brennan and I exchanged a glance, then I nodded and took his hand and we rematerialized down onto the beach.

CHAPTER FOUREEN

When we appeared on the beach, mere feet from the Fury, I could feel her. Raw power, familiar and ancient.

"You are supposed to be in the old Nether," I said calmly. Before me stood the third Fury, the one we no longer spoke of. Alecto, the Fury who had betrayed her sisters, who had set the entire path of Mollis's life in motion by helping Hermes, who had been both Alecto's lover and one of Hades' many enemies, hunt her down. She stood before me still wearing the black uniform she'd worn for her entire existence, a uniform she no longer had any right to wear.

"It's amazing the help you can get when an usurper sits on the throne," she said. She held Sean's arm in her hand, tugging at him as he tried to get to his father.

"She inherited the throne from her father, and you were after her long before that," I said. I heard Brennan roar behind me, and Alecto snarled. She began to run, and I followed. I could see her focusing, preparing to rematerialize, but, after several moments, nothing happened.

"She's too tired," Sean shouted to me, and she reached down and slapped him just as Brennan got past me. Both of us lunged at her, and just before Brennan's jaws snapped, barely missing clamping onto her leg, she rose into the air, pulling Sean with her.

Brennan landed, roared up at his son, who was flying higher into the sky with Alecto, her enormous wings flapping.

"Papa!" Sean shouted.

I watched in frustration as she flapped, then turned. Even at this distance, I could see the sneer on her face.

"What's wrong? Can't follow?" she taunted. "Wingless freak. You truly are worthless," she said with a laugh.

I snarled in frustration and heard bones popping, and then in an instant, Brennan was streaking into the sky, having traded his panther form for his hawk form, an enormous black bird with a sharp beak and deadly talons. Alecto was still much larger, and a Fury to boot, but I knew that we did not have many options, and of the two of us, he was the only one who could fly.

Alecto had apparently exhausted herself fleeing, and didn't have enough strength now to rematerialize. We had to keep it that way. We could not let her escape with Sean.

I watched as Brennan dove at her, ripping his talons across her face and I knew that my job was to be ready to catch Sean should she drop him in the fight. She was over the water, her wings taking her ever higher into the bright sky.

As I watched, Brennan tore at her again, and she struck out with a screech, hitting him. He somersaulted through the air, then came back around for another attack. She struck out at him again, missed, but then I saw Brennan freeze, and he gave a bone chilling screech as he plummeted, seeming to not be in control.

She was in his mind, then, I realized. I ran forward and caught the enormous hawk just before he hit the ground. He was shaking his head, fighting for control of his mind. I saw it in his eyes when he came back to himself. I was fairly sure I could see a glow of icy blue light form their depths, and I felt my heart soar. This was his immortal Aether side coming out, pushed as he was into the most desperate of emotions. He gave a few quick flaps, and was soaring toward her again, screeching. Sean was screaming, crying as she jostled him in the air. When she struck out this time, I heard a crack, and then Brennan was flailing, falling, his right wing hanging at an unnatural angle. I raced to where he was falling, caught him again, and as soon as he was on the ground, he began shifting back to his human form.

"Phone," he said, his voice harsh with pain. I dug my phone out of my pocket and handed it to him.

Calling for back up. Why did I never think of things like that?

It wouldn't be enough time, I realized, as she gave a few strong flaps, trying to get away from us during her reprieve.

I stared, gripped my dagger's handle, calculated the distance and paid attention to how she was moving.

"E…" Brennan said. I ignored him, and let the dagger fly. It struck, just under her wing on the side opposite where she held Sean and she screamed.

It gave me a chance to act.

I looked at where she was, focused, then rematerialized.

I had a fraction of a second when I appeared in mid-air. I stabbed her through the back of the neck with my other dagger, and when she let go of Sean in her pain and rage, I grabbed him. We were falling, fast, the rocky shore coming closer before my eyes. I closed my eyes, focused hard, and was rewarded in the next instant by the feel of the ground under my feet as I reappeared in the place I'd stood just moments before.

Alecto had just splashed into the river. I handed Sean to his father, then ran forward and dove into the raging river, determined not to lose her after all she had put us through.

"Eunomia!" I could hear Brennan bellowing. I turned just as she stabbed one of my daggers into my stomach.

"You think that's the first time I have been stabbed?" I asked as I grabbed hold of her long black hair, pulling hard. We wrestled, and she did her best to push my head under and disorient me enough to allow her escape. She was bigger than me, a more powerful build.

It was not the first time I had fought someone bigger than myself.

I let go of her for a fraction of a second to pull the dagger out of my stomach and slice it across her throat as she lunged for me.

The water around churned red with our blood. My body ached.

I pulled my arm back and plunged the dagger once more into her shoulder. Her motions slowed.

This would not kill her, of course. Only Mollis could do that. But it would slow her down. It would hurt like the Nether.

I only wished I could hurt her more.

I could feel my own strength giving out. Too many jumps, too many wounds from a Netherblade. I grabbed the back of her uniform and made for the shoreline. After a few feet, I felt a strong arm around my waist, and Brennan and I stumbled out of the river together, Alecto still gripped tightly in my hand, my daggers still leeching the strength from her as she bled.

Once we were on the shore, I shoved Brennan away and vomited. Water, blood. I still held onto Alecto, refusing to let her go.

I heard the "pop" sound that signified the appearance of an immortal.

"No!" I heard Tisiphone's enraged shout. And then Alecto was being yanked from my grip, and I looked up blearily to see Tisiphone punch her sister, hard, in such a way that Alecto's neck snapped on impact.

It did not stop the enraged Fury.

"You betrayed my daughter not once, but over," a punch, "and over," another punch, "and over again!"

With the final punch, Alecto's face was almost indistinguishable.

"Where is my grandson?" she asked, but Alecto was limp in her hands. Tisiphone shoved her down in disgust. She put her hands on Alecto's forehead.

"Call Molly again," she told Brennan.

I heard Brennan speaking into his phone again, and closed my eyes, unable to keep them open anymore. A few moments later, I felt a tiny, warm hand on my forehead. I opened my eyes. Even that bit of motion hurt. And when I looked around, it was to see Sean sitting on the shore near my head, his hand on my forehead as if checking for a fever.

"Hello," I said to him, not knowing what else to say.

"Hi," he said, watching me with the same serious appraisal I often seemed to get from his father. The boy had Brennan's eyes, for sure. "You saved me," he said.

"You helped save yourself. I was impressed by how you did not panic. And it was helpful knowing she was too tired to disappear."

He straightened his back, puffed out his chest a bit. "You got hurt," he said a moment later.

"I will heal, little panther," I assured him. "I am just glad we got you back safe."

He removed his hand from my forehead, then put his hand in mine. To my left, I could hear Mollis and Nain talking to Tisiphone, having arrived after Brennan's call. Brennan was beside me now, his hands moving over my body, checking me for injuries.

"I am fine," I told him.

"Obviously," he said, gently tracing his fingers across the cut on my throat. "Christ, Eunomia. You are completely insane."

"I would not have hurt him," I said, thinking he meant the dangerous way in which I had distracted Alecto.

He stared. "I know that. I mean that whole 'oh, I'm just gonna reappear in mid-air even though I can't fly and then kick someone's ass when I get back down' thing," he told me. "You're..." he swallowed. "Thank you. How many times are you going to save my life?" he asked softly, and I knew what he meant. If anything had happened to his son, it would have ended him.

"As many times as I need to, Cub," I murmured, looking up at him. "You are worth saving."

He bent down, and gathered me gently into his arms, and he cradled me in one arm as I healed, and Sean remained beside me, holding my hand. I looked past Sean to see Mollis standing over Alecto, and Alecto screaming as Mollis forced her way into her mind. The demon paced, clearly hoping Alecto would reveal some hint about where baby Hades was.

"This was a good night. Your New Guardians found Michael, and now we have Sean. Hopefully this nightmare will end soon. Really, we should just send your team out after Hades, huh?" Brennan asked with a smile. I gave a weak nod, still full of pride for my team. I was too full of emotion at the moment, and it was wearing on me. It was almost scary, how much I was feeling. I closed my eyes, afraid I would begin weeping, and if that happened, I most certainly did not want an audience for it.

"You should have Asclepius look at your arm," I said.

"I will. I think they're just about finished here."

"There he is!" I heard Artemis shout after another "pop" sounded.

"Gram!" Sean shouted, and then he was up and running. I heard Artemis squeal in delight at the sight of her grandson.

"Who's more beat up, you or her?" I heard Asclepius ask Brennan.

"Her," he said, while I answered "him" at the same time.

Asclepius chuckled, then I felt his warm, almost uncomfortably so, hand on my neck.

"This has stopped bleeding. Where else…"

Brennan lifted my hands from where I had them folded over my stomach, revealing the gore there.

"It is fine," I said.

I felt Asclepius pulling up my shirt, revealing my stomach.

"This is still bleeding," he muttered. "Would you stop getting yourself stabbed and cut, just for a week or two?" he asked me, and I glanced up to see him smiling.

"I will try," I said wryly.

"This is going to burn a little," he warned me, and I shook his head.

"Heal him first," I said.

"He has a broken arm. It's hardly the end of the world, and he will be good as new within seconds. You, however, are in agony and the sooner we get it closed up, the sooner you'll begin getting your strength back," he said sternly.

"Stubborn immortal," I muttered.

"Reckless, insane, Guardian," he shot back. "Have you no sense of fear at all?"

I raised my eyebrow. "I think given my record, it is they who should fear me."

Asclepius chuckled, and I glanced at Brennan to see him grinning and shaking his head.

"Tell me again how I'm the cocky one in this relationship," he said, his gaze meeting mine.

"I only speak the truth, Cub," I told him, and it ended on a gasp as the searing heat from Asclepius's healing power tore through me when he settled his hands over my stomach wound. After what felt like an eternity, the sensation passed.

I gasped again, felt my stomach turn with nausea. I glared up at Asclepius. "Whoever coined the phrase 'the cure is worse than the disease' clearly met with your healing at some point."

"You're welcome, Guardian," he said, grinning down at me.

I took his hand in mine. "Thank you, friend," I said to him, and he looked pleased. I sat up. I was still tired, but most of the pain was gone. I watched as Asclepius started talking to Brennan. I looked around. Sean was still in Artemis's arms. I had the feeling she would refuse to let him go for a long time. Nain was still pacing, Mollis was standing over Alecto's unconscious body, and both she and Tisiphone had that blank look on their faces that signaled that they were breaking into someone's mind. Clearly Alecto's.

Nain saw me looking, and walked over to me. I held out my hand, and he pulled me into a standing position.

"You're fucking amazing, E," he said, hugging me.

"We'll find your boy as well," I promised him. "We will."

He nodded. I have seen the demon angry. I have seen him worried about Molly. I have seen him broken, when we lost her to the Nether. The way he was now, it was clear he was walking the edge of control. His skin was almost completely red, halfway between his human and demon forms. That only happened when he was not focusing on controlling himself, which almost never happened.

I leaned in. "She needs you to be strong now. I know he is your son too. But she is going through everything you are plus blaming herself because once again, someone is using those she cares for to weaken or harm her. Do not lose it, demon, or so help you I will make you hurt like you've never hurt before," I hissed.

I stared at him in shock. It had done its job, though. The redness left his complexion, and his eyes stopped glowing. He took a breath, then nodded.

"Whether they find anything useful from Alecto or not, we will find him. You have gods searching the entire face of the Earth for your boy. We tend to be a stubborn lot, if you hadn't noticed."

"I noticed," he said. "Hephaestus wants to see you when you get a chance. Your team did good."

I smiled. "They did."

"Taught by the best," he added, and I shrugged. Brennan approached us then, draping an arm around my waist. Sean was on his other hip, his head resting sleepily on his father's shoulder. We stood, watching, as Mollis and Tisiphone both worked, trying to break into Alecto's mind. Even as weak as she was, Alecto was clearly putting up a fight. The sensation of power swirling around the Furies as they worked, as Alecto battled Mollis and Tisiphone in a war none of us could actually see, was enough to make it feel as if we were standing in the midst of a raging storm. Alecto screamed in rage, and, in the next moment, the Fury disappeared.

Mollis gave an enraged shriek, and there were several moments of chaos during which we searched for any sign of the Fury.

"How was that even possible?" Tisiphone asked, clearly upset and confused. "She did not have enough power to rematerialize away. She was barely hanging on to life by that point."

"I know," Mollis growled.

Then she walked over to us, her gaze empty. She shook her head. "We got nothing. I couldn't bust my way in. Couldn't see a damn thing about her deeds, the one and only time I've ever actually wanted my dad's ability to see everything to finally work, and it didn't fucking work with her."

"We will find him. My New Guardians said they ran from a woman with long black hair. We suspected Megaera. We know now that it was very likely Alecto," I said, "and knowing now who we are looking for will only help."

"It will only make her more careful. She's lost two of them now. The likelihood that we'll get that lucky again…" she shook her head. "I was counting on her knowing something," she said. "When Bren called and told me who you had, I thought this was it. I thought I'd have him back…" she trailed off, and when I think most people would have began crying, Mollis released an enraged, anguished scream that raised the hair on the back of my neck and made my ears feel as if they were going to burst.

It was not a sane sound. It was not a controlled sound, and when it ended, and she turned and looked at me, her eyes were glowing white, a snarl on her lips.

I had seen this look before. I saw it the night Nain had died. She had gone on, afterward, to end dozens of lives in revenge for her husband's death.

Even with what she had gone through then, I knew this was so much worse. Mollis's family was everything to her. Everything. She had never had one before, and I knew that losing her family was the one thing that could actually break her.

And if I knew it, her enemy likely knew it as well.

"Mollis. I'm going to tell you what I told him," I said, pointing at her mate. "If you lose control now, you lose focus. You can destroy all manner of things, and it still will not lead you to him. We need to be smart. We need to be organized. We need to keep our shit together now," I said, using a phrase I knew she would understand, because it is one she used often.

Her breathing was harsh, her power swirling around us giving the sensation of being caught in a tornado.

"Mollis!" I shouted. "Think of him now. You can destroy things afterward."

She stared at me, and I felt her power dial down.

"I thought I'd get him back, E," she said, and her voice was full of pain, disappointment, fear. I went to her and put my arms around her.

"Go," I told everyone around us. They hesitated, and I glared. "Go back to Detroit. Now."

One by one, they all disappeared, immortals rematerializing the mortals back to our home city. Then it was just Mollis and me, and once we were alone, the first few sobs tore from her throat. I held her, and she cried, occasionally screaming out in anguish as sobs wracked her body. Her grip on me was almost suffocatingly tight, as if she was trying as hard as she could to hold onto some vestige of sanity, and I was it.

I let her get it out. I knew Mollis. There were several things the two of us had in common, and one was the inability to allow ourselves to show this kind of emotion in front of others. I often felt as if I showed strong emotions, if I cried, if I screamed, it showed a certain weakness that would only worry those around me, and I did not want that. We, Mollis and I, were accustomed to playing the strong one, to pretending to be the one who has everything figured out, even if, internally, we were as lost as anyone else. We just refused to let others see it, needing the facade of strength the way a child needs a security blanket.

Eventually her sobs slowed, though she still held me.

"We will get him back," I whispered. "We will get him back, and we will destroy whoever took him. I promise you that from the depths of my soul, demon girl."

She nodded against me, still crying. After a moment, she straightened, wiping the tears from her face. "I need to get back. I need to find him," she said, and there was that steel in her voice again.

I nodded. "We will find him," I said again.

"You need to rest. I want you to go back to the loft. Nain probably took Brennan and the rest of them there already. I'll feel better with everyone in secure locations. The time for trying to lure the betrayer is over."

"It clearly was not Tisiphone or Megaera," I said.

"Thank god," she breathed. "I have never seen my mother that pissed."

"Well, you did not think you got all of your rage from Hades, did you?" I asked with a smile. She hugged me, hard.

"I love you, E. Thank you for always being my rock."

I hugged her back, a lump in my throat, tears stinging my eyes. "I love you too, Mollis." I pulled back, wiping my eyes, and she was blinking back tears again as well. "Now let's get back and find your son."

"But you're going to rest for a while first. The rest of us have this," she warned, and I nodded my assent, smiling.

"Maybe just a short one," I said. She took my hand, and we rematerialized, appearing back in the loft.

And just like that, I was home again.

CHAPTER FIFTEEN

I paced the loft, from the dining room, through the training area, to the living room windows, and back. As good as it felt to be back, to be surrounded by my friends and family, it did not change the fact that things were very much a mess. Mollis, Nain, Tisiphone, the Bloodborn, Triton, and anyone else available was out searching for Mollis and Nain's son. I had slept through the night and most of the day, and now it was night again. Mollis had insisted on the fact that I should remain at the loft, getting at least one more night to recuperate, and though I felt like arguing, I knew I was only going to be a detriment in my current state. My body was still sore where Alecto had stabbed and cut me. My back hurt, and that stupid ache in my wings that were no longer there plagued me. Another night of healing, and I would be much closer to full strength. Besides that, Quinn was still recovering, and I did not want him to feel as though I expected him out working again.

So, I stayed in the loft at Mollis's insistence, and I ate, and I slept. Brennan and Sean were there as well, though Brennan had been in and out all day and we had barely managed a quick kiss between him caring for his son, helping Mollis and Nain, and my much-needed resting periods.

With all of the insanity happening, I almost felt guilty admitting that I felt better than I had since before we had left for Japan. I was back in the loft, the charade Mollis and I had been playing mercifully at an end. It struck me that I should likely be irritated that we had apparently gone through all of that for nothing, but I was too happy over the fact that our betrayer was not Megaera or Tisiphone. Of course, Alecto and whoever was working with her were still out there.

You take the good news where you can, and try to hold on to it. This was one of those times.

With the recovery of Michael, and now, Sean, there was added security at both Hephaestus's home and at the loft, protecting the children from further danger. Zoe was at Hephaestus's home, an enraged, protective Mother Gaia watching over both her and Michael. I almost hoped our enemy would take a chance and try it. They would find themselves in a world of pain if they tried to cross Gaia. She would not allow herself to be taken unaware twice.

The previous night, I had changed out of my soaking wet clothing and into a pair of pajama pants and one of Mollis's tops, a strappy thing that allowed me to see every scar on my shoulders and arms, including the new ones I'd earned at Alecto's hands, angry pink slashes across my flesh. My hair was wet, slicked back after my shower. Artemis had been there for a while, holding her grandson, and had apologized profusely for any time she had ever been "bitchy" with me. She had then gone out with the rest of them, hunting those responsible for taking Sean and the others.

At the loft, it was me, the remaining imps, Brennan, and Sean. Rayna's people guarded the exterior and roof, along with a veritable army of shifters, who reveled in the fact that Brennan's son had been recovered and seemed to have made it their own personal mission to ensure nothing happened to him again.

Brennan came out of the upstairs room, and one of Mollis's Netherhounds loped up the stairs and walked past him, into Sean's bedroom. I watched as Brennan patted him on the head respectfully. I heard Brennan thank him, the one Mollis called "Kurt."

Brennan walked down the stairs, and I wrapped my arms around myself.

I went to him, put my arms around him. He wrapped his arms tightly around my body, lifting me up against his chest, off of my feet. He buried his face against the side of my neck, and I felt the harsh, wracking breaths that signaled that he was finally breaking, after it was all done. I understood. He had been all about finding his son, then dealing with the aftermath and trying to give Nain the same gift he had been given. Other than that one night I had cajoled him into resting with me, he had not rested a moment since Sean had gone missing, refusing to allow himself to be distracted by the terror he had been feeling all that time. Now, with Sean safe, it was all crashing down on him.

I held him, and kissed his cheek. "It is all right, my love," I whispered against his skin. "It is all right."

He simply held me tighter. We stood there, in one another's arms, for a very long time.

"You saved him, Eunomia," he said finally, his voice muffled, his face still buried against my neck. "I had a few bad seconds there, where I envisioned him falling when she dropped him— "

I squeezed him. "I would have done anything to keep it from happening. I am glad I was quick enough. I wish I could have gotten to him sooner."

"The wing thing," he said, pulling back so he could look into my face. "She was taunting you with that."

I nodded.

"You do the impossible. You amaze me more the longer I know you."

"I am just glad I was there to help you," I said. "There is nothing I would not do for you, Brennan."

"Yeah?" he whispered.

I took a breath. "I would do the impossible, every moment of every day, if that was what it took to show you how much I love you," I said, looking into his eyes. In the next instant, his lips were crashing down onto mine, and I was consumed, helpless against the rush of emotion, of desire, of pure white hot need that ran through me, and finally, I refused to run from what I was feeling for him. I kissed him back, hungrily, lips, teeth, tongue expressing things words had not been able to. He held me tightly against his body, and I reached up, tangling my fingers into his hair, bringing him closer, needing his touch more than I have ever needed anything in my entire existence.

"Eunomia," he groaned, trailing his mouth to my earlobe, then down the side of my neck, licking and biting the place where my neck and shoulder met, and I moaned.

"Yes," I murmured, my voice hoarse, throaty to my ears. He kissed, bit me again. It felt like every atom in my body screamed for him, every touch of his lips, every nip of his teeth, driving me closer to insanity. "I need you now," I told him.

A low growl escaped him, and I took his hand, pulling him up the stairs to the room next to Sean's. I closed the door behind him, and immediately grabbed the hem of his t-shirt, pulling it over his head, exposing the expanse of muscle and golden hair I had been fantasizing about for far too long. He held me, his fingers biting into the flesh at the sides of my waist, his breathing shallow, harsh as I kissed my way down his throat, licking the spot at the base of his throat where I could feel his pulse jumping. His collarbone, his chest. My lips closed over one of his nipples, and I sucked, hard, and the low, needy growl I earned in response only encouraged me to do it again.

"Do not expect me to be patient," I told him.

He let out a low chuckle, which turned to something else when my hands reached for his pants. I unsnapped his jeans, slowly, deliberately pulled down his zipper. "Thousands of years of existence, and I have never wanted anyone the way I want you," I told him, keeping my gaze locked onto his.

"Eunomia," he murmured. "I— " his words turned into a groan when I reached into his jeans, cradling his hard length in my hand.

"You were saying?" I whispered with a smile, and I earned a low, almost pained laugh in response as my hand worked over his hot length.

"Fuck," he groaned, pushing his hips toward me.

"Yes, that is the general idea, my love," I said.

In the next instant, my top was off, my breasts bared to his gaze.

"Perfect," he breathed. I was warm all over, hot desire curling inside me, my body already aching for him. His gaze was almost scary in its intensity, the animalistic need of it.

My hands went to my waistband, and I started slowly pulling my pants down, swiveling my hips in a way that had him groaning as he watched. When they finally dropped to the floor, I stood before him, watched as he stared possessively.

"Let me worship you the way you deserve," I said softly. I pushed his jeans down and off of him, and then gave him a gentle push, and he settled himself onto the bed, keeping his eyes on me the entire time.

"I'm pretty sure you're the one who deserves to be worshipped," he said. I got into bed with him, my body straddling his. I kissed him, and lost track of time as I relished the feel of his mouth on mine, his naked body beneath me, his hands expertly caressing my breasts. I kissed and nibbled his throat, his jawline, his shoulders, and the entire time, his ceaseless caresses, from gentle rubs to firm tweaks, continued.

I felt as if I was about to lose my mind completely.

I kissed my way down his chest, sliding my body further down, licked my way down his stomach, his thighs.

"Eunomia," he growled. And when I took him into my mouth, a sound of such complete hunger escaped him that it set my entire body into chaos. I relished the taste of him, the sounds he made, the feel of his hands in my hair, the way his hips bucked as I tried to express without words how much I wanted him.

"Come up here," he said hoarsely, and when I did, he rolled us both over, pinning me beneath his large body, his eyes locked onto mine. His breathing was harsh, and I could see, just a bit, that same edge of the power he held within him. It was time that he finally let all of that break free.

I knew what he wanted, what it would take to show him how completely I was his.

"You want to take me, don't you?" I asked. He clenched his teeth, swallowed hard. "You want to mark me. That predator, that wild animal inside you needs it, doesn't it?"

I heard a low growl from him, and he pushed his hips toward me, his hardness pressing into my lower belly.

"I want you to mark me, Brennan," I told him. "I want everyone who looks at me to know who I belong to. You are an immortal. The only being I have ever known who is my equal in every way. You are the only one I want, now and for the rest of my immeasurably long life."

His breathing was labored, and...oh, there it was.

It was only so long before his immortal side started truly showing itself. His eyes glowed, bright blue in his desire, evidence of the same power any of the Aether immortals have, and in that instant, I knew I had been right about him and the long life he had ahead of him.

Gods, it was beautiful.

I opened my legs to him, and it was all the encouragement he needed. He held himself above me on his elbows and tangled his fingers into my hair. "I love you, Eunomia," he said softly.

"I love you, Brennan. I need you." Words I had never said to another soul in the entire length of my existence. "I have never needed anyone the way I need you." He kissed me, and then trailed hot kisses down my throat, to the side of my neck where his teeth gently clamped onto me, and I could feel his hardness, his heat pressing against my opening as I writhed in need.

"Please," I moaned.

He entered me, slowly, tenderly, filling me, stretching me, his teeth still clamped onto the side of my neck, his fingers tangling almost painfully in my hair as he tried to keep control.

We groaned together as he filled me, and then he stayed still, letting my body adjust to him. And I needed it. "Well-endowed" did not even begin to describe him.

"How do you always know what I need, Eunomia?"

"I pay attention," I said, gasping as he began moving his hips. He went back to sucking and biting the side of my neck as his hips pumped, as my body rose up to meet his. He lowered one hand from my head to my breast, which he rubbed and tweaked. My entire existence was rooted to those three places on my body: my neck, where I could feel him marking me, my breast, which was in tender agony from the way he touched me, and the feel of him thrusting harder and harder into me as he drove us both nearer to release.

"Oh, gods, I love you," I whimpered as he thrust into me, slowly, agonizingly, filling me and then receding almost completely, making me feel every single inch of him. It was a sweet agony, and I never wanted it to end.

I could feel sharp canines against my neck as he pushed into me harder.

"Oh," I gasped, and then my release tore through me, endless, crashing over me with the strength of all I felt for him, multiplied millions of times over. He moved harder, less controlled, and then I felt a sharp pain at the juncture of my neck and my shoulder as his canines punctured my flesh, marking me, his teeth clamped onto me as he took me. I cried out again as a second orgasm pulled me under, and I heard him growl my name against my neck, felt him stiffen and then lose all control, as his own orgasm tore through him.

He was tireless, and even after his release passed, he kept thrusting into me. He kissed my neck and shoulder tenderly, licked the tender flesh there as if trying to soothe it. He only stopped for as long as it took to roll us over so that I was astride him again.

"Ride me," he said, and a shiver went through me at the tone, at the way he looked at me. My body was practically limp with exhaustion, yet I did not want it to end. I rested my hands on his chest and started moving my hips as he thrusted into me. He looked me over for a long moment, his eyes still glowing with that beautiful blue light. He cupped my cheek, then ran his hand down to my chest, gently cupping my breast and rubbing his thumb over an aching nipple before running his knuckles down my stomach until his fingers slipped between us.

"You're never getting rid of me now, Tink," he told me, a cocky grin on his face. "You're mine." He touched me in ways that overwhelmed me completely, the pleasure almost too much to handle, and he watched my expression.

"Brennan," I whimpered.

"Say it," he growled.

"I'm yours," I moaned. "I love you. I'm yours." I threw my head back as another wave of ecstasy rolled through me, and I heard a low chuckle as he watched me shudder in pleasure. When it was over, he settled beside me, pulling me into his arms. I wrapped my arms round his waist, trying to get my breath.

I lay there with him, and felt his hands running up and down my back, his heart beating against my cheek, his scent surrounding me. Tears flooded my eyes, and my breath hitched.

"What's wrong?" he asked quietly. "Are you okay?"

I held him tighter. "Just emotional, Cub," I said. "I love you so much," I whispered.

"I love you too," he murmured. "This… what we have between us, there's no coming back from. You've ruined me, Eunomia. There'll never be anyone else."

"There better not be," I muttered. "It took me thousands of years to make my way to you. I am never letting you go."

"Good. For the first time in a very long time, I'm looking forward to the rest of my life. We're gonna make this good," he promised me as his fingers lazily trailed up and down my spine. "This is everything I ever wanted, and I swear I'm going to make sure you know every day how much you mean to me. I'm looking forward to days lived by your side, and nights when I'm going do nothing but worship you and revel in your moans when you beg for me."

My heart was pounding. I knew he meant it.

"You have brought me low, my love. I have never begged in my life," I said sleepily.

"I love it when you do," he said against my shoulder as he kissed me.

"I'll likely do it often. If you are really lucky, I will make you beg as well."

"And I'm looking forward to it," he said, and I could hear the smile in his voice, and I smiled and let sleep pull me under.

CHAPTER SIXTEEN

The days stretched on, each day feeling a little more desperate as we still lacked any sign of baby Hades. I had very little time to spend with Brennan. I spent every possible moment tracking Mollis's son, and when I was not doing that, I was hunting souls and undead.

There were far too many of them, and, as I had first suspected upon seeing the undead corpse at Rayna's home, the undead threat had most certainly reached Detroit. The few days my team and I had taken to recuperate had resulted in a flood of unchecked undead activity in the city. Now that we were back to work, my New Guardians and I mostly seemed to be keeping it under control, but every time it felt as if we had gotten them all, there were more.

"We all know where this is goddamned coming from," Quinn muttered as we returned from turning yet another wandering soul over to Tisiphone.

"Whitechapel," I said. Too many of the undead we fought in Detroit had been from Whitechapel. My Guardian senses registered that immediately and I had found, to my delight, that Quinn and Claire both seemed to be gaining that particular skill as well. The others said they sometimes felt inklings of knowing, but they were not quite there yet.

"Fucking Whitechapel. And they're being brought here to keep us scrambling. Why?" he asked. The rest of the team was in my apartment. Erin was holding a cloth to her arm.

"I'm bleeding!" she said, and, despite her words, she was grinning. "Blood. Look!"

I had to laugh. The New Guardians' reactions to their increased physical bodies was entertaining, if nothing else. They had all spent so long as nothing more than energy. It felt strange to them, now, to be seen by others. They had just gotten accustomed to the immortals being able to see them, and now, it appeared, most humans could see them as well. Since the day we had watched Mollis destroy Mary, my team had not only grown closer, but more dedicated as well. It seemed that the embracing of their roles was resulting in them gaining fully physical forms, as well as Guardian powers to go with them. I could not have been more pleased with the way they were advancing. They were quickly becoming among those I truly trusted and admired, and the prospect of working with them for the rest of my days made me quite happy.

"Do you want a bandage?" I asked her with a smirk.

"No! This is glorious. I've never been so happy to see blood in my life!" Annie and Cathleen laughed, and Quinn merely shook his head.

I turned back to Quinn. "I agree with you. Do you want me to send you all to Whitechapel again to continue your work there, or would you prefer to remain here until this situation is handled?"

"What do you want, boss?"

I considered our options. Keeping Detroit undead-free would be wonderful, but I could not just allow the undead to continue to overtake the cities they were already in. "We need more Guardians," I said, rubbing the back of my neck. My mind raced. There had been thirteen of us originally. Knowing Nyx and her love of balance, it was quite possible that there would be enough New Guardians out there somewhere to make it thirteen once again. Quinn stood silently at my side, and after a few moments, I looked up at him.

"You were able to sense all of the others. The other New Guardians," I said. "You sensed Annie just as easily as I did."

"True. We can all sense one another, just like you can sense us. It's weird. You'd think we just feel like the other souls."

"But you don't," I continued for him, nodding. I glanced at the rest of my team. My team, who were coming fully into their powers, who were beginning to feel more like the Guardians I had spent my life with than anything else. But different, too. The same, and different.

Better.

I came to a decision. "If I sent you out to start searching for other New Guardians," I began. "Could you do it?"

He stared. "Uh…"

"You know how to rematerialize. You and Claire are both quite good at it now."

"Well, yeah," he said, and I smiled.

"We need more."

He took a breath. "I want to do this for you, lass. I do. But here's my thing: how the fuck do I know if they're any good or not? Right? Say I come across one of us, one who feels like the rest of us do. Dead, but overlooked by the crows and the old Guardians because our energy signature is just different enough to make us invisible to them… what if I bring 'em to you, and they're not on our side? What if they're more like the things we're fightin' against?"

I nodded, understanding his concern. The incident with Mary, as well as the general discomfort that we now had with trusting anyone, thanks to having not one, but three, betrayers somewhere in our midst, had us all second-guessing *what* we knew, as well as *who* we really knew. "If you find them, I can take them to my Queen or her mother. They can look into their minds. If there is even a shred of doubt, then they will be imprisoned. If they are like the rest of you, then we will take them in and train them."

"I'm in, then," Quinn said, nodding. The rest of the team approached, each with determination in their eyes, nods of agreement.

"We're all in," Claire said.

"Good. Bring any you find to the Netherwoods. Directly to the palace. Even if Mollis or Tisiphone cannot see you right away, there are demons there who will help you contain any who happen to be troublemakers."

"You will come after us if you need us, though, right?" Erin asked. "You're not just going to go out hunting on your own."

"You just do not want to miss out on the fun," I joked.

"I do not see how any of this is fun," Cathleen said, brow furrowed.

"I— never mind," I said, smiling to myself. The day when I was the one who was not taking something completely literally had finally arrived. "If I have need of you, I will find you. Quinn and Claire both have phones now. It will be easy to keep in contact with one another. And the same goes for you. Do not run into undue danger. Be careful. There are enemies afoot, and they would not hesitate to destroy you if it would cause more chaos, which it would."

"We will," Claire promised. They started preparing to leave, pocketing phones, putting shoes back on. I watched them with some amusement. Tisiphone had taken them under her wing, providing them with new, modern wardrobes. Erin and Claire both had a very feminine style that suited them. Cathleen was very much a jeans and t-shirt kind of woman. Quinn reminded me of a lumberjack. Annie had a classic, demure style that suited her quite well.

As I looked them over, Annie saw me watching them, came to me, and pulled me aside.

"I cannot do this," she said quietly.

"Why not?"

"I am not the fighter they are. What if we come up against trouble and they have to depend on me and I'm not bloody good enough?"

"You went with them before, to hunt," I pointed out. "And I recall Quinn saying something about you stabbing away at Alecto when she tried to attack Quinn back in London."

"Yes, but that was before I heard about what the Fury was able to do to you. She sliced your neck. Stabbed you in the stomach..." she trailed off, shaking her head.

I could have smacked myself. Of course. The stabbing would have triggered horrible memories for her. And those particular injuries were too similar to the ones that had killed her.

"You are strong and you are a quick learner. And you have a good head on your shoulders and often see things others do not." I had to remind myself that, like all of my New Guardians, she had not had a happy life. Annie, in particular, was not especially brimming with confidence. During her natural life, she had had issues with drinking, was spurned by everyone she attached herself to, and occasionally turned to prostitution in Whitechapel in order to earn enough for food and lodging. Murdered and mutilated by the one known as "Jack the Ripper," but who I knew as Eveline Noonan. She had spent her entire time as a soul in hiding, haunting the place of her death. "And no one will harm you."

"Yeah?" she asked in disbelief. "I've heard that before."

I met her eyes. "If you would prefer to let all of this go, to be sent to your final judgment and what comes after, I will escort you to my Queen myself. I well understand being tired and fed up. There is no shame in it."

"You would let me do that?" she asked quietly.

"Of course. Or you can go back to what you were doing before I found you."

She gave a small shiver. "No. No, I hated that. There is nothing worse than not being seen. You start to wonder if you are insane. To be able to see everyone around you, to hear them, and know that none can hear you... no. I do not want that again." She put her arms around herself, over her stomach, a stomach that had been ripped open in her murder, her intestines and uterus removed from her body. "I want to help," she finally said.

"Any help you give me will help me find your murderer more quickly. I want you to know that," I told her. She met my eyes and nodded. "And Quinn is like a very large, very mean guard dog. He would rather be hurt himself than see any of you harmed."

"That's the truth," Quinn said from my left. I glanced at him, and he was looking at Annie. "I promise it, Annie."

She took a breath, and gave another small nod. "Then I will go with them to find more of our kind. Do you truly think we will find any?"

"I certainly hope so," I said. I shook hands with each of my New Guardians, and watched as they joined hands and then, they were gone.

"Nyx protect them," I murmured, closing my eyes. I opened them and glanced at the clock on the wall near my kitchen. I had promised to meet Brennan at his office so we could go out together in search of baby Hades. We would meet up, and then check in with Tisiphone to see where they needed eyes.

It was likely pathetic that I was excited, almost gushingly so, over the prospect of seeing him despite everything else that was going on. I checked my hair, reapplied lip gloss, and focused on rematerializing in the building downtown where the Supernatural Affairs Division was located.

When I appeared in Brennan' office, I could hear that the department was much busier and more chaotic than it had been at any other time I had been there. People rushed back and forth in the corridor outside his office, and I could hear phones ringing, voices speaking. To be fair, it was not all that unexpected; everything was a mess.

I sat down, knowing Brennan would be in when he was able. He was expecting me. I only waited for a few moments, when the door opened. Instead of Brennan, however, it was Jamie, his partner and right hand. She had started as his assistant, but her investigative skills and experience in alleviating tension when out on calls soon proved to be too much talent to let go to waste. She was an agent, and typically worked with Brennan on the cases they were handling.

She was also the Detroit area's only female shifter alpha. Her father had been the pack alpha before her, but had fallen fighting at Mollis's side. From what I had heard, it had been hard-won, but she had faced every challenge to her leadership brilliantly.

I smiled when she walked in and noticed me. She was dressed, as Brennan usually was, in a dark suit, though she wore heels. I was pleased for some reason to see that the bubble-gum pink hair she had had when I first met her was back. She had gone back to her natural shade for a while, but clearly felt more comfortable in her role now. It absolutely suited her, setting off her dark complexion in a really stunning way.

"Hey, E!" she said in greeting. I stood and we embraced. "How are you?"

"I do not even know how to answer that question right now," I told her, and she nodded.

"Seriously. What a mess, right?"

"Anything new?"

She shrugged and sat down with a sigh of relief. "Other than pretty much every church in town denouncing our girl as some kind of plague on our society that caused all this mess, you mean?"

"Morons," I muttered.

"Amen."

"We have been on top of the undead situation here," I said.

"Yeah, but they've seen it now. And now that they have, everyone's paying a hell of a lot more attention to the word of undead in Europe and Asia. Shit is bad in London."

"If I never hear about London again, it would be a beautiful thing," I said.

She let out a short laugh.

"It was much worse in Japan and Paris before as well, but the creation of undead in those areas seems to have halted. Their focus seems to be London. And that is where I will be as soon as Mollis's son is found."

"She's not doing well, E," Jamie said quietly.

"I know."

She grimaced. "No, she's really not good. You haven't seen the news yet this morning, have you?"

A sense of dread settled over me. "Do I want to ask?"

She shook her head and took her phone out of her jacket pocket. After a moment, she handed it over to me. There was a video from one of our local news stations on the screen, paused.

"My day is going to get much worse after I watch this, is it not?"

"Oh, for sure," she said.

I pressed "play," and the video started, the view swinging quickly from a busy rush-hour traffic scene on Jefferson to Mollis, standing in the middle of the street, cars squealing to a stop around her.

"Yeah, get your phones out. Film this," Mollis shouted, and she sounded more unhinged than I have ever heard her.

"Damn it," I murmured.

Jamie put a hand on my arm, as if to comfort me. I continued to watch, and Mollis shouted again, her voice amplified unnaturally.

"Listen up, all of you. Now. My son is missing. Someone has him. If I don't get him back in the next two days, this whole fucking world is going to burn. It's in all of your best interest to find him. You fear me? You worry about what will happen if I go bad? You're about to find out unless I get him back," she finished, her voice thundering as people in the crowd screamed.

And then Mollis was gone.

Jamie and I sat in silence.

"We're gonna lose her, E," she said quietly. "She's on the edge."

I did not respond. There was nothing left to say. It was quite likely she would never follow through the threats, but the fact that they had been made would only make it that much harder for the mortals to feel safe around us.

We were sitting in silence when the door opened and Brennan walked in, Sean on his hip. I looked up at him, met his eyes.

"She hadn't seen the video yet," Jamie told him.

He leaned down and kissed me quickly, and Sean waved at me.

"Nain has her in the Netherwoods now with Tisiphone and Megaera," Brennan said. Artemis and Asclepius appeared with a "pop" just then, along with two imps and a demon.

Artemis greeted me and Jamie, then held her hands out for Sean. He clung to his father for a moment, refusing to let go, and it was only after some soft words from Brennan that the boy finally let go and went to his grandmother.

"We are going immediately to Mollis's palace," she told Brennan.

"Good. Thank you," he said. Artemis leaned down and pressed a kiss to his forehead. "Be good for Gram, buddy," Brennan said to Sean.

206

"I will," Sean said. In the next moment they were gone, and Jamie was heading out into the reception area to take care of something.

Brennan sat across the desk from me, his eyes on me, and I could not look away from him.

He was about to speak when his office phone rang, and he gave the machine an "are you kidding me?" look.

"I have to take this. It's one of our guys in L.A.," he said apologetically. I nodded, and he picked up. I listened as he greeted the other agent, then there were several long moments of quiet as Brennan listened to the report. His head slumped forward in the way it always did when he received news he was not happy about. Finally, he said, "okay, thanks. Let me know if there are any developments," then he hung up.

"Yeah, word is getting out. They found three more partially eaten bodies today in Palo Alto," he told me.

"So this is definitely no longer a European and Asian issue. Or even just a Detroit thing. They are here now," I said, and he nodded. "I will be leaving after this last shift looking for Hades. This needs to be contained, and as much as I want to be here for Mollis— "

"You're the only one who can really put a dent in it all. I know," he said with a small smile. "Just be careful."

"Of course. Are you almost ready to leave?"

He nodded, and then sat there, watching me. I felt my entire body warm under his gaze. No matter how insane our life was, he still managed to make me feel alive.

"I miss you, Tink," he finally said.

"Timing is not on our side, Cub," I answered. "But I am not going anywhere, so..." I trailed off with a shrug, and he smiled.

"Neither am I." We spent another moment, both of us simply enjoying the silence and the comfort of being in one another's presence. "Did you get my text earlier?"

I rolled my eyes. "Yes. Thank you for making me blush while I was in the middle of giving my team instructions."

He laughed, and I shook my head. "I considered sending a pic of my — "

"Do not say it," I warned, and he laughed. "I have no interest in seeing a picture of it, I want it in person," I added, and he groaned.

"That makes two of us." He patted the top of his desk with his hand. "Desk is sturdy," he said, and I shook my head.

"The world is falling apart around us and you want a quickie on your desk?"

He grinned. "Stress management is important at times like this."

"Ridiculous male."

He laughed then, then leaned forward and took my hands, resting our hands in the center of the desk. "The only time I laugh lately is when I'm with you. You know that?"

I squeezed his hands. "Nice save," I told him, and he laughed again. Gods, his laugh. Warm, deep, and that flash of teeth, the way his eyes crinkled at the corners. I would never tire of it. "We should check in with Tisiphone so we can begin searching again,"

He nodded, and we both stood up. He shrugged into his jacket and was straightening his tie when Jamie opened the door, a stunned look on her face. She seemed to be carrying something heavy in her other hand.

"Jamie? What's up?" Brennan asked.

"Uh. We found Hades," she said.

Brennan and I both turned, and I immediately assumed the worst. I knew from Brennan's expression that he believed the same.

"Where?" he asked.

"Someone left him in the lobby," she said, and when she opened the door, I saw that she held a large basket in her other hand, and in it, Hades was nestled amid several blankets. There was a sheet of paper tucked into the blanket. Jamie set the basket on Brennan's desk, and I plucked the note out, unfolded it.

Neat script met my eyes.

He has met his purpose, and now you may have him back.
There is a certain joy in knowing that every time you look at your son, you will see your undoing.

Brennan was reading over my shoulder as he dialed his phone. He met my eyes.

"Molly, we have him," I heard him say, and there was a scream at the other end of the line. "Someone dropped him off in my building. There's a note."

The next instant, Mollis and her husband were standing in the office with us, and Mollis was rushing to her son. She picked him up and held him close, sobbing uncontrollably as she kissed his forehead.

"He's here. He's alive," she wept, and Nain folded both her and their son into his embrace. The three of them stood there, Mollis's sobs the only sound in the room, the demon's harsh breaths as he dealt with his own emotions.

"He's here," Mollis whispered again.

Brennan and I exchanged a glance. I knew he was thinking the same thing I was. It was all too perfect. Too easy.

"Guys," Brennan said. "We should have him looked at. Remember what happened with Sean," he said quietly, reminding them that his own son had been ensorcelled in the womb, designed to be used against the team. A weapon. "He's back safe with us, thank god. But we need to know if there's more. Look," he said, handing the note to Nain.

Nain took it, looked it over, and snarled. "No one saw who left this?" he growled.

Jamie shook her head. "It was nuts. I was by the front desk talking to our receptionist. Place was empty. Nothing, nobody there but us. And then I heard a hiccup or something, and I turned around and there he was, on the floor by the entry door. He hadn't been there two minutes before, when a couple of our guys walked in."

"Did you feel anyone nearby?" Brennan asked, referring to someone with powers.

"Didn't see anyone, didn't feel anyone, didn't hear anyone. Didn't even smell anyone, and I tried. Instinct, you know," she said to Brennan, and he nodded. "Nothing. I can go down and sniff around as my wolf, though."

"That would be great. Thanks, J," Brennan said and Jamie nodded, patted Molly on the back, and left the office.

"It's really not surprising, since we can be pretty sure we're dealing with some type of immortal who can rematerialize," Brennan said, and I nodded.

"We really should have him looked at," I said gently.

"Babe?" Nain asked, looking at Molly.

"Persephone would be our best bet. She was the one who figured out what was up with Sean and how to get rid of it," she said softly. "She's still avoiding me, though."

"I will go," I said, remembering the friendly, if odd, discussion I had had with Persephone at the sushi restaurant what felt like years ago, now. "I will be right back."

I rematerialized to the Netherwoods, and, as I expected, I could see Persephone kneeling beside Hades' monument, black dress and veil covering her body. I walked toward her, not trying to be overly quiet, trying not to startle her.

"Persephone," I said softly.

She raised her head and looked at me. "Eunomia. What can I do for you?" she asked, and her voice was dead. Empty. She looked exhausted. I pitied her, knowing that, if I ever lost Brennan, I would be just as empty.

"I am sorry for intruding. Mollis's son has been found."

She gave a small nod. "I am glad. Surely, Mollis is elated."

"She is, but we have some concerns about what may have been done to him while he was gone. There was a note," I said. "We remember what you did for Brennan's son, and Mollis and her mate were wondering if you would please come and look Hades over."

She bowed her head again. "It hurts me to look at that child," she said softly. "I see his grandsire in him. His eyes," she added.

"I understand," I said. "And I know you have already been through so much pain. If there was anyone else who understood spells as you do, I would ask them. Please."

She sighed.

"It is bad enough that I have to see his namesake. I do not want his daughter, her mate, or the Furies around when I do this. You may be present. But I cannot handle seeing the whole happy little family right now."

I nodded. "Let me go relay that to Mollis so she can clear out. Will you wait here for me?"

Persephone nodded, and I reappeared back in Brennan's office. Mollis and Nain were hesitant, but eventually left Hades in Brennan's arms and retreated into the waiting room. I went back and found Persephone again, then took her to Brennan's office.

"Lay him on the desk," Persephone said as soon as we reappeared. Brennan obeyed, laying the infant on the desk and unfolding the blankets around him.

He was wearing nothing but a cloth diaper, the rest of his tiny body bare. On his chest was an angry red scar in the shape of an "X."

"Shit," Brennan breathed upon seeing it. He exchanged a glance with me.

"Whoever did that is going to pay," I said. Then a thought struck me. "Does Sean have a scar like this?"

He shook his head.

Persephone ignored both of us, approached the desk and stood over the baby. Hades had been fussing, but now wailed, loud, angry screams at such a pitch that it hurt my ears. He kicked his pudgy little legs furiously, his face red with the force of his cries.

"He usually does not cry like this," I said, going to him and resting a hand on his little arm.

"He has clearly been through horrors we cannot even imagine, if that scar is any indication," Persephone muttered. "Now be silent," she said to me.

She put her hands over Hades' head, hovering just above him, and she closed her eyes, focusing. Slowly, her hands moved in the air over his body, from his head to his toes as he wailed. After a few more passes, she opened her eyes and pulled her hands back to her sides.

"There is nothing there," she said numbly. "No curses, no spells. He has been returned clean."

"Well that is a relief, at least," I said, glancing at the scar on his chest, having a feeling I knew what it meant. Brennan wrapped Hades up again and cradled him in his arms, gently bouncing his body to soothe the child. "Thank you," I said to Persephone.

"I will be going now. I am glad he was returned safely. Please tell Mollis and Tisiphone I said so," she said, and I put my hand on her arm.

"I will do so. Please know that if there is ever anything you need, we are all here for you. You do not have to mourn alone."

She patted my hand gently. "I will remember that. Thank you, Guardian." With a nod, she was gone, most likely to continue her vigil at Hades' monument.

Brennan and I exchanged a look.

"Nain is going to want to murder someone even more when he sees this," he said, nodding down toward Hades, whose sobs had mostly stopped under Brennan's soothing care.

"As do I," I said. "It is sick. It is…" I could not even continue, shaking my head in rage.

"I know. We'll figure it out. We'll make them pay," he promised. Then he opened the door and called Mollis and Nain in.

"There's good news and there's bad news," Brennan said once the door was closed behind them again.

"The good news is, there is no curse or spell on him," I said.

Nain glanced at me. "And what's the bad news?"

Mollis was holding Hades, and I went to them and pulled the blanket back, showing them the mark on his chest.

Mollis froze at the sight, then focused and went into her son's mind.

"Erased," she whispered. "Everything since he was taken is gone except the memories of pain."

Nain roared and slammed his way out of the office, tearing the door from its hinges in his rage.

"We will find whoever did this, Mollis," I promised her. Her eyes glowed bright white, cold and deadly.

"Yes, we will. I don't care what it takes, we're going to find who did this to my son."

And with that, she stormed out, following her husband.

I turned to look at Brennan, who was typing something on his phone. "Heph says Michael doesn't have any scars either," he said, shoving his phone back in his pocket. "Just so we're on the same page: this is related to the undead shit, right?"

"I think so, yes."

He stood, thinking. "I think they took all three to cause as much chaos as they could. It feels like Hades was the actual target."

"Perhaps. Or perhaps they would have done the same to Sean and Michael, had they had a bit more time."

"Either way, they did that to Hades first. Us all being insane with worry, our forces split three ways gave them the time they needed to do what they did... how is he not dead? I mean, I'm glad he's not, obviously! But you'd think he would have died in the process of having his heart taken from him."

I nodded. "Yes. Even being immortal, he likely should have ended up locked away in the old Nether." It was what we assumed happened to all of the immortals not killed by Mollis herself. The mortal realm was physically closed off from the realm of the gods now, thanks to Mollis' grandmother, Nyx, who had permanently destroyed the gateway between worlds. However, the essence of a god, that thing that makes us immortal, is not a physical thing, and it cannot be destroyed by anyone other than Mollis. Always, when our physical bodies had failed us, our essence had returned to the Aether and Nether to allow us to resurrect. New bodies, same essence. It happened rarely, and had never happened to me, but Ares and Athena had each had their physical bodies fail them. Within days, they had been walking around in the Aether as if nothing had happened.

Having a heart removed certainly would qualify as the body failing. And not only had he not died, but he had grown a new heart, apparently.

"Molly was tortured and killed over and over again in the Nether," Brennan said, deep in thought. "I know Ares did a whole bunch of bad shit to her, stuff she shouldn't have been able to live through. That's what eventually drove Ares insane enough that he finally just gave up and decided to bury her alive."

"But Mollis is all god. Baby Hades is half demon," I said, thinking.

"Yeah, but the Nain has shared Molly's blood who knows how many times through the demon marriage bond, right? Everyone pretty much assumes he is immortal now because of it," he pointed out.

I shook my head. "Mollis's blood in Nain protects Nain. We have no idea if it would carry over into the child she created with him. It feels as if we are missing something."

"They could have had someone healing him as they did that to him." He was pacing, thinking. "Like life support or something...shit. You don't think Asclepius would do something like that, would he?"

"I cannot believe that. But I will look into it. It is a good thought. And, truly, even the idea of some form of life support that the humans use... if they had access to the types of things humans are hooked up to during surgeries, perhaps it would have been enough to keep him technically alive." I breathed out. "Too many questions, Cub. I do not like it."

"That makes two of us."

"Well. They will not be answered by standing here. I have work to do," I told him. He came to me, folding me into his arms.

"Be careful, Tink," he murmured against my neck as he kissed me.

"You too. Please," I added, needing to know how badly I needed him to be safe.

He pulled back, took my chin in his hands. "I promised you there would be no getting rid of me. I meant it. Now keep up your end of the bargain, all right?"

I nodded, and kissed him, closing my eyes and losing myself, for just a moment, to the beauty that lived in every touch, every kiss we shared. "Call me if I am needed," I murmured against his mouth.

"You're always needed," he said with a small smile. "I'll call if there are any problems."

I kissed him again, then took a breath and rematerialized away.

I had the nagging feeling that the key to so much of what we were facing could be found in Whitechapel, and the murderous soul who called it home. It was time for me to find her, and put an end to her madness.

CHAPTER SEVENTEEN

It was after dark when I appeared in Whitechapel. I had stopped by my apartment to grab the sword Mollis had given me. Hades' sword. I had my two Netherblades sheathed in the harness under my leather coat, the long sword of Hades strapped to my back. I pulled up my hood, fastened the cowl over my face.

It felt like coming home, just me and the hunt, and with all of the chaos, I needed it. I needed to not have my team around me, giving me more people to worry about. I needed to not have Brennan and his distracting body and the way I loved him overwhelming me.

Me, blades, and my prey. I had two out of the three, and I held out hope that I would find she who was responsible for creating nothing short of an undead army. Mollis had seen Eveline in Alecto's mind, the only thing she had been able to see.

As I walked the damp, deserted streets of Whitechapel, it felt as though I was surrounded by souls. Too many. The stench of death hung in the air, and most of the buildings were dark.

Not a sound met my ears.

The traffic lights cast ghostly red and green haloes onto the slick pavement. Automobiles sat parked at the curbs.

Dread filled me. Surely it could not have gotten this bad already?

The only answer I really needed surrounded me: the scent of decay, so many energy trails of lost souls that I could go in any direction and be lead to not just one, but several of them. It threw my senses off. Too many, so that everything was just a jumble in my mind.

I took my phone out of my pocket and dialed Quinn's new phone number.

The phone rang, over and over and over again and then finally kicked me to voicemail. "Quinn, it is me. When you get this, please bring the team to Whitechapel. We have quite a bit of work ahead of us here." I hung up, put the phone back in my pocket, and unsheathed one of my Netherblades.

I knew I should be getting to the souls that wandered. They would only be turned, in time, to undead. But I also knew that, for the area to be in such a state, my prey was here as well. Eveline had surrounded herself with death, by the abominations she had created, undoubtedly with knowledge gleaned from Alecto and whoever else still hid in the shadows.

Cowards, I seethed to myself as I walked. What honor is there in attacking this way? In using the souls of those you have murdered to cause chaos? To bring infants and children into your fight?

I could feel myself getting angry, and I shoved it down. Anger was a distraction.

The first undead leapt at me from the shadows between two tall, narrow brick buildings, and I stabbed out at him, catching him in the shoulder. I pulled my blade loose, then drew it hard across his throat.

He fell to the ground, head hanging limply.

I took a breath and continued, following the energy signatures, going in the direction in which there was the highest number of them.

She would have her minions around her, I thought with a sneer. Pathetic.

I knew this was not a fight that would be easy. With any luck, my New Guardians would get there before things got too bad.

I considered my course of action. I knew it was more than I could handle alone. I was perfectly confident in my fighting abilities, but there were only so many enemies even I could face on my own. What happened in Japan had been a good reminder of how horribly things can go when I am unprepared and undermanned.

I was pulling my phone out of my pocket, ready to hit Mollis's number, when I felt a presence I knew well behind me. "Triton?" I asked, pausing in my dialing.

"Oh, I'm glad you're here. I hoped I'd find you," he said, a bit out of breath. "I knew from Artemis that you would be here. Are you crazy coming here alone?"

I smiled. "I was about to call Mollis," I said. "Even I know when I am overmatched."

"Well, I'm here now," he said with a smile. "And she's currently torn between holding her son every second and trying to calm the humans after that outburst she had a few days ago."

I grimaced. "So you are offering to help me?"

He smiled again. "It has been a long time since I've gotten into a good brawl, little ghost."

I looked around. "I do not know that even the two of us will be enough. I can feel so many of them."

"Well, you said your New Guardians are likely on their way, right?"

"He did not answer when I called. Perhaps they do not have a signal where they are. I left a message," I said with a shrug.

"Well, they'll come when they get it. Let's just see how much damage we can do in the meantime."

I nodded and started walking with him though the damp, foggy, empty streets. He was a comfort beside me, a sign of normalcy. He looked so relaxed in his usual jeans and white t-shirt, though his shoulders were tense and his eyes scanned the shadows.

I could appreciate him now for the friend he was, without any other stupidity attached to it, and I was grateful.

"Thank you for being here," I said to him. "You were one of my very first friends, and it is lovely to be able to spend time with you again, though a meeting over coffee would have been quite a bit nicer."

He responded with a small nod, and glanced away.

We were on a narrow road, tall, narrow buildings flanking each side. It took me a moment to realize where we were: we were approaching the place where Eveline had murdered her first victim, leaving the woman to be found by whoever happened to pass by. That had been one of the things that had so disturbed people at the time, even beyond the brutal murders themselves. The way the victims were left, exposed, leaving them no dignity even in death, had been sickening. And planned. None of it had been an accident. Eveline was nothing if not manipulative. So of course she would lure me here, of all places. Back to the place where her "fame" had begun.

Such an egomaniac, I mused to myself as we walked forward.

I listened carefully now. Energy signatures converged, distracting in how many of them there were.

Triton put a hand on my arm. "Eunomia, stop. It's a trap," he said in a low voice, and at that moment, undead flooded from every doorway in the immediate area, all headed toward me.

I had a single instant to register the guilt on Triton's face before he disappeared behind the dozens of undead flowing toward me.

I want numb. Cold.

I would process it all later.

And, oh, how it would hurt when I did.

For the moment, I let myself sink into numbness. I let myself become the hunter I had been created to be. I drew my second Netherblade and went to work, slashing out at those undead closest to me, amid them, souls who were not quite finished becoming undead, stuck somewhere between being a soul and one of the horrid creatures.

I slashed, and I stabbed, and it was not long before I was covered in the sticky grayish blood of those I fought.

They had no weapons, using only their hands and teeth against me. My arms and back burned, my flesh scraped and torn under the assault of ragged fingernails.

Any who tried to bite me were immediately stabbed through the eye or the throat.

When I had a chance, I slipped one of my Netherblades into the sheath and drew Hades' sword. It allowed me to cut wide paths of them down. Heads fell to the ground, undead bodies were rent in half, and soon I was standing amid the rotting remains of those I had cut down, while others continued to come for me.

My arm began to tire, and I traded the sword for my second dagger again now that I had eliminated most of them.

I was not foolish enough to believe I was finished.

Every time I thought I might have a moment to call Mollis or Hephaestus or any of them to come and help me, another group surrounded me, excited even more by all of the death around us.

A few, disgustingly enough, began to devour the flesh of their fallen comrades, too distracted by the availability of flesh to bother with me.

Too many, though, seemed to recognize the difference between living and unliving flesh.

I was aware that Triton was nowhere to be seen.

Lying, cowardly, betraying piece of... no. I pulled myself back from thinking about him. Not now.

It just went on, and my arms grew more tired, though I had no major injuries. At least there was that. If I could just fight free for a moment... if I dialed Mollis, that would be enough to make her send the imps to look for me, and then she would come.

To my surprise, the advance of the undead slowed, and after a moment, I sensed why.

Eveline stood before me, as buxom and gorgeous as she had ever been in life. She wore a smirk, and her posture was one of smug confidence. She was powerful. I could feel immortal power in her, and my suspicion was confirmed. This was who had received the heart of the second god we had found in Japan. The goddess of winter's heart was what fueled the piece of absolute trash that stood before me. She, who had caused so much death and chaos.

My entire body went cold, and I lunged toward Eveline.

She held a dagger.

A Netherblade.

I snarled at her as we circled one another, each of us occasionally stabbing, lunging forward, trying to gain an advantage. It became clear, very soon, that while she was powerful and most certainly not new to using a knife, she was not a skilled fighter. We circled one another, and I pressed my advantage.

All of a sudden, she laughed, and my hand froze, as if encased in ice, around the hilt of my dagger.

She smirked. "Three times, eating the heart of Winter does wonders. I wonder what abilities the lucky one I gift your heart to will gain after you work so hard to grow your heart a third time? Perhaps we'll keep you alive so you can see for yourself."

I stabbed out with the other hand, the one that was not frozen, and she cried out in surprise as blood flowed down her chest.

I stalked forward. My hand had begun to thaw, and I could feel my fingers again. She was backing up, looking nervous, and I felt a cold smile spread across my lips. I sheathed my dagger, with the intention of taking my phone out and finally getting Mollis or one of the others to come. This had gone on long enough, and I was smart enough to know that I was weakening.

I heard a "pop."

In the next instant, Alecto was beside me, her hand in my pocket, and then she was back at Eveline's side.

A sense of foreboding settled over me when I saw that it was my phone she had I her hand. "We can't have you calling for help again, can we?" she asked. "You should have fallen to dust in Tokyo, zealot." She slammed the phone to the ground with enough force to cause it to shatter on the concrete.

"You mean the way so many of yours did?" I taunted, and Alecto's lip lifted in a snarl. Eveline laughed, a deep, throaty sound that echoed around us in the emptiness. Smug once again, now that she was no longer facing me on her own.

"Posturing now? Really? You are even more ridiculous than I remember," she said.

I did not hesitate. I had a Netherblade in my hand and I hurled it at her.

It hit her, planting itself deeply into her left eye socket, and she screamed in agony. In the chaos, I threw the second one, and it hit home at the base of her throat.

Mercifully, it cut off her screams, unable as she was to draw breath. I knew it would not keep her down permanently. Even now, Alecto was jerking the dagger from her eye, and she was scrabbling at the one in her throat, trying to pull it free. It would keep her weak for a little while, though.

Alecto lifted her lip in a snarl at me, flipping my Netherblade in her hand as she reached into her own sheath for a second Netherblade.

"This was your sister's. Thank you for ensuring I have a matching pair."

"You are pathetic," I said as we began circling one another. I was very aware of more undead gathering around us, of Eveline having yanked the other blade free, of her sitting up, trying to regain some of her strength. I tried to make sure I was aware of Eveline so I could prepare to position myself well in case she tried that freezing trick again. Hopefully, the Netherblades had weakened her for a bit.

"Are you really still on about Mollis murdering your pathetic, impotent little lover?"

Alecto growled at me, stabbed out, and I avoided it easily. Furies always had preferred swords. She would be dangerous with the daggers, especially since they were Netherblades, but not nearly as much of a threat as she would be with sword.

"Impotent? Please," she muttered.

"He was unmanned by a woman who had not even fully come into her powers yet," I taunted. "He had you doing his dirty work for him, while he hid in his hole like some kind of rodent. Hermes always was a joke, though, even at the height of his power."

She leapt at me again, and I swept out hard with Hades' sword, catching her across the stomach. She screamed in rage and leapt aside, then at me again.

"You think it's really about that now?" she sneered.

"Or maybe someone is just upset that her niece sits on the throne," I taunted, and she stabbed out again. I avoided most of it, but she managed to slice into my right shoulder, and it burned. I swung out with the sword again, and she rematerialized away from me, going back to where Eveline was now standing.

"Together," Eveline said, and Alecto nodded.

I had a moment to think of Brennan, a moment to realize that I might not make it out of this alive, before they were on me.

CHAPTER EIGHTEEN

We fought.

We fought, and the clang of blade hitting blade, the occasional grunt, the sound of our labored breath and the scuffle of our shoes on wet concrete were the only sounds to be heard. The time for taunts, for posturing, had passed.

All I could do now was fight for the chance to remain in this realm, to avoid my life in the mortal world coming to an end.

The prospect of an eternity trapped in the Old Nether, among the rampaging souls and the monsters that now called it home, cut off from Brennan and everyone else I cared for, was what kept me fighting. It was what kept my sword arm working, even when my muscles began to burn, even when it began to feel numb under the weight of Hades' sword.

I bled.

The cuts I had received from the Netherblades wielded by Alecto were numerous, and Eveline had produced a normal dagger from beneath her voluminous skirts as well. Together, they pushed their advantage relentlessly.

They were like sharks who smelled blood in the water, strengthened and frenzied, having found more energy in the sight of my blood.

I caused damage as well. Alecto lost two fingers on her left hand, leaving her unable to use both daggers, which gave me some respite. She had slashed across my throat, and I had returned the favor.

I swung at Alecto, overstepping my balance, and she took advantage of it. She plunged the Netherblade into my stomach with all of her strength, so deeply that I felt the blade scrape my backbone.

With a gleeful shriek, Eveline stabbed her blade through my chest, scraping rib, and I gasped, unable to draw breath for a moment, realizing she had struck a lung.

I was weakening. And no one was coming. I stumbled, fell back, and Alecto was on me, holding my arm, and I scrabbled at her hand, trying to get loose.

Eveline stood above me, and yanked my head up by my hair, forcing me to look up at her. I grabbed for her hand, but she paid me no mind.

"This will be so satisfying, you absolute nuisance," she gloated as she raised a Netherblade.

"Yes. It will," I managed in a gurgly voice, and with the last of my strength, I focused, holding on tightly to both of them.

I held with all my strength, and found myself praying to Nyx that I had managed to maintain enough strength for this last desperate move.

I focused, and I felt us falling away.

And in the next labored breath I took, I felt the cool stone of Mollis's office floor beneath my back, a crackling fire to my right. I smiled as my appearance was met by the sound of confused shouts and Alecto's enraged scream.

I felt Mollis nearby, saw Eveline's head fall from her body under the black flames of Mollis's sword, and then Alecto was pulled roughly away from me, and I heard her cursing me, almost incoherent in her rage.

I turned my head. I was on the floor in Mollis's office in her palace in the Nether. Rematerializing there had been my last chance, and I was just grateful it had worked. I knew Mollis and the demon spent most of their time there. I was glad I had guessed right that they would be in this particular room. Several demons, Nain, and Mollis had jumped into action at my appearance.

I saw that Zoe and baby Hades both slept on one of the sofas, blankets tucked around them.

Tisiphone came into the room, and she and Nain had Alecto cornered while Mollis came to me.

"E. E, you stay with me, you crazy, insanely brave bitch," she said, and there were tears running down her face.

"Triton," I managed through a throat that had been slashed again in that moment before we had managed to rematerialize.

"Triton is in danger?" she asked, and I shook my head.

"Was there," I managed.

I gave her a helpless look, and opened my mind, and she saw.

"I will fucking kill him," she growled. "Asclepius is here," she said with relief as the healer god bent over me.

"Great Gaia almighty, Guardian," he grumbled. "Did we not just talk about this?"

I watched his face as he lifted my shirt. He and Mollis exchanged a look.

"My blood again, your healing," Mollis said.

"Mollis..." Asclepius began, and he was stopped short by the feel of Mollis's power roaring over us.

"We will fucking save her, Asclepius," she shouted, even as tears rolled down her face.

I felt myself fading.

The room started getting dark, their voices farther away, echoey in the darkness.

"E, don't you fucking dare!" I heard Mollis scream. "Now, Asclepius!"

I felt the burning pain of his healing, of her blood flowing into my wounds, and still, everything felt further and further away. I was being pulled away, my physical body failing, my energy gathering, freeing itself from the body it had called home for nearly twenty-five thousand years. There was no more feeling. There was no more pain, no more burning. I could not feel Asclepius's hands on me anymore, Mollis's blood burning me. There was no cold, and no warmth.

"Eunomia."

His voice, faint, so faint I thought I imagined it. If I could have wept, I would have. The one thing I wanted, the one thing I needed to hear, so I could remember it.

"Eunomia, you promised me eternity," he said. I focused on his voice.

"You promised me forever, and you promised me that you would make me beg. I am begging you right now, sweetheart. Don't go anywhere. Don't leave me." His normally strong, calm voice broke on the words.

I wanted to scream. I wanted to rage. I wanted to claw my way back to him.

"You are mine, Eunomia. You are not the type who breaks her promises. Come back to me, Tink. Please," he said, and all that mattered anymore was his voice, even as I felt that pull on me, even as I felt myself drift further away. Even as I became more detached from life on the mortal plane, I realized that I had never wanted so desperately to be there.

"Eunomia."

I focused on him.

"I love you."

I held onto his voice, and I felt the pull on me slow, just a little. He kept talking, and I stayed, held by nothing more than the sound of his voice. It felt as though I was lost at sea, waves crashing over me, and his voice was the one thing enabling me to stay afloat, no matter how desperate it all seemed.

And still, he talked.

He sounded closer, and I swore I could feel his warm breath on my ear.

"I love you so much."

He sounded more solid.

"Stay with me. Don't make me live without you," he said, and I could feel his face against mine, his harsh, ragged breaths on my ear. I could smell him.

I gasped in a painful breath, gulps of air as if I had been drowning, and I heard Mollis crying, Asclepius's instructions to keep working, that I was not out of the woods yet.

But I knew better. I looked up at Brennan's face, and I smiled, and tears flooded my eyes when I saw his beautiful blue eyes overflowing with tears.

"You are never getting rid of me," I whispered in a ruined voice, and he rested his forehead against mine, and I focused on him as Mollis and Asclepius healed my torn body.

I stayed conscious though most of the healing, and told an exhausted Mollis, mentally, because my voice was not yet reliable, about what we had found in Whitechapel. I told her that if she heard from my team, they needed to go there. I told her that Alecto was working for others, that they had to try to find out who. I told her that we had more work to do.

She told me to sleep, and that she loved me, and that if she saw me up and around anytime soon she would kick my ass.

I smiled and thanked her for all she'd done, and I felt Brennan lift me into his arms and carry me through the palace. I felt Artemis, as well as Sean, nearby, and Artemis set a hand on my arm and murmured a few soft words to me, meant to soothe.

When we got to one of the many guest rooms in Mollis's palace, Brennan set me on the bed and I tried to sit up.

"No," he said, holding my shoulders down gently. "Asclepius said to stay still a much as possible." He took a breath and shook his head. "Why didn't you call for help?" he asked.

"I did try," I rasped, raising an eyebrow. "The bitch broke my phone."

He laughed, and, once he started, he could not stop, and I found myself smiling at the obvious release of all of the tension and fear I had caused him.

"Come and sleep with me," I said, and he nodded.

"Let me clean you up first, okay?"

I gave a small nod, and he gently, slowly peeled my torn, bloody clothing from my body.

"We'll get this fixed. Or have a new one made," he said, looking at my destroyed coat. I smiled. I liked that he understood what it meant to me. "Maybe with more chainmail embedded in it next time," he said with a raised eyebrow as he tossed it on a chair nearby.

Once I was free of my clothing, he brought a washbasin and a washcloth from the bathroom and set it on the nightstand. He sat on the bed beside me and slowly, gently, cleaned the blood and gore from my body.

"They wanted my heart," I said. "They were going to use it."

A look of rage crossed his face, though his hands remained gentle on my body.

"All I could think of at the end was you," I said, my voice hoarse, reedy sounding. I wondered if it would ever be normal again.

He met my eyes. "We agree that we belong to one another, yes?" he said, and though the words were gentle, I could hear the anger beneath them. I gave a tiny nod. "Then I think we can also agree that we are partners, in every way. That when you fight, I fight by your side, and when I fight, you fight by my side. There is no more of this 'this is my problem not yours' or 'I can't be distracted' bullshit. If we belong to one another, we do it fully, taking all of the risks and dangers of our lives together."

"The way Rhiannon and Sean did?" I asked in an almost imperceptible voice. I knew he could hear me, even as quiet as it was.

He nodded. "The way my parents did." He ran the cloth over my stomach, which was still quite sore from the healing. The cloth came away deep red, and he rinsed it, and wiped me again. "And if we die, we die the way Rhiannon and Sean did, fighting for one another's lives."

"And if we leave a son behind? A son who needs his father?"

His eyes met mine again. "My parents died heroes. I've had a good life, no matter how much I miss them. Sean will have the same. And I have no intention of either one of us dying. You're not getting rid of me that easily."

I smiled, looked down and watched, mesmerized, as he washed my abdomen, my hips. Scars crisscrossed over my stomach, my ribs, my thighs.

"My body is not the most attractive thing I have ever seen," I said, for the first time ever wishing I did not have the numerous scars I had earned in battle.

He washed the last of the blood from me, and then lowered his face to my stomach, his lips trailing over every line there, every ragged scar, from my stomach, down to my abdomen, my thighs, then back up to my arms, my neck. He ended on the one he had left the night he had marked me.

"You are the single most beautiful sight in this world or any other. You are a warrior, a hunter, a goddess, and I am overwhelmed by how stunning you are," he said, meeting my eyes. "You are the product of every scar you wear. How can I find them anything but gorgeous?"

I blinked tears back from my eyes. "You are very good at sweet-talking me," I whispered, and he smiled.

"It's easy to do when every word is the truth." He shucked his own bloody clothing, leaving them on the floor, and climbed into bed with me, pulling the heavy down comforter up over us. He gathered me gently into his arms, and kissed me, and it healed me in a different way. "Now sleep."

"Stay with me," I murmured, closing my eyes.

"Always."

CHAPTER NINETEEN

The next morning, I woke in his arms, his lips on my neck. I smiled and laced my fingers with his, and he kissed me. There was a whole new, even deeper feeling to our kisses now, to every touch we exchanged, and I knew it had a lot to do with the promise I had made him, by the fact that in the end, it was him that brought me back. We lay in bed for a long time, alternately kissing and dozing. We did not bother speaking, because everything we needed to say to one another was being said in other ways.

Later in the day, he finally got up and dressed, and he brought me a t-shirt and pajama pants and helped me slip into them. I insisted on getting up and sitting in one of the chairs in our room, and though I could tell he disapproved, he did not argue.

"I'm going to go check on Sean and get you something to eat," he said,

"I do not know how much I will be able to keep down," I said, my stomach still burning from the injuries it had received.

"I'll bring it anyway. Tea?" he asked, and I nodded, smiling at him. He dropped a quick kiss on my lips, then opened the door. He looked out into the corridor, said a few words to someone, then looked back at me.

"Quinn has been out here waiting to see you."

"Send him in," I said with a smile.

Quinn strode into the room, and Brennan left, closing the door behind him.

"Boss," Quinn said, coming and kneeling on the floor in front of me. "Jesus Christ, boss…" he trailed off, and bent his head, seemingly overwhelmed.

"Are all of you all right?" I asked.

He looked up at me, an incredulous expression on his face. "You're askin' about us? Are you serious?"

"Of course," I said, and then smiled at the fact that he seemed unable to process it all, as he sputtered, and shook his head. Finally, he gave up and looked at me helplessly.

"I'm so sorry, boss. I didn't even hear your message until after you didn't need us anymore." An expression crossed his face. "I'm so sorry," he repeated.

"Where were you?" I asked.

"Mostly in the States. We were in a lot of rural areas. Maybe that's why the call didn't go through," he said. "Boss, if we'd have gotten the call, we would have been there for you. After we checked in here about you, we went to Whitechapel. We're only back here now because we had more souls to turn over."

"I know you would have come, Quinn," I said, and he took a deep breath. I held my hand out, and he took it.

"I can't believe you faced that shit alone," he muttered.

"It is not your fault. I did not expect the situation to be as insane as it was. And truly, I do not know that it would have made any difference. They wanted my heart, and they wanted to end my interference."

"Well, they failed on both fuckin' counts, then," he said, and I smiled. "We also brought you another New Guardian. Your Queen checked her out. She seems like she'll do real well with us."

"Where did you find her?"

"New Orleans," he answered.

"I am looking forward to meeting her. Thank you."

He nodded. His hand was still clasped with mine, and he looked up at me and met my gaze. "I hope you know, boss… you've given me what I lacked all that time I spent in death. I have a reason for being around now. And every good thing I manage to do, every soul I am able to bring to their final judgment… it makes the nightmares all a little less powerful."

"Your heart is finding a way to heal. Work is good for that, sometimes," I said softly. "I am grateful to have you on my team."

He nodded, and just then, the door opened, and Mollis poked her head in. Quinn gave my hand a squeeze and got up, bowed to Mollis, then left so Mollis and I could talk alone.

Mollis entered the room and began chiding me for being out of bed, and I waved it off. She dropped to her knees in front of me and hugged me, careful not to squeeze too tightly.

"You are nuts, you know that?" she said when she pulled away.

I smiled. "I will tell you what I told Brennan: I did not intend to face them on my own. I called my New Guardians, and then I tried to get an opportunity to call you. Triton lured me into a trap, and Alecto broke my phone."

"Fucking Triton," Mollis snarled. "I never saw that coming. That time he met with us in my office, there was nothing in him that indicated anything like that."

"Perhaps they convinced him afterward," I said with a small shrug. I really did not want to discuss Triton. That one hurt too much, and would likely still hurt long after my body had fully healed. My sisters' betrayal was nothing to me compared to his. He had been my friend, my confidant, my first love, even if he did not know it. How could I have judged him so wrongly?

"Your team did get your message, but by the time they did, it was all over. They're freaking the fuck out, worried about you, but they're doing what you wanted. After I gave them an update on you, they went to Whitechapel. I spent all morning judging the souls they keep bringing me. Tisiphone, Meg and I have been very busy."

"Is it making things better for you?"

"It is," she said, nodding. "It looks like a good number of the undead fell at your hand, though your team has brought several down as well. Hephaestus wants to see you," she said, and I was reminded that Brennan had said the same thing after I had saved Sean. "I'll send him in next, if it's okay?"

I nodded. "Have you found anything out from Alecto?"

"We know for a fact that they're working for someone else. They had orders to do everything they have done. Alecto kidnapped Sean herself, right out of Brennan's house. She was the one who was responsible for watching Michael at the time your team found him and escaped with him, but she was not the one who took him. That was someone else."

I nodded, thinking it all through.

"So they had orders. Any idea from whom?"

Mollis shook her head. "It's the weirdest fucking thing, E. Nothing in Alecto's mind is erased. She couldn't do that to herself, so I felt lucky when I was finally able to break in, right?"

I nodded, urging her to continue.

"She took orders from a being she could not see or sense, but who she could hear. The being felt extremely powerful and somehow familiar to her, and it promised her revenge. It promised her that they would take my throne from me. As if I even want the fucking thing," she said. "If they weren't evil assholes, I would give the damn thing to them, you know?"

I gave her a smile. "I know."

"So they had these promises from this invisible being, who I guess had to be an immortal of some kind, if they respected its power that much. And they worked with it, and took orders from it. The undead were created specifically to fuck with me and keep you busy. And then you kept being really good at your job and messing up their plans and slowing down the building of their army. So then they got orders to kidnap the kids. Alecto took Sean, like I said, but she didn't know which of the beings took Michael and Hades, though she seemed to have the feeling that the being she was taking orders from was the one who took Hades. It seemed to know our schedules perfectly, and the kidnappings were planned down to the second. And it did what the invisible being wanted it to: it threw us off of Eveline and her undead-making operation in Whitechapel, and in the time when we were all scrambling for the kids, she went nuts making more undead."

I sat quietly, listening and putting it all together. "But it was not all a distraction. They used Hades' heart, demon girl."

She nodded, rage crossing her face. "They did. I'm not sure yet if that was just a bonus for them, another immortal heart to put into a fucking undead who will come at us soon, or if it was more personal."

I had my own suspicions about that one, but I did not voice them. She knew as well as I did that it was no accident that of all three children, it had been her child who had been mutilated and tortured.

"So we need to track down this shadowy troublemaker and whichever other immortals it was working with. We can likely assume that Triton was one. Have we tracked down Eros yet?"

She shook her head. "I have the imps and Netherhounds looking for both of them. Once Artemis feels up to it, I'm going to ask her to start tracking them as well."

I nodded. "There are too many unknowns out there, devil girl. It troubles me that we have not heard a single peep of Hera or her whereabouts since the day Hephaestus sent Zeus back to the Old Nether."

"I know," she said. "Too many questions. What else is new?" We sat in silence for a few moments. "We'll work on tracking them all down. And we'll continue with the accounting of the other immortals and lesser gods that Artemis and Brennan started. That was a rather brilliant idea of yours, and I want to make sure we see it through."

"And I have many, many undead to hunt," I said.

"Not anytime soon," she argued.

I shook my head. "Once I am up to it. Which will not take long. We both know that now that they are out there, they will only continue making more. The undead plague will spread." A thought hit me. "Why did the creation of undead seem to halt in Tokyo and Paris all of a sudden?"

"Oh, that. Apparently Eveline is a bit of an egomaniac? You probably noticed that."

"Yes, I noticed that," I said wryly.

"Anyway, she wanted Whitechapel to go down in history again. She asked the shadow or whatever the hell we decide to call it, to send the other undead to her city and she would create an undead army there. I guess the shadow must have been suitably impressed by her insanity and dedication by then, because her wish was granted and all of the undead created in the other cities ordered to converge on Whitechapel."

"And some were sent here as well," I added, and she nodded.

"So I have undead to hunt. And we have a shadowy figure to reveal, lying, cheating betrayers to track down," I said, thinking of Triton. "Things are not yet calm, demon girl."

"Not yet," she sighed. "Someday, E."

"Someday," I agreed, patting her hand. Another thought came to me. "Do we have any idea where Megaera was going all those times she could not be found?"

Mollis laughed then. "You wouldn't believe it if I told you."

"Try me," I said.

She laughed again. "Megaera has a boyfriend!" she exclaimed as if she was still in disbelief.

"No," I said.

"Yes!"

"Who?"

"The alpha of the Detroit pack," she said with a grin. "She was ashamed of her need for a man. She was the only one of the Furies who had managed to hold on to what we are supposed to be, and she was annoyed by what she saw as her weakness." She was still smiling. "She introduced me to him today. She has good taste."

"He must like his women mean," I said, and she laughed.

"Maybe," she agreed. She sobered again. "There was also one final thing I was able to get from Alecto before I killed her."

I steeled myself, the worried look on Mollis's face telling me I was about to hear something I would rather not. "And?" I asked.

She got up and paced across the spacious room. "There were thirteen original Guardians," she began, and I nodded, even as my heart sank. I wanted nothing further to do with any of my sisters, or to hear about them. More than anything, I wanted to forget their betraying existence entirely. "You captured Delo, Anthousa, and Kleio. I destroyed them, as we discussed," she mentioned, and I nodded. "I was able to verify that I did manage to actually kill six of them in the Nether. They are entirely dead. Alecto and her people did look, but it looks like those six died before the others learned how to fake their deaths."

The sisters who had stayed alive, despite being cut with Mollis's blade, had faked their deaths by rematerializing and holding a glamour to make it look as if they had fallen to dust before her. It was a rather ingenious move, and one that I did not believe they had come up with on their own.

"That leaves three of us," I said, and Molly nodded.

"Right. That leaves you. Two of your sisters are unaccounted for. Alecto didn't know anything about Amalia or Zara."

I did not respond.

"Neither of them were involved with Alecto's plot with Hermes, either," Mollis continued, watching me slowly.

"Yet neither of them has presented themselves to help, knowing they are sorely needed," I said. "So at the very least, they are cowards. And just because they were not directly working with Alecto it does not mean that they were not still working against you."

"But there's the possibility that they weren't working against me. And, whether they were or not is irrelevant. They are loose ends that we need to tie up."

"You want me to find them."

She smiled. "When you get a spare minute, you know," she joked, and I shook my head. She sobered again. "If they're cowards, then whatever. We'll just know where they are and to check on them if we need to. If they're working against me, then we bring the pain." She paused. "But it's entirely possible that they're out there, and not evil jackasses, and maybe they need help."

We sat in silence for several moments. I was relieved to hear that the whereabouts of most of my sisters was known, and that they no longer marred the name "Guardian." But that possibility, even the slight one, that the ones who still remained were not working for the enemy was almost too much for me to take in just then.

The silence was interrupted by another knock at the door, and Hephaestus poked his head in.

"There's my little nightmare," he boomed, and I smiled. He was carrying a large duffel bag, and he set it on the floor as he came to me. Mollis got up, and then Hephaestus crouched in front of me and took my face between his palms, placing a warm kiss on my forehead.

"You scared the shit out of me," he said. "And I am going to rip Triton's fuckin' head off as soon as I get a hold of the bastard."

"I love you too, you great oaf," I said, and he grinned, then took my hands in his.

"I tried to get a second to see you before everything went nuts," he said, and I nodded.

"I know. I meant to come and see you."

"Well. I decided to come to you. I don't want this to wait." He paused. "Your team… they did real good, E. My son is home because of them, and the only reason that is possible is because they were trained by the best."

"They were fairly amazing before I met them," I said with a smile, touched by his words.

"But you're the rock. You're what inspires them. Hell, you're what inspires me sometimes. You were my only friend for so long, and I hope you know what a gift that was."

I blinked back the tears that threatened. "Your friendship was a gift as well. And continues to be," I told him.

He grinned. "My stories. You love 'em."

I rolled my eyes, and he laughed.

"I went to work making these right after your team brought Michael home," he said, dragging the bag over and unzipping it. He handed a leather sheath to me, and I looked at him questioningly. I put my hand around the handle that was sticking out of the top of the sheath, and pulled out a dagger, its black metal blade gleaming in the warm light of my room. I could feel its power, and I stared at Hephaestus.

"I have six of those," he said. "Made by my my own two hands of metals found only beneath the soil of the Netherwoods, blessed by the Goddess of Death Herself."

I shot a surprised look at Mollis, and she smiled.

"I cannot believe…. Thank you," I said, awestruck.

"I have no idea if they are as good as those I created before. I don't know if the metal here is as strong as it was there," he cautioned. "Though we did test them out on one of the undead Molly was about to destroy, and it seemed to hurt a lot."

"I do not know how to thank you, my friend," I said to him, and he grinned.

"All the thanks are mine to give, E. Thank you and your team for finding my son."

I nodded, and he leaned forward and hugged me, being careful not to hug too hard.

He glanced at Mollis, then back at me. "I should go now. Meaghan is still not quite comfortable when I'm away, after all of that."

"I completely understand. Thank you again. And give my regards to Meaghan," I said, and he pressed another kiss to my forehead, and then he was gone. I sat admiring the blade for a few moments. My team would be honored, as was I.

Mollis and I sat in silence for a few moments, and she ran her fingers through her hair. "Your team is looking for more New Guardians?"

"When they are not hunting down and destroying undead, yes."

"They brought one for me to look at, and she seems like she'll fit in really well with you team. She's staying in one of the rooms downstairs. I figured you wouldn't want her out hunting until you'd gotten to know her a bit."

I nodded. "I will pay a visit later as well."

"No rush. Seriously, rest up, E. It's not like she's going anywhere." She sighed. "I think I need you in Whitechapel when you're able. As much as I love having you here, that area needs a calming presence, and I can't think of anyone better suited to it than you." She grimaced. "I know you miss the loft. I know how much that meant to you, to be home." She met my eyes. "But I think you've changed too, since you've come back. Maybe you're starting to realize that home means something a little different to you than it did before."

Brennan's face came to mind, and she smiled, having caught it.

"Exactly," she said softly.

"His work is here," I reminded her.

"We both know he hates his job. Take the man with you. He has no reason to keep that job anymore. We're out in the open. He bought us time and privacy, and it was exactly what we needed. Now he can move on."

"We will see," I said noncommittally, and she rolled her eyes.

"Good talk, E," she said, and I shook my head.

"I hate Whitechapel," I told her.

"I know. I'm sorry."

I waved it off. "Make sure you keep in close communication with Rayna. They are running into the undead too, and it is affecting their people."

"How?"

"It seems to kill them. The blood, I suppose."

"Oh, shit. Yeah, we'll have to get the word out about that. I'll make sure to keep Rayna updated."

I nodded. "And keep yourself together, demon girl. The only reason I am not fighting you on this Whitechapel thing is because I know so many are in that area. Perhaps our shadowy figure still lurks there, as well. But I will not be here to talk you down. If you need me, do not hesitate to come to me."

"I won't. I am getting better. Your team is making a difference, and... I don't know. Things changed the moment I had Hades back. I feel more focused than I have ever felt in my life. It was like I was given a second chance, and I'm not going to waste it."

"Good."

"Keep your ass safe, E. Don't make me go through that again," she said. "That was a nightmare."

"Trust me, I will do my level best not to get my ass handed to me. Seriously, do you people think I do this on purpose?" I asked her, and she laughed.

I sat there for a while with my best friend, knowing life was sending us on our separate paths once again, and hoping that when it was all over, we would find one another still sane and whole.

EPILOGUE

I stood in the living room of Brennan's home, looking at the piles of boxes heading to storage, the suitcases piled by the door, awaiting our departure. His household... our household, packed up and ready for the next stage of our journey. We would be leaving in the morning.

Sean slept in his room, and Artemis and Asclepius were out, taking advantage of the quiet to enjoy one another's company. We had returned to the loft earlier in the evening for a going away dinner, the entire team gathered around the gleaming dining room table, children laughing and running around us all as we ate and talked and laughed.

Brennan carried one last box into the room and set it by the front door. We had a flat waiting for us in Whitechapel, and had been rematerializing things there throughout the past couple of days. A shifter from one of the packs would be moving into Brennan's childhood home, and I knew that while Brennan would miss the house, he also wanted to give the shifter and his young family a chance to live in a place that had brought him so much happiness. In the past few days, he had cut so many ties to things that had once bound him to Detroit, and while I was concerned at first that it would cause him sadness, he seemed to lighten with each tie he severed.

And I realized how badly he had needed to cut himself loose from certain things. There was a new energy to him, an enthusiasm I had not seen before. Perhaps he had been like that earlier in his life. He had spoken before about how he had once loved travel. It seemed like a new chapter for him.

And for me, I thought as I watched him head back into his room, the room we had been sharing for the past few nights after I had finally convinced Mollis that I was more than well enough to get up and get back to work.

Brennan came back into the room and sat on the sofa beside me. I climbed onto him, straddling his lap and resting my arms around his waist.

"I was never one of those touchy-feely types," I said as I rested my head on his shoulder. He settled his hands on my hips.

"I'm a bad influence on you," he said, a smile in his voice.

"No. Never that," I told him, and he squeezed my hips gently. I pressed my lips to the side of his neck, then nuzzled him, and he gave my hips a squeeze. How I loved the warmth of his hands on me.

"Eunomia," he said, and I looked up at him, leaning back so I could see his face, the tight anxious tone of his voice drawing my concern. Despite his enthusiasm for this next part of our lives, he had been progressively more nervous all day, and I had attributed it to the fact that we would be leaving home, family, and team behind.

"What is it, my love?"

He dug into his pocket, and when he pulled his hand out, it was closed around something. I looked at him questioningly.

He slowly opened his hand, and in his palm sat two silver bands, a matching set. I met his eyes, even as my heart pounded.

"These belonged to my parents," he said. "Ada told me, once I was old enough to understand, that they would have wanted me to have them, to give to the woman I was going to spend my life with."

"I... Mollis did not wear this," I said, knowing that the only ring she wore in her time with Brennan had been Nain's.

"No. She didn't. I think maybe I knew even then... like I said before, it was instinct and automatic and I still don't understand it all. I think somehow I knew it wouldn't last forever."

"And you think we will?" I asked softly, almost afraid to say the words.

He tilted my face up, drawing my gaze away from the rings. "I know so. What about you?"

I smiled, and picked up the larger of the two rings. I held his left hand in mine. "It goes on this finger, yes?" I asked, double-checking.

"Yes," he answered, the slightest of smiles on his lips.

I slid the band onto his finger, ran my fingertips over it. The sense of rightness, of home, was so strong my heart felt full. "You are mine, for the rest of our impossibly long lives, and even after that, Brennan Matthews," I said, meeting his eyes. These were the only marriage vows we would ever need, these simple words said between the two of us. There was no magic here, no instinctual or blood bonds. Just the two of us, and the knowledge that, strange as it seemed, as different as we were, our devotion to one another was complete, and pure. I was his in a way I never would have imagined, not in all the years of my long existence. And he was mine.

He picked up the other ring and slid it onto my ring finger. "Yours, Eunomia," he said. "And I swear I'm going to be the man you deserve."

"Just be yourself, husband of mine. It is all I want from you."

He grinned, and leaned forward and kissed me, and I started to believe that perhaps life in Whitechapel would not be too horrid, after all.

* * *

Clouds passed across a waning moon as a figure moved through the dark, silent forest of the Netherwoods. Or, it may have been a figure. It was more the sense of something being there, the feeling that there was more than the things that could be seen with the naked eye. Maybe it was the way the grasses moved, as if something or someone had brushed past them.

Another figure joined the first, this one in shadow.

"I am sorry. We failed to destroy the troublesome Guardian," the unseeable figure said.

"It is of no matter," said the other in a gentle voice. "Damage has been done, and that is always to our advantage."

"She will continue to be a problem," the first argued.

"She is of no consequence," the shadowy one said calmly.

"She will hunt the undead. We know this. All of our hard work will be undone. She has taken our servants to the pretender who calls herself a Queen."

The shadowy figure laughed, and its laugh was bright and clear and did not at all fit its dark presence. "Oh, my dear, she is nothing. A gnat against the likes of us. Our goal is in sight."

"Do you forget what she is? She is unstoppable. A psycho even among the psychos she calls friends. A zealot," this last said with obvious distaste.

"Ah, but a zealot can be put to work."

"Not this one. She cannot be bought, swayed, or turned. It has been tried, and it has failed."

The shadowy figure laughed again. "Perhaps not before. But everyone has a weakness, darling, and we finally know hers."

After a moment, their soft laughs whispered through the woods, and then, as if they had never been there at all, they were gone.

The End

Eunomia will return in *Zealot,*
the third book in the *Hidden: Soulhunter* series.

Never Miss an Update!
Sign Up for Colleen's Newsletter at
http://bit.ly/colleensnewsletter

Visit **http://www.colleenvanderlinden.com** for news and upcoming releases

LETTER FROM THE AUTHOR

Thank you so much for reading BETRAYER. I absolutely loved writing this book, and I hope you loved reading it! If you have a moment, your reviews on Amazon would be hugely appreciated. Of course, I also love hearing from you via Twitter (I'm @C_Vanderlinden over there) Facebook, or via email. Please let me know what you think!

I have several people I want to thank. First of all, I want to thank my readers for your enthusiasm and support. You make this so much fun for me, and I could not keep doing what I do without your support. Thank you!

I want to thank my husband Roger, who is an amazing partner and who is my first reader and layout genius and cover designer and... he is wonderful.

Thank you to my kids for reminding me to stop staring at the computer every once in a while, and for listening to Taylor Swift's "Bad Blood" with me so often. That helped. A lot.

Thank you to Elizabeth Hunter for beta reading and assuring me that this book does not suck. Thank you as well for making me laugh and helping me feel a little less crazy. You're an inspiration and a wonderful friend. The beards and man buns were, of course, for you.

Thank you to my amazing, wonderful beta readers. This book is much improved thanks to your feedback! Many thanks to the lovely Susan Cambra, Rachel Scott, Brenda Hopkins, Sarah Leenart, Jayna Longstreet, Kathie Littlemore, Kristin Driscoll, Jo Dawson, Sarah Wicks, and Amber Hegarty. Let's do this again soon, ladies!

I want to give a final word of thanks to the authors of the many, many Jack the Ripper websites and articles I used as research during the course of writing BETRAYER. Ripperologists are truly a passionate group, and I learned many more details than I could have ever wanted to know about Jack the Ripper, but it all went into making my fictional embodiment of the Ripper as real as possible.

XO,
Colleen Vanderlinden
Detroit
June 24, 2015

ABOUT THE AUTHOR

Colleen Vanderlinden is the author and publisher of the *Hidden* series, which currently includes *Lost Girl*, *Broken*, *Home*, *Strife*, and *Nether*. She lives in the Detroit area with her husband, children, and two lazy cats. She enjoys reading, obsessing over comic book characters, gardening, and playing *World of Warcraft*.

Learn more about Colleen at her website, colleenvanderlinden.com, contact her via email at email@colleenvanderlinden.com, or follow her on Twitter and Facebook.

The Hidden Series
Book One: Lost Girl
Book Two: Broken
Book Three: Home
Book Four: Strife
Book Five: Nether
Hidden Series Novellas
Forever Night
Earth Bound

The Copper Falls Series
Shadow Witch Rising

The Hidden: Soulhunter Series
Guardian
Betrayer

Never Miss an Update!
Sign Up for Colleen's Newsletter
http://bit.ly/colleensnewsletter